The Courageous Bride of Charleston

STAND-ALONE NOVEL

A Christian Historical Romance Novel

by

Chloe Carley

Table of Contents

Let's connect!

Impact my upcoming stories!

My passionate readers influenced the core soul of the book you are holding in your hands! The title, the cover, the essence of the book as a whole was affected by them!

Their support on my publishing journey is paramount! I devote this book to them!

If you are not a member yet, join now! As an added BONUS, you will receive my "Colorado Reborn" prequel Novella:

FREE EXCLUSIVE GIFT
(available only to my subscribers)

Click the button below to get the FREE BONUS:
https://chloecarley.com/ccbbse

Letter from Chloe Carley

"Once upon a time..."

...my best childhood nights had started with this beautiful phrase!

Ever since I can remember, I loved a good story!

All started thanks to my beloved grandfather! He used to read to my sister and me, stories of mighty princes and horrifying dragons! Even now, sometimes I miss those cold winters in front of the fireplace in my hometown, Texas!

My best stories though were the ones from the Bible! Such is the spiritual connection that a sense of warmth pass through my body every time I hear a biblical story!

My childhood memories were not all roses, but I knew He would always be there for me, my most robust shelter!

Years passed by, and little-Chloe grown up reading all kind of stories! It was no surprise that I had this urge to write my own stories, and share them with the word!

If I have a God's purpose on Earth, I think it is to spread His love and wisdom, through my stories!

Now, it is your time to read my **New Novel "The**

Courageous Bride of Charleston"!

Brightest Blessings,

Chloe Carley

Chapter
One

"Sir! The roof, sir! The roof! Stand clear!"

No sooner had the warning boomed out than the creaking timbers of the house gave way and the entire top floor of the grand building came crashing in on itself. The townsfolk fled in screams of terror and pain as splinters of molten lead and darts of wood rained down on the crowd. They had gathered on the edge of the peninsula in the small riverside town of Georgetown, South Carolina to watch the devastating fire.

A stout man dressed in the traditional red jacket of the volunteer fire department stood bellowing orders by the entrance of what was once the driveway of this fine summer residence. His brass buttons gleamed a burnt copper in the light of the fire. This was Clayton Stringer.

"Mr. Paxton, sir a lot more water is needed," he said. "Blast it all man, are we still relying on buckets in eighteen-ten? Good Lord, it will never subside at this rate."

A young man, dressed similarly but with the addition of a large black bowtie, sprinted past hauling two buckets weighing heavy with water and silt. He set one down at his feet and held the handle of the other between his two hands, then he spun around and flung his load into the flames. The fizzle and hiss of the cold water hitting the crackling wood was all but lost as the towering inferno blazed on. Discarding the empty bucket, he reached for the second, but again his actions barely even raised a wisp of steam. He collected the buckets and dashed back past Clayton who was still screaming for all he was worth.

"Where the blazes is that engine?" Clayton was shouting now.

A young boy started jumping up and down in excitement, pointing to something moving in the distance. "I see her! I see her! It's Bessie!"

As Clayton squinted, a large shire horse came into view pounding down the street. A pump and engine were rattling and careering along behind her on an old wooden cart.

"Thank the good Lord," he muttered to himself.

But she had arrived much too late.

A terrifying scream came from the crowd, but it was quickly stifled by an earth-shattering boom signaling that the fire had reached a gas supply pipe. The windows of the lower floor blew, spewing out a mixture of shattered glass and burning debris. Clayton threw himself to the ground and covered his head with his hands as bits of charred wood and metal clanged and clinked off his protective hat. With a yell, three men carrying a large hose pushed past the crowds of people who were now fleeing in the opposite direction, terrified by the blast and wanting to get to safety.

Clayton got back on his feet and began to give the order to two hefty men manning the pump. "On my mark gentlemen and heave..."

The great pump wheezed into action. The two red and black-clad firefighters heaved and pushed at the heavy engine using the swaying weight of their bodies to keep a steady rhythm. The water slowly began to be sucked up into the hose and fed down to the men waiting in front of the desecrated remains. Clayton heaved a hefty sigh as he watched the water spewing forth, calming, cleansing and finally controlling the blaze. A nasty smell of singed timbers and wet ashes wafted through the air, tickling each nose with its foul stench.

A figure made her way gingerly up towards Clayton holding her handkerchief to her nose in a vain attempt to keep any impurities in the air from reaching her sense of smell. Clayton immediately reached out to take her elbow, guiding her back the way she had come and away from the distressing wreckage.

"My dear, this really is no place for a lady," Clayton told her. "Please stand clear until the flames have subsided. It is a blessing that none were hurt and we should not want a casualty now."

The lady, clearly shaken and in terrible shock, tried to speak. Her words muffled by her handkerchief. "But... Mr. and Mrs. Johnson sir," she finally said.

"Who?"

He stopped as she gripped his arm, her swoon took her legs out from underneath her and a little sob escaped her lips giving away her grief. Clayton turned to a young boy hanging around the engine horse. The young boy appeared to be desperately trying to get the horse to notice him.

"You there!" Clayton called to him. "Kindly fetch me two buckets and I shall thank you to leave my horse be."

The boy jumped and ran into the street and grabbed two buckets, delighted to be involved in the big event. "Here's your buckets mister, shall I fill 'em with water for you?" he asked, a huge grin plastered across his dirty face.

Clayton, still clutching the arm of the grief-stricken woman, huffed his annoyance at the plucky youngster. "Certainly not," he replied gruffly. "Set them here, upturned if you would," he pointed to the floor just in front of them with the toe of his boot.

The boy did as he was told, a baffled look on his face. His expression seemed to say: Why on earth would he want them upside down?

"Out of the way child, this lady has been taken ill. Find a physician," Clayton ordered as he carefully maneuvered his charge onto one of the upturned buckets. He seated himself on the other and proceeded to tap her lightly on each cheek as he rummaged in his belt pouch for a bottle of smelling salts.

The child raced off full of self-importance, pleased that

there might actually be an emergency after all and he would get to play a part. Clayton held the smelling salts bottle under the nose of the semi-conscious woman moving it back and forth in an attempt to rouse her.

"Now ma'am there's no need to take on so; no one was hurt. The property is a summer residence I believe so the chances are good that it was empty."

Her eyelids flickered as she started to come around. She opened her eyes wide and gripped Clayton's arm again. "Sir, Mr. and Mrs. Johnson. Where are Mr. and Mrs. Johnson?"

Clayton took her hand and placed it carefully on top of the other and rested them in her lap. "Now, now, explain to me quietly and calmly. Let us start by telling me first whom you are and then we shall move on to Mr. and Mrs. Johnson."

The lady choked back a sob and, shaking her head, she tried to compose herself. "Sir," she started shakily her voice soft and faint. "I am Mrs. Cartwright and I am in the employ of Mr. and Mrs. Johnson. I am charged with keeping the house clean and livable in their absence," she stopped and moved her watery, tear-soaked eyes up to look at Clayton.

"Sir," she continued, "they arrived this very afternoon."

A look of horror washed over Clayton's face as the realization of Mrs. Cartwright's words took hold. He left her still sobbing on her makeshift seat and dashed back to the house. The fire had now gone out and had left the house a burned-out shell which was still smoking and cracking as the wood shifted and eased itself, cooling down after the extreme heat of the fire. He grabbed one of his firefighters and pulled him to one side.

"Don your gloves and steel yourself, hardy Mr. Paxton. I've just been informed that two people were in residence."

Mr. Henry Paxton hung his head. This was the part of the job he hated most. They optimistically called it searching for survivors but casting his eyes across at the desolate scene, eerily silent and still, he knew in his heart that all they were likely to find were bodies. A ripple of whispered voices ran around what was left of the crowd of horror-struck onlookers as Clayton and Henry carefully picked their way through the wreckage looking for anything that might still be counted among the living.

***

"Sit still child. Honestly, if the good Lord had wanted us all to be jack in the boxes he would have put springs on our bottoms and cushions on our heads."

Clara Johnson's young governess gently unrolled the wet rags and paper that held each lock of Clara's golden hair tightly in place. Clara flinched as another perfect ringlet was released from its pent-up state and fell down to bounce in front of her pretty pale blue eyes.

"But it's hurting me, Nursie," she complained as once again she shifted uncomfortably on her stool.

"Well, your mother requested ringlets Clara so ringlets you shall have. And they look so pretty on you."

Clara had been in the care of Miss Orm since her birth five years previously and no one was more adored nor more precious to Miss Amelia Orm as Clara was. Clara was a bright, young, and happy little girl. She was also the spitting image of her beautiful mother with thick golden curls, full pink lips, and sky-blue eyes, which Amelia affectionately called, 'laughing eyes'.

The last curl was unfurled and Amelia picked up the twists of paper and rags and, after kissing the top of Clara's head by way of an apology, sent her out into the nursery to play.

"There we are Clara Elizabeth all done. Am I forgiven?"

Clara turned and ran back to her beloved governess, her arms stretched wide embracing Amelia in a warm hug. "Oh, Nursie you know you are."

And with that, she ran off. Eager to see how Mr. Flopsy and Mrs. Mop were getting on with their tea things. Amelia smiled to herself as she watched the little girl serving tea to her dolls. Sadly, their cheery morning was cut short by an unexpected ringing of the front doorbell.

Miss Nancy Whigg, the Johnson's housekeeper, pulled open the heavy wooden door of the grand Charleston house to find a very lavishly suited young gentleman accompanied by an officer of the law. She directed her attention to the policeman as suspicion and panic were already starting to form in her stomach.

"Can I help you, officer?" she enquired politely. "I'm afraid the master is currently holidaying with Mrs. Johnson, but we are expecting them back tomorrow."

The policeman raised a hand stopping her full flow. "I'm afraid this is a matter of some delicacy ma'am. It may be better if we step inside."

Nancy moved back to let them in closing the door behind them and giving a quick warning glance to the peering faces of their neighbors across the street. *Nosy Rosetta Bragstock,* she thought bitterly, *it'll be all over town by dinnertime.* She put Rosetta to the back of her mind, promising her a public snubbing the next time they met. She turned her attention back to the two men waiting in the lobby and motioned for them to go through to the parlor.

"If you'd like to take a seat through there Mr. erm…" she stopped, leaving her sentence hanging in mid-air as a reminder to the two gentlemen that she still didn't know who they were.

"I'm dreadfully sorry ma'am, I'm Officer Walker." He removed his helmet and gestured towards his companion. "And this is Mr. Samuel Farnsworth."

On hearing his name Samuel too removed his light brown bowler hat and bowed slightly. "How do you do?" he stammered.

Samuel was a nervous man by nature but this visit was making him particularly uneasy and his stomach was beginning to feel unwell. Nancy gave them both a thin-lipped smile and again nodded towards the parlor door.

"Very good I shall inform Miss Orm of your arrival."

16

Samuel looked up, startled. "Miss Orm? So sorry, w-w-who is this 'Miss Orm'?"

"Miss Orm is the Johnson's governess sir, as I already informed you, Mr. and Mrs. Johnson are away and, in their absence, all dealings are with Miss Orm." With that, she turned on her heel and marched off up the stairs to find Amelia, a feeling of discomfort and dread looming over her. She rapped smartly on the nursery door.

"Miss Orm?"

Amelia came to the door holding a piece of chalk in one hand and a block of slate in the other. The letter 'D' clearly etched out in white chalk emblazoned across its face.

"Yes Nancy, we were just practicing letters," she answered happily, but her cheery smile faded as she looked at Nancy's frowning face.

"There's a police officer and a Mr. Farnsworth waiting in the parlor," she replied, dropping her voice so as not to alarm Clara.

Amelia nodded and turned to call back into the room. "Clara dear I'm just going with Nancy as I have a visitor. Make sure that Mr. Flopsy practices his letters neatly in my absence, won't you?"

Nancy allowed herself a little smile as she thought about how much Amelia suited her job. She remembered thinking to herself when Clara was born that she really hoped that Mrs. Johnson wouldn't pick a stuffy old nurse for her. She cast her mind back to the day Miss Orm had arrived. She had expected a thin, scary, old crone with a hooked nose and thin lips who hardly ever smiled. But when the young, willowy creature with the warm smile and deep, soft brown eyes had stepped out of the coach, Nancy knew then that they had been truly blessed with sweet, kind-hearted Amelia.

Clara's reply filtered back from somewhere inside the room. "Of course, Nursie."

Amelia quickly checked her glossy, black hair was still secured in its tight bun before closing the door and following Nancy downstairs, apprehensive as to what a police officer would want with them. Crossing the room, she introduced herself smiling warmly at the two waiting gentlemen.

"Sorry to have kept you, gentlemen. I'm Miss Amelia Orm. I deal with family matters in the absence of Mr. and Mrs. Johnson."

The two men rose from their seats waiting for Amelia to settle herself before lowering themselves back down. Officer Walker cleared his throat.

"I'm sorry to have to inform you, ma'am of a terrible accident that befell the summer residence of Mr. and Mrs. Johnson the night before last," he darted his eyes up to look at Amelia. All the color had drained from her face. He dropped his eyes back to his hands and pressed on with what he had been dreading all morning.

"And that Mr. and Mrs. Johnson perished, along with their property at approximately 11:35 P.M. last Friday evening." He paused for a breath before continuing, "The volunteer fire department of Georgetown do not suspect any foul play ma'am and have informed us that the fire was likely caused by a faulty gas lamp."

Now that his speech was out at last, he looked at Amelia expecting her to have broken down or at worst, fainted. But she sat, composed and elegant, contemplating what to say next. After what seemed to Officer Walker like an age she finally broke the silence.

"Thank you, officer," she said, her voice cool and tempered. "I realize how difficult imparting such terrible news must have been for you and I appreciate your coming in person."

This was true as Amelia felt that to have read such a thing in a letter would've been too awful and cold for her to bear. She looked down at her hands clasped in her lap thinking how cruel and unfair life was that her beloved Clara was now orphaned. Samuel let out a nervous cough alerting Amelia to his presence.

"Forgive me dear lady but there, erm, are some i-important matters we must discuss with you. I realize of course that, erm, this is not the most, erm..." He stopped and glared earnestly at Officer Walker for help.

Amelia cut in. "Yes, yes I understand sir please continue. It is, as you say important."

Her clean, emotionless tones were doing nothing to calm poor Samuel's nerves and for a moment he wondered whether it would've been better had Amelia taken on in sobs and tears. He reached for his case.

"I believe there is a child, a, erm, d-daughter? One, C-Clara Eliza-beth Johnson?"

Amelia looked at him and for a moment a flash of emotion passed across her passive eyes and she swore to herself that whatever else, she would see to it that nothing but the greatest good was to happen to her Clara.

"Yes, that's quite correct. She is a five-year-old infant and is currently in my care."

Samuel nearly flinched at the look of defiance in her eyes. He looked away and busied himself with his papers. "She, erm, that is to say, Mr. Johnson left us a letter, erm, m-ma'am," he stuttered his way through his sentence as he fished out a well-fingered paper and handed it to Amelia. She took it from him as calmly as she could.

"Forgive me for appearing rude sir, but who are you?"

This completely threw poor Samuel who gripped his case and cast pleading glances at Officer Walker who, taking the cue, cut in.

"Pardon me ma'am this is Mr. Farnsworth. He is your late employer's lawyer."

Amelia smiled a cold smile at Samuel, any trace of warmth and cheer form her previous demeanor now gone. She looked down and read the letter.

July fifteenth, 1805

I, Willis Edward Johnson being of sound body and mind do

hereby transfer legal guardianship of my only daughter Clara Elizabeth, if in the unfortunate instance that anything should happen to myself or my wife Mrs. Joslyn Cornelia Johnson, to the Right Honorable Reverend Anthony Charles Cavendish and his wife Mrs. Cora Isabelle Cavendish.

> *And it is my fond wish that our faithful family retainer Miss Amelia Constance Orm, if still in our employ, not be removed from her post as governess to Clara.*

Amelia finished reading the letter and carefully handed it back to Samuel who immediately pulled out an envelope.

"All the p-p-possessions and, err, p-property belonging to Mr. Johnson, are now to be held in a, erm trust until Clara should turn, erm, tw-twenty-one or sh-should take a husband. Whichever event should occur first." He flicked through the pages of Mr. Johnson's will nervously, wishing that this could be over. "Y-you of course, a-and the staff have been re-remembered in the will and all settlements owing w-will be paid in due course."

He stood to leave, anxious to be as far away as possible. Preferably with a bottle of bourbon. Taking this as a cue Amelia rose from her seat.

"Thank you, gentlemen. As I'm sure you can appreciate there are matters that I must now attend to." She crossed the room and pressed the bell push to alert Nancy. "Miss Whigg will see you out."

She left Officer Walker and Samuel with Nancy and slowly walked up the stairs, unsure of what to say to Clara. She pulled herself up to her full height, pushed her shoulders back and entered the nursery.

Chapter
Two

"Goodness me things never change," Amelia commented as she pulled Clara's hair up into a neat roll and pinned it there while Clara flinched and fussed. "It doesn't seem like five minutes since I was putting your hair in ringlets, let alone thirteen years."

Clara smiled warmly at Amelia. She no longer thought of her as her governess, but more her closest friend. "Oh, but Nursie," she teased, "it's hurting me."

The two friends giggled as Amelia helped Clara to prepare for her guests waiting downstairs on the back lawn. Mr. Cavendish had gathered together some of his closest friends and family to help Clara to celebrate the transition into adulthood: her eighteenth birthday.

The Reverend Cavendish had been very good to Clara. He had taken her in and loved her as if she was his own daughter. He had wanted this to be a double celebration, announcing her engagement to his son Lawrence, but as far as Clara knew Lawrence had been so busy with his historic endeavors that he had not found the time to formally propose to her.

For as long as Clara could remember there had been talk of her marriage to Lawrence with Mr. Cavendish discussing the subject at length with Amelia on numerous occasions. Clara smiled at her reflection in the mirror. A slender, sylph-like, young woman smiled back at her. It was odd for her to think of herself as anything other than Lawrence's future bride for she had heard it so many times.

Amelia glanced at her suddenly thinking that no one had ever actually asked Clara if she wanted to be married to Lawrence. It had just been mentioned one day and Clara hadn't questioned it, but now she had another job to do: play hostess.

"Right then, Miss Clara Elizabeth, stand and let me look at you."

Clara stood as Amelia admired her handiwork occasionally hitching up her petticoat or smoothing down a hem. She stopped and clicked her tongue in annoyance at the stray hair that refused to stay in place. She groped for another hairpin from the china pot on Clara's dresser. Perhaps she was being a little too fussy this afternoon, but her work was on show to extended members of the Cavendish family and she wanted them both to make a good impression.

Clara tittered. "Dear, sweet Amelia, you always make such a fuss of me."

Amelia stood back, finally satisfied. "There, I believe you are all ready." She turned to pick up her purse and parasol just as a soft tap came at the door.

A male voice called out, "Clara? Are you ready?"

Amelia crossed the room to answer the door. "Good morning Mr. Cavendish she is all ready. If you wish to escort her down to the garden I shall follow along behind."

"Of course, ma'am."

Lawrence stood in the doorway looking stiff and awkward. His glasses were pushed up onto his head revealing his piercing silver-grey eyes, half-hidden beneath his dark wavy hair and his best suit draped over his tall, thin frame making it look ill-fitting and uncomfortable. But this was hardly surprising, Lawrence had always been far happier stripped down to his shirt and flannel pants, pouring over dusty old artifacts. Formal occasions bored him rigid and he had always thought parties rather dull and silly. However, had he not agreed, his father would've plagued him all evening and again the following day. Lawrence longed to get back to cataloging and recording his beloved antiquities.

At least this way he could spend an entire uninterrupted day with his work. And anyway, he had invited Professor Baxter and the delightful Sophie so at least he should have someone to talk to about far more important matters than bonnets and parasols. He offered his arm to Clara begrudgingly. If he had to do this damned silly thing he would rather get it over and done with as quickly as possible.

"Clara?"

Clara stifled a giggle as Amelia raised an eyebrow, giving Lawrence a reproachful look. "Begging your pardon Mr.

Cavendish but are you addressing Miss Johnson?"

Clara smiled as she mistook Lawrence's look of enraged annoyance for nervous embarrassment. He cast his eyes up to the ceiling in a gesture of exasperation. "My apologies ma'am." He turned to Clara bowing stiffly in an over exaggerated gesture that hadn't gone unnoticed by Amelia. "Please allow me to escort you, Miss Johnson."

Beaming at Lawrence's apparent good humor Clara graciously took his arm and the odd little party of three made their way downstairs to mingle with Clara's guests.

As they reached the entrance hallway Lawrence leaned into Clara to whisper in her ear. "You don't like all this stuff and nonsense, do you? Do you not find it all a tad…" He paused thinking of a suitable word. "Restrictive?"

Clara moved her eyes down to look at her gloved hand and then back up to Lawrence. "I would not wish to offend the generosity shown to me by Uncle Anthony," she replied.

Lawrence winked at her. "What a sweet little thing you are Clara Johnson, but I fear that you will find this party awfully dull."

They resumed their pace and crossed the airy entrance and out towards the double doors leading to the yard. Entering the garden, the Reverend Cavendish beamed proudly at his young son walking with Clara on his arm. But his pride soon turned to annoyance as he watched Lawrence seat Clara beside a distant aunt of his and immediately leave the garden.

"Goodness me how lovely you are Miss Johnson," the Cavendish aunt said as she leaned over and squinted at Clara through old, milky white eyes. "I remember your dear mother, there's a lot of her in you." She sat back, observing the party.

For a while, neither of them spoke. But just as Clara was about to turn to matters pertaining to the health of her companion, the ancient lady spoke again.

"Anthony tells me you are to marry Lawrence?"

"Yes ma'am," Clara replied. She expected a hearty congratulations, or perhaps the wisdom of a long-married woman on the subject of men, something which Clara herself had very little knowledge of at all. But instead, the aging matriarchic figure asked her if Lawrence looks at her. Clara thought this very odd, of course, he had looked at her. He had seen her almost daily for the most part of her life.

Confused, Clara leaned closer to her strange interlocutor so as to hear her a little better. "I'm afraid you have me at a loss ma'am."

The elderly aunt brought her face as close to Clara's as she could. "You think about it, my girl."

Clara was about to ask her to explain what she had meant a little more when Anthony suddenly appeared. A stout man of good standing, the Reverend Anthony Cavendish had a happy, if somewhat tired face. The many lines a testament to the long hours he had spent raising both Lawrence and Clara since the death of his beloved wife, Cora. To speak nothing of the problems of his parishioners that he had both listened to and tried to solve.

"Ah! There you are, Clara. Do excuse us Aunt Lucy, won't you? But there are some friends who have expressed an interest in Miss Johnson." With this, Anthony pulled Clara up by the elbow and whisked her away to the other side of the garden to introduce her to a cousin and his wife who had traveled all the way from Wisconsin just to meet her. "Clara this is a cousin of Cora's, Mr. Heeley and his wife."

Mr. Heeley nodded his head slightly in Clara's direction. "Delighted to meet you, Miss Johnson. You are set to marry Lawrence I believe?"

Mr. Heeley had a big booming voice and a beard to match. His wife Rebecca stood demurely at his side. Smiling when he smiled, laughing when he laughed but otherwise staying absolutely silent and Clara began to feel a little uncomfortable at what might be expected of her as Lawrence's wife. She smiled warmly at the Heeley's.

"Yes sir," she replied.

"Capital. Capital. Where is young Lawrence? He should be here introducing you to his family and friends."

Clara scanned the garden looking for Lawrence. But when she found him he was in active conversation with a pipe-smoking man in a tatty morning jacket on the other side of the garden. "I believe he is otherwise engaged sir," Clara motioned to where Lawrence was now sitting, beside a small, plump, plain looking girl, probably around her own age. The three of them were deep in conversation.

She wondered if perhaps Mr. Heeley was right and that Lawrence should be spending the afternoon proudly showing off his fiancée. She suddenly had a queasy and uneasy feeling in her stomach.

"Ah, so he is. Excuse me, Miss Johnson." He turned to his wife. "Rebecca?"

And without a word to Clara, she trotted off behind her husband. Clara watched her go. Again, stopping when he stopped, laughing when he laughed but never saying a word to anyone.

"Yes, it is a little bizarre isn't it?" A voice behind Clara made her spin round coming face to face with Amelia.

She nodded in response.

"Are you enjoying yourself, dearest?" Amelia asked. Amelia knew Clara better than anyone and she could tell that something wasn't right.

Clara, not wishing to offend Anthony, gave Amelia her best smile. "Of course. Almost everyone knows of my engagement to Lawrence and they all seem very friendly and welcoming," she trailed off as she noticed Amelia looking over in Lawrence's direction. She too had noticed how friendly the girl sitting beside him was.

Making a decision, she took Clara by the arm. "Come along Clara. I believe it is time we learned who Lawrence's companions actually are." She escorted Clara over towards

Lawrence and his two guests. As they neared they could hear Lawrence chattering away about a large building full of artifacts and antiquities from bygone years.

"And people will flock to see things that no one has set eyes on for decades, centuries in some cases. What do you think professor?"

The man in the tatty jacket took his pipe from his mouth and scratched his head. "My dear boy it is of such things as dreams are made surely. And open for general public viewing you say?" He stopped to bash the loose leaves of tobacco from his pipe before sliding it into his jacket pocket. "It would be a major feat if it could actually be achieved."

Amelia saw her opportunity and took it. "Pardon our rude intrusion, Mr. Cavendish, however, Reverend Cavendish has expressed a wish that all guests have a glass to partake in toasting the cake."

Lawrence grimaced. Another silly tradition that didn't mean anything. Clara and Amelia stood waiting for Lawrence to introduce them but instead, he excused himself from the conversation and stomped off in the direction of the drinks. Amelia turned to the girl who was awkwardly sitting on her chair, gazing after Lawrence.

"Excuse me my dear, but I must compliment you on your exquisite dress. I have been admiring it all afternoon."

The girl's cheeks filled with color as she smiled, lighting up her smooth, round face and causing Clara to smile too. "Thank you, ma'am, do you really like it?"

Amelia treated her to one of her warm smiles. The kind of smile she would reserve for little five-year-old Clara when she had done well with her spellings, or eaten all of her dinner. "I think it sets off your lovely green eyes beautifully," she replied.

This seemed to please the girl prompting the pipe smoking gentleman to speak.

"Yes, Sophie has always taken after her mother," he said, a look of pride crossing his face. He bowed lightly to the ladies. "Forgive me dear ladies, how rude of me. I'm Professor Baxter, formerly of the University of South Carolina."

Clara smiled. "The same institution that Lawrence attended?" she asked, delighted to find some common ground at last.

"The very same." Professor Baxter gestured towards Lawrence who was coming back holding a tray of five glasses of orange juice. "I'm afraid we know very little about Lawrence's family, my dear, as he talks incessantly of tombs and treasures lost beneath the sea eons ago."

Clara laughed. "Yes, that does sound very much like Lawrence."

Sophie grinned at Clara. "You and your brother are very alike. I shall look forward to getting to know you better," she said.

Just as Clara was about to question Sophie's statement, Lawrence thrust a glass into the hands of the professor and Sophie. "I meant to ask Professor, how are you finding your new post at the College of Charleston?" Lawrence asked, taking a large gulp of orange juice.

The old professor smiled. "Oh, fine dear boy, fine. I much prefer our residence in Charleston to the cramped lodgings of the horseshoe building in Columbia." He glanced down at Sophie who nodded enthusiastically. "But it has come a little too late for your good self I fear," he added.

Clara looked confused. "Pardon my ignorance Professor Baxter, but why do you feel that it has come too late for Lawrence?" she asked.

The professor threw back his head in a hearty laugh. "Because my dear," he explained, "Lawrence would have easily been able to travel from home had the college offered studies in archeology, and would not have had to live in cheap lodgings and survive on traditionally terrible student fare." He chuckled.

"I always quite enjoyed my on-campus meals. I feel I fared far better than William Turner who spent the entire duration of his studies eating nothing more than cheese," Lawrence winked at Sophie who blushed and giggled. He turned his attention to Clara. "I hardly came home pallid and ill, did I? Or perhaps you viewed me as a half-starved, mad-man with crazy hair." He ran his fingers through his thick, wavy hair making it stick out in odd directions as he pulled a funny face making both Clara and Sophie giggle.

Amelia rolled her eyes. "Mr. Cavendish—" she started but was unable to finish.

Anthony announced the traditional toasting of the birthday cake. "Miss Johnson, if you would be so kind as to cut the first slice?"

Clara giggled, her earlier conversation with Sophie temporarily forgotten as she took the cake slice from the cook and slid it into the cake. Anthony raised his glass in the air prompting his guests to follow suit.

"Many happy returns to Clara," he announced proudly, leading the party into a unified cheer.

Getting down from the raised dais that had been used as a stage for the occasion, Anthony Cavendish went in search of his son leaving his cook, Mrs. Dimbleby, to share out the cake. Mr. Heeley and his strange wife Rebecca moved to intercept him as he made a beeline for Lawrence and his Professor.

"Anthony," the large man boomed. "We have a business proposition for young Lawrence. Haven't we Rebecca?" He turned to his wife who nodded solemnly.

"Business proposition," she repeated dutifully.

Anthony smiled, Robert Heeley could talk and talk. His word with Lawrence would have to wait. "Robert, of course, my dear fellow. My apologies that I did not have time to speak with you properly earlier. It is nice to see you here sir, and your good lady wife. How are you Rebecca, my dear?"

Rebecca looked anxiously at her husband, clearly unsure as to what to say.

"She's fine." Robert waved his hand in the direction of his wife, dismissing the question as trivial. "I have been speaking with young Lawrence with regards to possibly funding his new venture, assuming of course that a moderate percentage of the ticket price were to find its way into my possession. He informs me that you, in fact, are in charge of the financing of this project and that any investment should be discussed with your very good self."

Anthony mentally shook the last of the booming tones from his ears as he prepared his response. "Mr. Heeley, Robert sir, that is a generous offer indeed. If you should like to step into my study after supper we shall discuss the matter further. As I am certain you can appreciate, a birthday celebration is hardly the suitable atmosphere for talk of business." Anthony extended his hand out to Robert who took it and heartily pumped it up and down.

"Capital dear fellow, capital. I shall look forward to it earnestly," Robert exclaimed.

Rebecca, who had been standing silently beside her husband, suddenly let out a small gasp. Her hand flew to her mouth.

"Rebecca, what is the matter with you woman? Can you not see I am talking?" But before he could berate her further, a loud voice screeched across the garden.

"Do excuse me Robert, Rebecca." He raced over to where Lawrence appeared to be being assaulted by an overtly irate elderly woman, beckoning to his cook as he did so.

"And another thing my lad, you do not speak ill of the dead! May you be struck down where you stand."

Mrs. Dimbleby took the arm of the woman and led her inside. "Come with me Aunt Ermentrude and I shall find you a small tot of brandy," she said, leaving Anthony to deal with Lawrence.

"I've never, not in all my days ever... Displaying unnecessaries like that? It's disgraceful, it's blasphemous, it's abhorrent..." Aunt Ermentrude was gently taken to the Orangery where she could sit and calm down in the company of a very fine bottle of Anthony Cavendish's best brandy.

Anthony practically pushed Lawrence into his study closing the door firmly behind him. He guided his son into an empty chair before seating himself behind his desk. He leaned forward placing his elbows on his desk for support.

"What did you say to your great aunt?" His voice was calm and deliberate which told Lawrence all he needed to know. He was in trouble and he needed to tread very carefully.

"Father, I honestly do not know what she is so upset about. She asked me about my plans and I simply furnished her with an answer." This, after all, was the truth, it wasn't his fault that Ermentrude was old and set in her ways. People needed to see what life was like before them. Studying the great artifacts of history could help people discover new and better ways of doing things. Or even discover new things altogether. This was the future, this was his vision and if he had to tread on the toes of a few old 'fuddy-duddy' women to achieve it, then so be it.

Anthony leaned further towards his son, his eyes narrowing behind his spectacles. "What *exactly* did you say to her?"

Lawrence shrugged. "All I said was that we had just had a very interesting artifact that had recently come to us for display in the museum that tells us a lot about how our ancestors might've coped with family planning."

Anthony let out a loud sigh as he pinched the bridge of his nose. Desperately trying to ward off the headache he could feel coming on and indeed always did when having these types of conversations with Lawrence. "And what, pray tell, was the artifact in question?" he asked tentatively, not at all sure he wanted to learn the answer.

At this point, Lawrence had the decency to look a little embarrassed. He dropped his eyes as he felt the hot blush of color fill his cheeks. "A chastity belt," he muttered almost inaudibly.

Anthony snapped his head up to glare at his son, praying that he hadn't heard what he thought he had. "I beg your pardon?" he hissed. His face turning crimson

Lawrence, admitting defeat and looking his father squarely in the eye replied. "I said a chastity belt, Father."

Anthony rose from his chair his face turning purple with a mixture of embarrassment and rage. "How dare you bring an item of that nature into this house. Is this what that museum of yours is to be filled with is it? Is this what your vision entails is it? Debauchery?"

Aunt Ermentrude smiled faintly to herself as Anthony's bellowed words echoed through the house.

"Father, Father, please! My museum is to be a place of learning, of paying homage to the great thinkers, innovators, and geniuses of a bygone era. The chastity..."

Anthony's voice reached fever pitch as he roared across Lawrence's explanation. "If you dare to utter the name of that disgusting piece of filth again I shall remove you from my house with my bare hands." He placed both his hands on his desk, breathing hard as he tried his best to calm down. "I have never been so embarrassed and ashamed in all my life Lawrence Cavendish. I have always held my head high in this town. A highly respected preacher with wholesome Christian values. But you are on the path to single-handedly ruining my reputation."

Lawrence looked dismayed. "Father, please, this was never my intention! I have always regarded you as a fine upstanding Christian. I would never wish to bring any such embarrassment upon you or to tarnish your good name."

Anthony sank down into his chair. His temper subsided and his energy spent. He regarded his son taking in the earnest and genuine expression of despair etched across his young face.

"I can see by your expression that what you say is the truth and I thank you for it. I blame myself. Your dear mother, may she rest in peace, and I have always allowed you the freedom to choose your own path and I have not ever imposed upon you the restrictions I ought to have done." He stopped and turned to look out of the study window before continuing, "I have, in a word, spoilt you."

Lawrence rose from his seat and crossed to the window to join his father. "No Father, you have always done your best to raise both myself and my sister to have the same values as yourself and we are forever grateful. As a matter of fact, Clara was only saying this very morning that she was grateful for all that you have done."

Anthony surveyed the party guests milling around his garden. "Look at all the happy faces, Lawrence. Everyone is here to wish Clara well and to offer their congratulations for your union to her."

Lawrence sighed and stomped back to his seat. "Father, please. Not this again. I have no intention of marrying Clara."

Anthony whipped round. "What's that?"

Lawrence continued. "You have raised us as brother and sister. I love Clara dearly and I want to see her happy Father, but I'm not the man for her."

Anthony could feel his temper rising again, he tried his best to keep it at bay. "But surely you can see that this is God's will?"

Lawrence scoffed.   "How is it God's will Father? Because she was sent to us after her parents' untimely passing? I do not see how raising Clara as my sister could possibly mean that we should be married?"

Anthony could see that he would need to explain a little

further to his son. "My child. I speak with the good Lord every day. It is my job to interpret his wishes through the actions that he has us perform throughout our lives." He lowered himself back down into his chair.

"When Clara's mother and father were blessed, it was a full two years after their union in the house of God. Everyone was beginning to feel that perhaps God had other plans for them than to start a family. But when Mrs. Johnson fell pregnant, Willis came to me and I made a promise to him and in the eyes of God." He paused to push his spectacles back up the bridge of his nose. "I gave my solemn oath that if anything should happen to either of them I would raise Clara as my own and take care of her future."

Lawrence cut in. "But that does not necessarily mean that she should be married to me..." he trailed off, catching sight of Anthony's expression.

"You were entering your fifth year when Clara was finally born. Willis came to me again and we discussed at length the possibility of joining the two families. I intend to honor his wishes and I expect you to do the same."

Lawrence was at a loss for words. Eventually, he found his voice and again beseeched his father. "But surely you would prefer Clara to be with someone who truly loves her? Someone who will make her happy Father?"

Anthony nodded his head. "Indeed, I do sir and I expect you to do your utmost to see to it that Clara is well kept. The wedding is planned for two weeks following your twenty-fifth birthday. I shall expect you to have opened your museum and be turning a tidy profit by this date. Enough in fact to have a home ready for yourself and Clara."

Lawrence rose from his seat, desperation lacing his voice. "But Father I cannot marry Clara."

Anthony could feel his temper raising once more. He desperately tried to keep his emotions stable. He had a garden full of guests that he did not want overhearing this conversation. "And why not? What good reason could you have for not honoring the wishes of your father?"

Lawrence swallowed hard. "Because I have feelings for another and I would rather myself dead than hurt my beloved Sophie!" At this Lawrence tore across the study and opened the door to leave.

Anthony called after him. "If you defy me in this Lawrence, I will cut off all financial aid to the museum."

Lawrence froze his hand still on the door handle before throwing the door open fully and storming out into the hall. Just as Clara emerged from the Orangery after having spoken briefly with Aunt Ermentrude, seemingly oblivious to the entire chastity belt debacle. But Clara, who would never condone the act of listening in at keyholes, had heard far more than Anthony Cavendish had intended. She made up her mind to seek Amelia's advice that evening when the two ladies retired to their side of the house.

Lawrence was somewhat surprised to see Clara, and, wishing to avoid another unpleasant confrontation with his great-aunt, took her by the arm and sped her down the hallway towards the kitchen.

"Lawrence, this is most irregular. Why are we absconding to the kitchen? The cake is in the garden and cook has cut more than enough for everyone to have their fill."

"I have little interest in the cake Clara, not nearly as much as in the avoidance of the beastly and deeply unpleasant Great Aunt Ermentrude."

Clara, shocked and a little taken aback by Lawrence's bluntness let out a nervous giggle. "You shouldn't say such things about your great aunt, she seems perfectly charming to me."

"You were not on the end of her sharp tongue," replied Lawrence as he swept Clara past the kitchen sink and out through the servant's door into the yard.

"Really Lawrence, all this to avoid making a simple apology? It does all seem rather excessive."

Lawrence grinned at her.

"Fun though eh Clara? Just like when we were children and cook would turn us out into the yard for stealing cherries from the pantry?" He darted back inside and came out again a moment later. "Close your eyes," he ordered, his mouth full. Clara did as she was bid and Lawrence popped a small, juicy cherry into her mouth.

Clara giggled. "Oh, Lawrence, you can be so amusing at times."

He smiled at her and, once again taking her by the arm, escorted her back through the yard and into the party.

Chapter
Three

"Well my dear, that certainly was a most enjoyable, if not absorbing, afternoon wouldn't you say?" Amelia crossed to the dressing table and placed the pot of hairpins in front of Clara's mirror. She picked up a brush and made her way back to where Clara was sitting on her stool in her night things waiting for Amelia to prepare her hair ready for bed.

"Yes, I spoke with a good many people and every one of them seemed perfectly charming." Clara stifled a yawn as Amelia pulled and plaited her thick hair.

"I saw you walking with Lawrence after the cake had been cut. A little improper to have been without your chaperone, but I could see you so I feel that there was little harm done."

Clara turned to her friend. "Amelia, may I confide in you? I'm afraid that I may have done something awful."

Amelia let her arm fall as she surveyed her young ward. "Of course, you know that I am always here should you need me. But what can you have possibly done that is so terrible?"

Clara dropped her head. "This afternoon, shortly after Lawrence had been accosted by his great-aunt, Ermentrude, I followed Mrs. Dimbleby into the Orangery to see if I could help to calm the old dear."

Amelia went back to her task, brushing out long locks of Clara's hair until it shone. "That's hardly awful, Clara. In fact, I would go so far as to say that it was the most decent thing to have done and I commend you for it, my dear."

"Thank you. But as I was talking with Aunt Ermentrude I was close enough to overhear Lawrence's conversation with Mr. Cavendish."

Amelia continued to pull on Clara's hair, tugging and plaiting the sections of gold which wrapped around her fingers expertly. She let out a small sigh. "Ah, now eavesdropping is another matter, Clara. We must not concern ourselves with the private lives of others."

Clara turned her head to look into Amelia's eyes.

"Will you please sit still? At this rate I shall have to start again," Amelia chastised her sharply, tired and annoyed to find that Clara had been listening in on other people's affairs.

Clara was close to tears. "I did not eavesdrop! But the door was open and Uncle Anthony threatened to withhold funding for Lawrence's museum if he should defy him."

Amelia went silent as she contemplated what this could mean. She sucked hard on her teeth. *Defy him? What could he have meant?* As far as Amelia knew Lawrence had given his consent to the betrothal to Clara and had been too busy with his museum to have worried about it all that much. But his eyes had undeniably sparkled when he had been talking with that girl, what was her name? Ah yes, Sophie. She needed more information before she could give Clara any sound advice.

"Did you hear anything further?"

Clara shook her head. "No, it was shortly after this that Lawrence took me back into the party." She looked down at her hands strengthening her resolve as she made up her mind to tell Amelia of her plan. "It is my belief that Mr. Cavendish wishes for Lawrence to keep me after we are married. And he intends for him to do this by means of profits taken from the museum."

Amelia nodded and sighed for a second time. "Yes, my dear that is usual within families of your class and breeding."

Clara thumped her hands down onto her knees.   "But I do not need to be kept. I am of the means to fund the museum and myself am I not?" Clara knew of her vast inheritance.

Amelia spun her around on her stool. "Clara, your wealth is held in trust which you cannot access until you marry and what you are suggesting is a very dangerous notion. Imagine your husband's social standing if anyone were to know the means by which he had funded his business? He would be a laughing stock. No one would agree to enter into business with such a man. Your money would not help him here." She held Clara's shoulder's gently as she explained.

"Your late father's factories are to be managed by your husband by all means and your inheritance will act as a sizable dowry, but if you were to offer any amount of money to your fiancé before you are officially joined in matrimony it would be most improper."

She rose, left the room and came back with the footstool from the shared sitting room. Easing herself down on it she continued to explain, "All you are likely to do Clara is to make Lawrence appear silly—and you yourself. It would look to others as though you had to buy yourself into a marriage and I will certainly not allow that. But as I say, your wealth is untouchable until you are married, so I should put the idea firmly from your mind." She spun Clara around again and continued with her braids. "Do you understand what I have told you?"

Clara stared into the middle distance as Amelia resumed her tugging. "I understand perfectly. But this does not alter my feelings on the matter and I may not currently have access to the means to support Lawrence's business, however, I intend to work honestly for it."

Amelia, having finally finished Clara's plaits rose and busied herself with turning down the bed. "And how do you propose to do that?" she asked.

"I shall work in one of my father's factories and donate the money as an anonymous benefactor."

Amelia whipped around and stared, open-mouthed at Clara. "You most certainly shall not," she managed finally. Aghast that Clara should even suggest such a thing.

"I do not see what is so wrong with my idea. Not only shall

I be of some small assistance to Lawrence's endeavors, but I shall also be learning my family trade first hand. Then, I shall be capable of managing my own factories and I shan't need to be kept."

Amelia was stunned. Clara had never spoken with such steely resolve nor such passion before. She had always been a compliant and passive child and Amelia wondered where this sudden defiance had come from. Was it simply fueled by her love for Lawrence, or was it something new? Was it that she really did feel that she needed a purpose in life, more than simply being a wife to Lawrence?

All the same, Amelia couldn't help but feel a little glimmer of pride for her charge as she realized, rather guiltily, that she had begun to consider Clara of no more worth than simply Lawrence's wife herself. All that being said though, she could never permit her to do this. How could she? Clara's upper-class upbringing and her lineage would never allow for such an endeavor. She had to forbid it. Her late employers had been good to her and she had received enough money to continue on as Clara's governess, plus a little excess that she had put away for her dotage. No, she would deny Clara her request.

"I am sorry Clara but I simply cannot allow for you to do any such thing. I have a duty to your late mother and father and also to your social standing. Not to mention my obligations to the Cavendish family. This would hardly be a fitting repayment to Mr. Cavendish for the kindness he has shown to you for the past thirteen years." She paused hoping that Clara was taking in the severity of the situation.

She continued, "Your reputation would be in tatters and then there would be slim hope of you attracting another suitor. You shall keep to your business and let Lawrence keep to his and that is my final word on the matter."

Clara knew when to push her governess and when not to. This was certainly a time to exercise the latter. She took Amelia's tone as her cue to retire. "Thank you for your advice Amelia, I shall think on what you have said most deeply. But as we are now both very tired I shall bid you a good and restful night," she crossed over and climbed up onto the soft, downy four-poster bed that sat at the far end of her room.

"I'm glad that you understand your position, Clara. God bless you child and keep you safe until morning."

Amelia had always tucked Clara into bed in this way, ever since she had first become the child's governess when Clara was only a few weeks old. She would swaddle her in muslin and settle her in her crib, kissing her forehead and bidding the good Lord keep watch over her until morning. Even though she was now an adult, Clara always felt that she would miss this little ritual, and it had become so habitual to Amelia that it would now be unnatural to her not to say it.

"Goodnight Amelia, God bless."

Amelia left the room, putting out the lamps as she went, leaving Clara alone in the darkness. She lay awake staring at the underside of the bed's canopy as her eyes adjusted to the gloom. How could she possibly implement her plan now? If it would be an out and out insult to her guardians then she could not. She would not do anything that hurt the reputations of her family and friends, but now that Clara had the idea in her head, she really wanted to see it through.

Originally, she was thinking only of Lawrence, but each time she thought of being kept her mind harked back to Mrs. Heeley who was dutifully trotting after Mr. Heeley, only ever having his opinions, only ever speaking to reiterate her husband's words, or out and out repeat them in some cases. Mr. Heeley. Even answered any questions directed at her. This may not be true of all marriages, but still, Clara disliked the notion that she may simply be Lawrence's chattel and nothing more. She allowed herself a glimpse of the future, imagining herself trailing around after Lawrence in much the same way as she had witnessed Mrs. Heeley doing, stopping when he stopped, laughing when he laughed, even if the joke was unfunny or his laughter inappropriate, and repeating some of Lawrence's endless chatter about artifacts and ancient mysteries.

She shuddered, and for the first time in her young life, Clara began to question whether she really wanted to be Lawrence's wife at all. She put the thought firmly from her mind. Uncle Anthony had been good to her and anyway, he had said that their union was foretold to him in a vision or some such hadn't he? In which case, if it is God's will that they be married then she would simply have to help Lawrence all she could. After all, was God really all that interested in the social standings of upper-class families?

Clara allowed herself a huge yawn, reminding her of what a tiring day she had had and how exhausted she actually was. As she closed her eyes, she let the exhaustion wash over her body, relaxing her muscles and allowing her to succumb to the peaceful state of slumber. However, just before she slipped off into a fitful sleep, an idea popped into her head. Was this a way forward? Was this a message from the good Lord, perhaps answering her prayers? Clara didn't know but tomorrow she planned on giving it far more thought. With that in mind, she drifted off happily, to sleep and to dream.

***

The following morning dawned bright and clear and Clara woke early having hatched her plan which, after breakfast, she fully intended to put into practice. She sat up in bed and pulled back the covers, swinging her legs around as she fished around underneath the bed for her slippers. A polite tap sounded at the interconnecting door between her room and the small sitting room both she and Amelia shared. Once upon a time, it had been her school room, a place of learning where Amelia could pass on all of her knowledge to her pupil, but for some years now it had been remodeled in keeping with Clara's age.

"Come in Nursie, I'm awake."

Clara berated herself for slipping back into calling Amelia by her old pet name, but it was an old habit that refused to die away and would sometimes resurface if she wasn't paying close attention. Such as this morning when she really couldn't find her blasted slippers. She allowed herself a cheeky smile. She suspected that even now she would've had slapped legs for that one.

"Good morning Cla-Clara! What on earth are you doing? Are you unwell?" Amelia stopped in the doorway to find

Clara's unmentionables gracing the air where her head would normally be.

Clara's muffled voice came from beneath the bed. "No, no, I'm not unwell, I simply cannot find my slippers. They were here when I retired I'm certain. But this morning they seem to have vanished."

Amelia tutted and rolled her eyes. "I really do feel we could do without the theatrics, Miss Johnson, certainly so early in the morning. I can see your slippers they are on this side of the bed and certainly not where you are clumsily impersonating a duck." She smiled to herself as she watched Clara clasp her hand to her behind in dismay and shuffle herself round to retrieve her slippers.

"I am most dreadfully sorry Amelia. What a sight for you to have seen!"

Amelia let out a chuckle. "Well, it was rather. However, you are now the right way up so shall we wash and dress for breakfast?"

Amelia crossed to Clara's closet and pulled out a clean dress, underthings, and petticoat. She carried them over to her screen and waited while Clara washed. As she passed each garment to Clara, Amelia asked her what she planned to do that day.

"I have a good many things that I wish to have done by the end of the day," Clara informed her. "I had promised Uncle Anthony that I would accompany him to old Mrs. Seabright's cottage this afternoon as she has been ill of late and I find

Uncle Anthony's work very interesting and worthwhile."

Amelia knew that this was true. Anthony Cavendish had always invested a great deal of his time and effort into helping the needy within his parish and Clara had always held him in very high regard for it.

"And what of this morning?" Amelia was always keen to encourage Clara to plan out her day. She was a firm believer in never wasting a moment of the time that you have on God's green earth as you will never be able to take it back.

"I have some correspondence to address this morning, and I really do need to visit Mrs. Bloomindale's."

Mrs. Bloomindale had been an excellent milliner for the best part of thirty years and Amelia had always purchased both her and Clara's various headwear from her little shop on the corner of Chalmers Street. Indeed, if Amelia had not become a governess she had always thought it would've been lovely to work in Mrs. Bloomindale's hat shop helping all the young ladies to choose the perfect headpiece for their coiffeur.

Clara emerged from behind her screen clad in her underthings and corset. Amelia pulled the laces tight to give Clara the desired shape and then tied them off, securing the garment in place. Clara then stepped into her dress. After setting her hair and donning her boots, Amelia deemed Clara fit to attend breakfast and followed her down to the dining room where Anthony was already seated.

Mrs. Dimbleby brought in two platters covered with stainless steel cloches and set them upon the dining table next to a tureen full of scrambled eggs. Clara drank in the delicious aroma of bacon and sausages, her stomach already reminding her that it had been hours since her last meal. The cook disappeared back into the kitchen and returned carrying a tray laden with four racks of hot toast and a silver butter dish. She placed these at equal intervals down the table and retired once more to the kitchen to brew two pots of tea and coffee respectively.

"Good morning Clara, I trust you slept well?" Anthony greeted his adopted daughter with a warm smile.

Clara returned the smile in kind as she took her place at the table accompanied by Amelia. "Beautifully thank you, uncle. Are you well?" Clara reached over and lifted the cover from the sausages, transferred two to her plate, and replaced the cloche.

Anthony beamed at his young ward. "Good to hear it, my dear. I am indeed very well for I have, this very morning, received news that my nephew Alexander is to be gracing us with his presence for an extended stay and it is my fond hope that he will help me in one or two matters pertaining to an obscure law that has been troubling me of late." He cut into his bacon hungrily and shoveled a large forkful into his waiting mouth before continuing, "Good morning Miss Orm. Am I to have the pleasure of your company at church this morning? My organist is still indisposed and the choir is in desperate need of your services."

Amelia smiled broadly, pleased at being asked back again. "Of course, sir, I shall be honored to accompany the choir."

"Excellent my dear lady, I shall be meeting my choristers at ten o'clock this morning and would deem it a pleasure if you would care to join me in a light stroll across to St. James'."

Amelia, her mouth full of hot scrambled egg, nodded her consent and swallowed her food as quickly as she could. "Thank you, sir, that is most kind." She turned to Clara. "I shall be passing the mailbox this morning, Clara dear, if you have your correspondence prepared I should be able to deliver it for you."

Clara placed her knife and fork neatly on the plate in front of her. "In which case, may I be excused as I really do need to write to dear Miss Fenton. She has been bedridden this last week and I really ought to see if she is any better."

Anthony gave his permission, so Clara left the table and made swiftly for the door, anxious to finish her letter before Amelia headed out with Reverend Cavendish for choir practice. As she reached for the door handle, however, Lawrence came bursting into the room. The door handle smashed into Clara's thigh sending her sprawling to the ground with a sickening crunch as she caught the corner of the sideboard on her way down.

"Oh, Clara, I am so dreadfully sorry! Have I injured you? Are you hurt?" Lawrence's face was full of worry and concern as he knelt down to assess any damage that he might have done and to help the poor unfortunate Clara to her feet.

"No, no, I'm fine..." Clara winced with pain as she attempted to reassure Lawrence that no harm had been done. Mrs. Dimbleby came bustling across the room followed by

Amelia and Anthony bringing up the rear.

"Lawrence, you have again disappointed me. That is twice in as many days now. How dare you tear about in such a manner! Young Clara here could be seriously injured," Anthony reprimanded his son.

"Let me help you, dear," Mrs. Dimbleby said as she fussed about Clara like a mother hen tending to her chicks.

"I really am most awfully sorry Clara, I do feel dreadful. Is there anything I can do?" Lawrence looked so forlorn and sorry for himself that Clara couldn't help but smile at the silly, sensitive creature, despite the awful pain welling up in her thigh.

"Would you be so kind as to carry Clara into the sitting room and place her on the sofa? I wish to inspect her for any injuries," Amelia asked Lawrence, who immediately scooped Clara up in his arms.

"Yes, yes, of course, Miss Orm. It is the very least I can do."

As Clara lay, held fast in Lawrence's arms, she was surprised to find that it didn't feel as she had imagined it would. For years, her dreams of being carried by Lawrence in such a way had always felt more, well, romantic. But this didn't feel anything more than one friend lifting another. There was care there, of course, there was, but not the love or excitement that she had expected there to have been.

Lawrence placed her carefully down onto the sofa in the main sitting room and promptly left, still feeling very remorseful at what had happened. He knew that perhaps he didn't pay enough attention to the world around him but his museum and his vision possessed every waking moment and it simply had not ever occurred to him that others may not share his feeling on the matter. He paced up and down in the hallway. Not daring to leave in case he should be sent to fetch Doctor Pearson.

"Stop pacing Lawrence, it serves no other purpose than to wear out a perfectly serviceable carpet." Anthony Cavendish had settled himself on the bottom stair and was watching his son twitch back and forth. Lawrence did as he was bid and promptly joined his father.

"Do you think I may have done her serious harm, Father?"

Anthony could see by Lawrence's expression that he was genuinely concerned for Clara's wellbeing. Perhaps the boy was coming around to the idea of marriage after all.   "Let us pray not. However, ladies are a delicate breed and we must assume that a physician may be needed and ready ourselves for such an eventuality." Anthony regarded his son, twitching and bouncing his legs up and down in worried impatience. Lawrence needed something to calm his fraught nerves.

"Cast all your anxiety on him because he cares for you," he recited.

Lawrence looked at his father, his eyes wide with hope at the reverend's wise words. "I Peter 5:7." He sighed and leaned on his knees in an effort to keep them still as father and son waited for news of Clara's condition. They had not the need to wait for long, however, as presently the door opened and

Amelia appeared. She was wearing her 'no-nonsense' expression that she used when dealing with the girls in Sunday school. Lawrence shot up from his makeshift seat on the stair.

"What news Miss Orm, is she alright?"

Amelia took a deep intake of breath. "Well," she said, letting it all out again in a protracted sigh. "There is no need for a doctor, but she is very shaken and I have no doubt that she will suffer some severe bruising. However, I do have some witch hazel and alcohol for the treatment of such maladies in the bathroom cabinet. If you would be so kind as to fetch it please, Mr. Cavendish? I have asked Mrs. Dimbleby for a basin of cooled boiled water and some clean rags."

"Certainly Miss Orm," Lawrence replied as he bounded up the stairs in search of the tonic Amelia had prescribed for Clara's bruising. He must be far more diligent in future. Dreams were all very well he thought, but hurting Clara had upset him far more than he had realized. He stopped at the bathroom door. Hurting Clara had been bad enough, but what if he had knocked into poor Sophie. The mere thought made him ill. It wasn't that he cared more for Sophie than for Clara, but Clara had always seemed more robust than gentle, sweet Sophie.

Grabbing the tincture from the cabinet shelf and dashing back down to the sitting room, he made his mind up to try to pay more attention to his surroundings. After all, his vision had already upset his father, threatened to ruin the good family name, and now damaged his sister, he could not afford any more unpleasantness on his account.

"Thank you, sir. However, I was beginning to think that you were unable to find it as you had taken so long." Amelia took the bottle from Lawrence's outstretched hand and disappeared back into the sitting room, closing the heavy wooden door behind her.

"Right then Clara dear, this may sting a little," she said as she tipped a few drops of the potion onto a sterilized rag and held it to the side of Clara's outer thigh. Clara flinched as a strange, sharp, tingling sensation spread out across her skin.

The bruise had already begun to show, a large purple and blue mark stretching nearly the length of her thigh. A knock sounded at the door.

"Clara is not in a suitable position to receive guests yet Mr. Cavendish," Amelia called out. "You shall be sent for once I have finished tending to the damage you have inflicted."

"It's Mrs. Dimbleby ma'am with a fresh basin of water, shall I bring it in or set it down out here?"

Amelia opened the door and took the basin from the cook. "Thank you, I dare say we shan't need anymore."

The cook nodded.   "Very good ma'am."

Chapter
Four

April seventeenth, 1823

Dearest Ophelia,

I hope this epistle finds you well and in a favorable state of health. I am writing to ask if you are in a position to receive Clara as your house guest on a matter of convalescence. She has recently been unfortunate enough to fall victim to an unpleasant accident that has left her shaken and delicate and I feel that she should benefit greatly from young Florence's companionship.

I look forward to your timely acquiescence.

Yours gratefully,

Amelia

Amelia sealed the envelope and looked in on Clara before accompanying Anthony to choir practice. Clara had been made very comfortable in the sitting room and would be attended to by Mrs. Dimbleby should she need anything further. After all, she should be back within the hour. Clara glanced down and took note of the addressee of the letter Amelia was holding. This had worked out far better than she had hoped. She had not wanted to lie to her family after all, but she had already decided that she would need to visit a friend in order to successfully implement the first part of her plan.

But now Amelia had actually insisted that she take an extended stay with Florence Kettering, one of her oldest and dearest friends. Perhaps this could be counted as a little divine intervention?

"I shall be out for no more than an hour Clara, shall you be comfortable until then?"

Clara smiled brightly. "Yes, of course, Amelia, I am most comfortable thank you and Mrs. Dimbleby has gone to fetch a tome she feels I may enjoy."

Amelia smiled, a book was always a worthwhile and pleasant way to pass the time. "Very well then my dearest, I shall take my leave."

***

It was a mere two days before Amelia received a reply to her letter offering their sympathies for Clara's unfortunate accident and stating that 'of course, she must come to stay' and that they shall expect her presently. As Amelia had no doubt that her childhood friend would acquiesce to her request, Clara's bags were all packed and ready for her to leave.

"Make sure to get plenty of rest and to offer our deepest

gratitude to Mr. and Mrs. Kettering." Amelia leaned into the cab to kiss Clara before sending her click-clacking her way across town to the home of Joseph and Ophelia Kettering.

The cabbie shook the reigns and steered his horse away from St. Michael's vicarage and on down Queens Street. Clara leaned forward a little in order to catch a view of the Dock Street Theatre. She squinted as they drove past, hoping for a glimpse of the performers in their grand costumes, but all she saw were closed doors. She stifled a moan as the movement of the cab jostled her, forcing her sore leg to press against the side of the seat. Suddenly, she was thrown to the right as the cabbie took the corner onto East Bay a little too quickly. Clara glanced up to watch the familiar pillars of the Exchange and Provost drift past as the cab clattered on towards East Battery and the seafront.

After what felt like an eternity, the cab driver slowed his horse as the handsome residence came into view. Ophelia Brown had married early and had chosen for her husband Mr. Joseph Kettering, a man some ten years her senior but who had great influence in the world of cotton manufacture. Indeed, it was Ophelia who had introduced her childhood friend Amelia to the Johnson household as Joseph and Willis had been business rivals, but also very dear friends.

Clara took the hand proffered to her by the cab driver as she stepped down awkwardly onto the cobbles outside 'Morning View House', her injured leg stiff and sore from the journey. It would be good to see Florence again. Indeed, Florence had been unable to attend her birthday tea due to her visiting an ailing grandparent and Clara looked forward to spending the next few weeks with her immensely. The cabbie picked up Clara's luggage and walked with her up the stone steps to the front door. He yanked the bell pull and they waited. The door was answered by a small girl, hardly older than Clara herself.

"Yes, ma'am?"

"I'm Miss Johnson, I believe I am expected," Clara replied politely as a friendly voice from inside rang out.

"Clara, my dear girl, how good it is to see you! Don't keep Miss Johnson waiting on the doorstep Prudence, she is our guest." Joseph Kettering was a slender gentleman with striking good looks and strong blue eyes. He wore his silver hair slicked back from his face and it was usual to see a broad smile playing on his chiseled features. He was the kind of man whose warm-hearted demeanor and an infectious smile spread out to all those near to him. Clara felt a glow of warmth as he greeted her fondly.

"Very good, sir." The small, spindly girl who was apparently called Prudence, stepped back into the shadows to let Clara and her luggage into a rather grand entrance hall.

"Good morning Mr. Kettering. Please accept my heartfelt thanks for allowing me here to convalesce, I am so looking forward to seeing Florence."

Joseph beamed at Clara as he tipped the cabby and picked up Clara's bags. "Nonsense, we are happy to have you here. Although I must confess when Ophelia received Amelia's letter we were all concerned as to what had befallen you, my dear. You must tell us all over luncheon," he headed towards the stairs but stopped suddenly, a look of concern crossing his usually cheerful face.

"Oh, my apologies my dear Clara. Are your injuries such that you are unable to manage the stairs?" he asked.

Clara smiled at his thoughtfulness and thought Mrs. Kettering truly blessed to have such a kind and thoughtful husband. "I believe that Amelia has exaggerated the extent of the damage. I have sustained some painful bruising but very little else. You need not worry about the stairs, Mr. Kettering."

The beaming smile returned to Joseph's face as he led Clara to the room that was to be hers for the duration of her stay. Clara tried desperately to hide the mounting pressure and pain she felt in her thigh from Joseph. However, she couldn't help wincing a little with each step. Joseph, with his back to Clara, didn't appear to notice.

"Ophelia and Florence are not currently at home, but I do expect them back shortly." Joseph stopped outside a closed door on the first floor of the house. "Ah, here we are my dear. Please, feel free to treat this room as your own whilst you are here. I shall ask Prudence to come and attend to your unpacking. Please take your time and come down to the dining room when you are good and ready. And may I say how lovely it is to have you staying with us." He set Clara's luggage down on the floor and turned to leave.

"Thank you for your kindness, Mr. Kettering," Clara called after him. He gave Clara a slight bow, making her giggle and left the room, closing the door behind him.

Clara looked around her comfortable bedroom. Her bed was much the same as the one she had at home, however, the canopy was a pretty periwinkle blue and not the swathes of white as she was used to. She grimaced in pain as she crossed to her luggage to retrieved her vanity case. The bruise on her leg making it painful to walk. Her undergarments had started to feel a little tight on that side too. She tried to put it from her mind as she placed her hairbrush and hairpins on the dresser and removed her bonnet, hanging it neatly on the stand by the window.

The room was big but felt cozy with a small en-suite bathroom discretely placed behind a large double wardrobe. Clara slipped out of her overcoat and placed it on the bed together with her gloves and parasol. She glanced in the mirror to make sure that her bonnet hadn't caused any of her hairpins to slip. Satisfied that she had traveled well and that she was of a fit state to present herself at lunch, she left the room.

Just as she was closing the door, Prudence walked up behind her. She stood to one side waiting for Clara to notice she was there. Clara turned in the direction of the stairs and jumped, giving a little yelp of surprise at the silent Prudence, waiting dutifully to enter her room and unpack her things.

"Please forgive me Prudence, but you startled me." She looked at the tiny maid. Her short, wavy, light brown hair stuck out from underneath her starched, white cap.

Prudence looked at her feet, embarrassed. "I beg your pardon, miss, but Mr. Kettering has asked if I would attend to you while you are staying here."

Clara smiled at the shy maid. "Thank you, Prudence, that would be most welcome. I am in need of a lady's maid and I believe that we shall grow to be good friends."

Prudence looked up at Clara and smiled weakly. This was the first time that Clara had got a good look at her face and she had to stop herself from recoiling in horror at an angry scar that ran the length of her cheek, stopping short of her eye. Surely the Ketterings hadn't been the cause? The wound looked freshly treated and Clara couldn't help but wince a little at the thought of how much it must have hurt poor Prudence to receive it. And here was she being pampered over her own tender bruise. She felt more than a little ashamed.

Prudence dropped her head again, realizing that Clara had noticed her disfiguration. She gestured to the door. "May I, miss?"

Clara stepped back to let her pass. "Yes of course. Thank you."

Prudence paused, clearly unused to being thanked, before opening Clara's bedroom door and shuffling inside.

As Clara was making her way gingerly downstairs, she wondered if it would be rude to inquire about Prudence and her horrific scar to the Ketterings. Deciding that yes it probably was, she filed it away to discuss with Prudence herself at a later date and turned in the direction of the dining room. The delicious smell of freshly baked bread, honey and warm scones greeted her as she pushed open the dining room door. She found the room empty, save for the Kettering's cook who was busily laying the table with a glorious spread of cheeses, baked goods, ships biscuits, and a large ham. She smiled warmly at Clara as she entered.

"Good afternoon miss, I'm Miss Parker. You look as though you could do with a good meal, my girl. There's plenty here. Mrs. Kettering asked for a spread of everything so you'd have a choice."

Clara beamed at Miss Parker. She was the sort of woman you would have expected to have been a cook by trade. A plump, jolly, middle-aged person with two sparkling eyes surrounded by laughter lines. Clara liked her at once.

"Thank you, Miss Parker, I'm a guest of Mr. and Mrs. Kettering. My name is Miss Johnson."

Miss Parker nodded as Clara lowered herself gingerly into a seat at the table and waited for the family to arrive.

"Would you be wanting strawberry or blackcurrant preserve, miss?" Miss Parker asked as she held up two identical looking jam jars.

"Oh, always strawberry, Miss Parker thank you," Clara replied solemnly. She could never understand anyone wanting blackcurrant anything, let alone preserve.

"Duly noted, very good, miss." Miss Parker chuckled to herself as she placed one of the jars down on the table in front of Clara and trundled her trolley back through the doorway and off towards the kitchen.

"Clara! How wonderful! You have arrived safely," a new voice called to her which was achingly familiar.

Clara jumped up from her chair, a hot twinge of pain shot down through her thigh reminding her to take more care. She carefully walked over to Florence. "Oh, Florence, it's so good to see you. My, you are looking fine my dear, are you well?"

Florence, a petite, willowy girl with a headful of dark curls, embraced her friend tightly before escorting her back to her seat at the table. "Wonderfully so, but what is this I hear of an accident? When mother read out Amelia's letter I very nearly hitched up my skirts and ran all the way across town to see you, Clara."

Clara laughed. Florence had always been flighty and enthusiastic. She loved her dearly.

"Clara, Joseph informed me of your arrival only moments ago. I am dreadfully sorry that we were not here to greet you," another voice called to her. Ophelia Kettering was what many would call beguiling. A true beauty in every sense of the word. She wore her straight, auburn hair long and let it flow loosely down her back making her, already willowy, figure appear even taller.

She elegantly glided into the room, the epitome of sophisticated grace. Clara had caught Joseph gazing in awe at his mesmerizing wife on more than one occasion. She had always thought it lovely to see. It made her think of her own marriage plans and also of the odd comment that old Aunt Lucy had made to her on the afternoon of her party. She wondered if this is what she had meant and she committed herself to observe any glances that Mr. Kettering made to his wife.

"Ah, the family are all seated. Good afternoon my dears, did everything go well with the dress fitting Florence?" Joseph asked.

Mrs. Kettering shot a warning look at her husband who seemed to understand and abruptly changed the subject. But not before Clara had picked up on the exchange. What was going on?

"My word, Miss Parker has indeed outshone herself this afternoon," he said as he bowed his head leading the small gathering into grace. "Now," he said, clapping his hands together for a good job well done, "I think I shall start with one of her delightful cream scones if I may."

Ophelia passed around the basket full of freshly baked scones still warm from the oven. "Please Clara, help yourself and make sure to eat your fill. You are here to convalesce are you not? We cannot have you losing strength."

Clara took a scone and broke it open on her plate ready to spread it with strawberry preserve and thick clotted cream. She took a large bite forcing the stiff cream to ooze out of the doughy sandwich. She allowed herself a few seconds, reveling in the texture as a large strawberry burst in her mouth sending sweet, sticky juice sliding down her throat. She replaced the sugary treat and reached for her napkin to deal with the excess cream.

"Oh yes, your accident," squealed Florence. "Do tell us what happened Clara."

Clara put down her knife as she relived the fall for the

Ketterings. "And so here I am," she finished. "Although I hardly feel that it was necessary to put you to all this trouble, Mrs. Kettering. I have suffered nothing more than bruising. Honestly, it is poor Lawrence whom I feel has suffered more. He really did feel awfully wretched and has been easing himself in and out of rooms ever since."

Mr. Kettering gave a hearty laugh. "Still, it is a blessing you were not injured further, my dear."

After the lunch, things had been cleared away and Clara had convinced Ophelia that she had indeed eaten enough, Florence and Clara were allowed to retire to the garden where the two ladies could chat more freely.

"I say, Clara, did he really scoop you up in his arms like that? How romantic."

Clara smiled weakly, giving a nondescript 'hmm' by way of an answer. She still wasn't sure how she felt about it all and was not about to say something to harm the carefully laid plans of her late father and her guardian—even to Florence. However, Florence hadn't noticed as she seemed a little preoccupied.

"Clara dear, I really would like you to be the first to know."

Clara looked into her friends shining eyes, getting caught in her euphoria and feeling herself starting to get excited. "Oh? And what is it that you wish me to be the first to know about?" she asked, but her face had already broken out into a big, beaming grin, even before the first word was out of Florence's mouth.

"I'm to be married, next month."

Clara squealed with delight and embraced her dearest friend tightly. "Oh Flo, that is truly wonderful news. To whom?" Although she felt immensely happy for Florence, there was a part of her, deep within herself, that wished it were her. She started to feel a little hot and nauseous but said nothing to Florence. It was unthinkable to ruin her moment.

"Mr. Owen Baxter. He is a senior executive within my father's firm. Father shall be making him a partner in the company once we are married. Isn't it fantastic?"

"Baxter?" Baxter, Baxter, there was something about the name that Clara recognized but she could not for the life of her remember why. Perhaps she had heard Mr. Kettering mention the name or maybe Florence had spoken of him to her previously and she had simply forgotten. She tried to put it to the back of her mind but she couldn't help feeling that the name was important to her for some reason.

Well, whatever it was, she felt sure that she would remember soon, and in the meantime, it really was wonderful to be with Florence again, she could see weeks of fun stretching out ahead of her. The familiar sharp pain pulsated through her leg causing her to bite her lip, not knowing how much longer she could keep her discomfort a secret from her friend.

"Yes, do you know of him?" Florence gripped Clara's hands in excitement.

Clara shook her head. "I don't think I do dearest, tell me all about it, how did he come to propose?"

Then, Florence launched herself into the entire story of how Mr. Baxter had been to see her on many occasions, at first to see her father on business but afterward mainly to see herself. Clara did her best to listen as she felt another wave of pain-filled nausea wash over her.

"And then, one afternoon, Mother invited him to stay for tea, after which she suggested we take a stroll around the gardens as it was such a lovely day. We stopped there underneath the Hawthorne tree and he asked me to be his wife." She paused, waiting for Clara to tell her how romantic it all was, but Clara had remembered where she had heard the name Baxter before.

"Clara dear, what on earth is the matter, are you feeling unwell? Oh, I am wicked to have kept you standing on your aching bruise while I prattled on about Mr. Baxter. Come with me." She led Clara to a long, low swing attached to one of the trees at the bottom of the Kettering's large garden as Clara tried in vain to convince Florence that she had not been taken ill, even though she was now beginning to feel very faint indeed. She lowered Clara on to it.

"Thank you, Flo, but honestly, my bruises hardly hurt at all now." This was certainly not true. The large black bruise on the outside of her thigh was currently throbbing and seemed to be straining against her pantyhose as the pain got more severe, but she really didn't want Florence feeling any worse.

"Tell me, is your Mr. Baxter related to a Professor Baxter of the University of South Carolina?" she asked as she sat further back on the swing. She could feel a strange hotness creeping up her body.

Florence tipped her head to one side as she pondered this question. "I don't believe he has ever mentioned such a connection no. Why? Whom is Professor Baxter?" Florence wanted very much to know if there were any relatives that she should be adding to the wedding guest list.

"A steadying of ancient history and archeology. He held a position at the institution where Lawrence received his education, but from what I understand he has moved now to the Charleston College."

Florence nodded as though making a mental note to speak with Owen about Professor Baxter the next time he came to call on her.

"Have you made many wedding preparations?" Clara asked. "You'll be wed at St. Michael's of course." She was now in constant pain accompanied by waves of giddy sickness as the swing moved gently back and forth. She tried to steady it with her foot.

Florence nodded earnestly. "Oh, of course, Reverend Cavendish has always delivered such engaging sermons and as Owe... I mean, Mr. Baxter is of St Michael's parish it is natural we shall be married there." Florence grabbed Clara's hands and, after giving them a squeeze, she delivered her second piece of news. "And Clara dear, you will be my bridesmaid, won't you? It has to be you. You must say you will or else I shall pout terribly." She contorted her face into a perfect pout making Clara giggle despite her mounting discomfort.

"Flo, you know I will! I couldn't ever say no to you, I would consider it an honor to accompany you as your bridesmaid." Clara, now feeling as though the world were spinning around her tried very hard to keep her expression cheerful. She would not have liked to have ruined Florence's big moment.

Florence gave Clara another smothering cuddle as a rumble of thunder was heard in the distance. "If I am any judge, I would say if we don't hurry back inside, we shall both be caught in a terrible downpour."

Clara grinned, but this quickly contorted into a grimace of pain as she tried to stand, her painful leg now looking quite alarmingly swollen. Her leg gave way underneath her and she fell to the ground.

"Oh no, Clara!" her companion cried at the sight. "Stay here and I will fetch Father to help," Florence told her as she hitched up her skirts and ran full speed back up to the house. Skidding into the kitchen, she almost collided with Miss Parker.

"Oh, Miss Kettering, you did give me a start. What on God's green earth are you doing throwing yourself around in that manner?"

"I'm so sorry Miss Parker, Clara has been taken quite ill, I must fetch Father." She dashed out and into the hallway. "Father! Father!" she called as she made her way to her father's study.

"Florence, what is the meaning of this, what has happened?" asked Joseph as he appeared out of his private study at the sound of his daughter's urgent call.

"Clara's leg has given way, it is swelling quite badly, she cannot stand."

Joseph raced out into the garden, catching Prudence as he did so. "Fetch Doctor Fletcher please, Prudence, and quickly."

Prudence nodded and darted out through the front door and off into town to look for Doctor Fletcher. Joseph raced across the lawn, the rain now starting to pound the ground with large droplets as the storm approached. He could see a figure lying on the ground and made for it.

"Miss Johnson? Clara? Can you hear me?"

But Clara could not respond. Picking her up in his strong arms, he marched back into the house carrying the unconscious Clara gingerly so as not to damage her leg further. He placed her on the daybed in the parlor and called for his wife. "Ophelia, we need smelling salts and clean towels, I fear this leg might be more than just a little bruised."

His wife appeared at the top of the stairs. "Joseph, what has happened?" she asked as she gracefully sped down the stairs giving the illusion that her feet hadn't touched a single step. Grabbing her purse from the closet beneath the stairs, she pulled out her bottle of salts and followed her husband to where Clara was lying, still unconscious and dripping wet on the daybed. A strange mixture of blood and pus seeping through her clothes.

She knelt down by Clara and took the stopper out of the bottle. She waved it under her nose and Clara's eyelids fluttered as she started to come around. Ophelia placed her hand on Clara's face and stared up at her husband in shock.

"She has a terrible fever, we need a physician."

"I have sent Prudence for Doctor Fletcher, my dear, all we can do now is hope and pray. We must put all our trust and faith in God for Clara is in his hands now."

"Is there anything I can do to help, Mother? Has she come around yet?" Florence, her pretty face full of concern for her young friend, lingered in the doorway, one ear out for Prudence returning with the doctor, the other for any news of Clara.

"That is very kind of you my dear, but I fear that none of us are of any use at all until Doctor Fletcher should arrive." Ophelia wafted her small bottle of strong-smelling salts under Clara's nose once more, but it did little good. She would stir and open her eyes for perhaps a few minutes before they snapped shut again as she lost consciousness.

"Florence, fetch a clean flannel from the bathroom and soak it with cold water and bring it to me. There's a good girl." Ophelia replaced the stopper in the top of the salts bottle and stashed it back into her purse in case they should be needed again.

Florence came dashing back, a dripping flannel held

between her two hands. "I didn't wring it, Mother, was that right?" she asked as she handed it over.

Thanking her daughter, Ophelia set to bathing and cooling Clara's skin in an attempt to lower her fever.

"Sir, Doctor Fletcher sir," a breathless Prudence called as she came hurrying into the parlor with Doctor Fletcher following close behind.

"Thank you for attending so quickly Doctor Fletcher, it is our guest young Miss Johnson. We understand that she has recently suffered a fall and has sustained heavy bruising to her thigh, however she was taking a stroll in the garden with Florence when she collapsed. We have been unable to rouse her." Joseph spoke quickly, anxious that Doctor Fletcher be informed of the facts but would not be delayed in administering treatment to Clara.

"I see." Doctor Fletcher knelt beside Clara. He felt her clammy skin. "This child has a fever, I shall need to see her bruising."

Joseph called to Prudence and the two of them left Clara in the capable hands of Doctor Fletcher. "Prudence, I fear that Miss Johnson shall be bedridden for the duration of her stay with us and it is my wish that you shall attend to her every need. I shall be excusing you of your daily duties to us so that you may be of constant service to Miss Johnson."

Prudence nodded. "Of course, sir, I shall be only too glad to assist the young lady."

Joseph smiled. Prudence was a good child and had been

invaluable to the household since she had first arrived. And there was no doubt in his mind that she would do Clara well. "I shall expect you to be a companion for Miss Johnson as Florence has her vows to prepare for," Joseph added solemnly.

Presently, the door opened and Doctor Fletcher came to speak with Joseph. "The extent of her injuries is severe. He left leg has some internal fluid forming underneath an abnormally large hematoma which must be drained immediately. I shall require a number of items from my surgery."

"And you shall have them, sir. Tell me what is it that you require and I shall fetch them myself," replied Joseph, already pulling on his over jacket and reaching for his hat.

"Good man," said Doctor Fletcher, scribbling out a list which he gave to Joseph. "Speak with my housekeeper she shall direct you."

Taking the list, Joseph called for Prudence to accompany him. "I may need some assistance in the form of an extra pair of hands." Prudence dutifully fell in with her employers' step as they dashed up the road to Doctor Fletcher's surgery.

"She's waking, doctor," Ophelia called as Clara's eyelids began to flicker. She let out a soft moan before again slipping back into unconsciousness.

"It would be far better for all concerned if she were to remain in her current state while I perform the procedure as she will be less likely to experience pain, nor to move thus making it harder for me to drain her properly." Doctor Fletcher removed his coat and turned up his sleeves.

Ophelia turned to a very pale Florence. "Fetch a basin, a kettle of boiling water and one of cold, and a bar of honey soap from Miss Parker. Then take three clean towels from the laundry," she ordered in a voice that told Florence that time was of the essence here.

"Of course, Mother." Then Florence sped off, eager to do all she could for Clara.

"How did the young lady sustain her injuries?" Doctor Fletcher enquired of Ophelia as she carefully exposed Clara's sore swollen leg ready for Doctor Fletcher's treatment.

"She was knocked down onto a hardwood dining room floor by a heavy wooden door as an overenthusiastic family member crashed through it. I believe her thigh bore the brunt of the door handle and the corner of a heavy wooden piece of furniture."

Said aloud it sounded comical, but if Doctor Fletcher had found it funny he didn't allow himself even a hint of a smile as he surveyed his patient. A knock sounded at the door as Florence and Miss Parker arrived with the items asked for.

"Begging your pardon ma'am, but I believe the good doctor's items may have arrived also." As soon as Miss Parker had spoken Prudence entered holding a large bag.

"Excellent, place it there, young miss." Doctor Fletcher turned to the waiting crowd. "I shall require two to assist me and everyone else may retire, but I must inform you that the nature of this procedure is not for the faint of heart."

Ophelia, concerned for the delicate disposition of her daughter, volunteered herself and Prudence.

"I shall need you, Mrs. Kettering, at Miss Johnson's head and Prudence, I shall need you to hold this bag as high above your head as possible whilst balancing atop this chair."

Prudence leaped up onto the chair as Ophelia braced Clara's head against her lap.

"I need you to keep the bag as high and still as possible Prudence and Mrs. Kettering Clara may react, if she does I wish for you to try and calm her as much as possible as I need for her to be as still as she can be." With his patient braced and his hands and tools clean, Doctor Fletcher set about the task of draining Clara's pulsating leg.

Chapter
Five

The procedure had been fairly straightforward from what Prudence could see. The difficult part had been holding the bag up there for over twenty-five minutes as Doctor Fletcher sliced into Clara's leg. Mrs. Kettering held Clara's head and stroked her hair, speaking kindly to her throughout as the young doctor inserted tubes at strategic points around the large swelling.

"When you go through deep waters and great trouble, I will be with you. When you go through rivers of difficulty, you will not drown. When you walk through the fire of oppression, you will not be burned up—the flames will not consume you," Ophelia recited as she continued to stroke Clara's golden hair.

"Ah, Isaiah 43:2." Doctor Fletcher nodded in approval. "'Tis a good choice ma'am, but I have always felt that Jeremiah 30:17 is a far more appropriate passage in times such as these."

Ophelia smiled warmly as she leaned in towards Clara's ear to recite the familiar words. "For I will restore health to you, and your wounds I will heal, declares the Lord."

At this, Clara woke, stared at Mrs. Kettering in wide-eyed horror, and then immediately fell back into her sleep like state. Prudence knew more than anyone what Clara was feeling and she felt immensely sorry for her. She set her mind to holding the bag as still as she could while Doctor Fletcher continued drawing fluid from Clara's leg.

"That's excellent Prudence, my dear, you are doing a fine job and we shall soon have Miss Johnson sutured and bandaged," he praised.

Prudence beamed at the doctor's kind words of encouragement. She had not heard many words of kindness in her young life and it made her more determined than ever to make sure that she was the best possible ladies' maid she could be to Clara.

As the doctor pulled the last tube from Clara's thigh, he prepared his needle and got to work with mending the holes he had made. The work was fiddly and intricate but he continued tirelessly until it was stitched, cleaned, and bandaged. Then, Doctor Fletcher allowed Ophelia to re-dress Clara's leg.

"I believe that her fever should break now Mrs. Kettering and I shall take Prudence aside and teach her how to clean and dress the wounds as it is paramount that she avoids infection at all costs." He washed his blood-stained fingers, adjusted his shirt sleeves and cleaned and packed his tools.

"We are most grateful for your time and skill Doctor Fletcher. If you present your bill to my husband he shall pay you directly." Ophelia did not feel that she could leave Clara and continued to sit cradling her head in her lap, gently stroking her hair.

"Thank you, ma'am. I would strongly suggest that Miss Johnson keeps to her bed for at least three weeks. However, I shall be back within two to make sure that the wounds are clean and healing well and to remove the stitches." He turned to leave but stopped and cast his eyes up to where Prudence was still perched atop her chair, the bag high above her head and a pained expression gracing her face. He let out a loud laugh.

"My dear child, you can drop the bag now. Goodness me what devotion you have shown to your mistress. I do believe that I was right to have given that job to you." He was still shaking his head and tittering to himself when he left the room, only to be immediately set upon by a hysterical Florence.

"Oh, Doctor Fletcher is she... Has she... May I see her?"

Doctor Fletcher clasped her shoulders and told her that although her leg will now heal with care, she may be out of sorts and her fever still needs to break. "However," he added, smiling kindly at Florence. "I believe she shall make a full recovery."

Florence turned and collapsed into her father's arms, sobbing with relief.

"Now, now, don't take on so, Clara won't want to see you in such a state," said Joseph kindly, dabbing at her face with his clean handkerchief. "Why don't you run in and see if you can do anything for your mother while I settle our debt with Doctor Fletcher here."

Florence nodded and walked solemnly into the parlor. Doctor Fletcher gave Prudence a large pot of green substance which was to be rubbed onto the wounds three times daily and fresh bandages applied on top.

"On no account should the stitches be allowed to moisten or be washed with water," Doctor Fletcher warned as he pulled a bottle of rubbing alcohol from his large black leather bag. "This is to be used to clean the wounds before treatment and dressings can be applied."

Prudence took the bottle proffered to her by the doctor. "Yes, sir." She nodded solemnly, eager to make sure that she remembered everything correctly.

The doctor turned his attention to Joseph. "The emergency procedure, plus the cost of diagnosis and after treatment, shall be three dollars, sir."

Joseph counted out the money and handed the paper bills to Doctor Fletcher who took them and stuffed them into his inner jacket pocket.

"Many thanks, good sir, I shall take my leave. However, should you have any concerns, do not hesitate to send for me." Then Doctor Fletcher donned his hat and left Clara's wellbeing in the hands of the Ketterings and their staff.

Making his way back to his parlor door, Joseph knocked and waited, unsure as to what state Clara might be in.

"Come," Ophelia called brightly. Joseph pushed open the door and entered. Ophelia looked up at her husband and smiled. "She is still a little hot but the good doctor feels that her fever should break soon." She paused to look down at Clara, now sleeping peacefully. "I fear that she may be out for quite some time yet, but should wake with little to no memory of the procedure," she finished. Florence, who had seated herself as close to her stricken friend as possible, looked up at her mother, her eyes filled with tears.

"Oh, Mother, I am truly sorry, what a terrible thing to have happened, and all because I made her stroll too far in the garden. Prattling on as I was about Mr. Baxter, never giving one thought to her discomfort. Do you think she will ever forgive me?" Florence unpinned her handkerchief and taking the small, white lace square, dabbed at her eyes. She looked across at the shape of Clara's elevated leg beneath the blanket.

"Now, Florence, how could you be to blame, after all my dear, you did not inflict the wounds upon Clara yourself did you?" Ophelia reached down and took Florence's hands in her own. "Come now, it was simply the unpleasant outcome of an unfortunate accident, and now I do believe it is time that we transported Clara to bed." She turned to Prudence. "Pru..." she stopped. "Where is Prudence?"

But Prudence was already on her way upstairs to prepare Clara's bedroom in readiness to receive her patient. Sliding his strong arms beneath Clara's slight frame, Joseph lifted her carefully and easily from the makeshift operating slab that had once been the Kettering's parlor day bed and carried her gently up to her room. On entering he found that

Prudence had already opened the windows wide and turned down the bed. He placed Clara down onto the sheets and left the room as his wife, daughter and Clara's new ladies companion set about making her comfortable and getting her into her night things.

***

Clara didn't awake again until the next day when she felt dreadful about the whole situation. "Please accept my sincerest apologies for having put you all to so much trouble and please forward the doctor's bill to Amelia as I have no doubt she would be distressed to find you out of pocket on my account." Clara was sitting upright, her injured leg stretched out in front of her.

"I shall do no such thing, Clara. Doctor Fletcher's bill has been paid and we shall have no more talk of troubling us. Joseph was a very close friend of your father's and I am certain that he would deem it an honor to be of use to Willis' daughter in her hour of need." Ophelia smiled kindly at her before turning to her young maid. "Prudence here is to be your companion whilst you are bedridden my dear. Should you need or want for anything, Prudence shall see to you. Indeed, she was instrumental in administering the treatment that may well have saved your leg."

Prudence, unused to so much praise and attention, dropped her head as Clara turned to her.

"Prudence, I am forever in your debt and I am now certain that we shall become the dearest of friends." Clara beamed at her new companion warmly as Florence squeezed her hand.

"We shall have to get you fitted for your dress soon Clara and..." Florence trailed off as she noticed the look on her mother's face.

"I am dreadfully sorry Florence," Ophelia began, "but Doctor Fletcher has prescribed complete bed rest for Clara for at the very least three weeks." Florence gasped as she realized what this meant. "And so, it is with no little amount of regret that we must find another to act as a bridesmaid," she finished as Florence's eyes filled with tears.

"My dearest, I am truly sorry, what a terrible thing to have happened! I am to be so involved with the wedding preparations that I cannot spare more than an hour each day to come and see you, dearest heart." Florence leaned over and kissed Clara's forehead tenderly.

"Florence, it is I who must offer you my apologies as I was so looking forward to being involved in your lovely wedding." She turned her attention to Ophelia who was busying herself with moving furniture closer to Clara's bed in order that she should have everything she needed.

She placed a small golden handbell on Clara's nightstand, instructing her to ring if she should need anything, and that Prudence had been moved into the adjoining room. Clara looked across at the timid little maid and found it quite admirable that she had done all that she had for her over the last few hours. She owed her a great debt, that she knew.

"We shall leave you in Prudence's care, my dear, as I have some correspondence to deal with. Mr. Cavendish should learn of recent developments and I should expect a visit from

Amelia. Make sure that you rest Clara, Ophelia leaned over and kissed the top of Clara's head. "Florence my darling, please go to the kitchen and explain to Miss Parker that Clara is to have all meals prepared on a tray and to ring for Prudence once the food is ready." Then she left, leaving the door slightly ajar indicating that she expected Florence to follow forthwith.

"Please try and rest Clara, I shall not enjoy a single minute of my wedding preparations if I thought that you were not comfortable," Florence told her and looked into Clara's eyes earnestly.

"I am sure that Prudence will see to it that I am adhering to Doctor Fletcher's advice," Clara replied and watched Florence leave the room, letting the door fall closed behind her. She glanced across at Prudence who was still standing silently at the foot of the bed. "Pull up a chair Prudence and sit on this side of me. I should like to learn more about you." Clara watched as Prudence carried her dresser stool up to the side of her bed and set it down.

"That's better," she said as Prudence slowly lowered herself down, feeling very self-conscious and nervous. "Now, tell me, honestly now my dear, what is it that Doctor Fletcher has done to my leg? Mrs. Kettering did tell me, but I was still very confused and I am ashamed to say that I hadn't the faintest clue what she had meant."

Prudence smiled weakly as she tried her best to explain what had been done. "Well, miss, he bid me stand on a chair and hold a bag filled with fluids above my head as he..." she trailed off, afraid that the more unsavory aspects of Clara's treatment might bring on a relapse. "Forgive me ma'am, but my concern is for your emotional wellbeing. I do not want to shock or offend you in your fragile state." Prudence looked down at her hands clasped in her lap.

Her scar was clearly visible to Clara and she thought again about where she might have received such an angry and disfiguring gash. Although she thought it rude, she was incredibly curious to know what had happened and she was just trying to think of a way to broach the subject when she caught sight of her old bonnet hanging on its stand on the other side of the room. This triggered the memory of her plan and she berated herself that she would not now be at all able to implement it. She looked at Prudence and wondered whether she could discuss it with her, after all, she had only known her a few hours. Still, she was her companion and as such, she should be able to trust her. If only she could be sure it was the right thing to do.

In these situations, she usually would've asked Amelia's advice or taken Florence into her confidence, but as neither were an option to her now she figured that she would either have to take a chance and speak with Prudence about it or battle it alone. She decided that taking Prudence into her confidence might be the better option, but how could she approach the subject?

Prudence looked at her mistress, clearly deep in thought and mistook her expression of anguish over her unenviable decision for one of dis-ease pertaining to her recent operation. She decided to try and change the subject lest Clara asked her to describe the second stage of the procedure.

"Did you travel far to be with us, miss?" Prudence's soft, high voice pierced through Clara's daydreaming and brought her back to the present. She started guiltily.

"Oh Prudence, I am dreadfully sorry. I was engaging my mind on a matter completely unrelated," she admitted. "No, not very far as it happens. I live with the Reverend Cavendish and his family in the parish of St. Michael's across the other side of town in Queens Street." Clara asked her where she had originated from.

Prudence sighed deeply. She liked Clara and she was honored with her new role as her companion, but she really hadn't wanted to share her personal circumstances. But when you are asked a direct question by your mistress it is unwise not to answer.

"I have always lived in this part of town, miss."

Clara mistook this to mean that she had always lived with the Kettering family, but Prudence quickly corrected her.

"No mistress, I had only been in Mr. Kettering's employ for a number of weeks before your arrival." Prudence scanned her mind to try and find a subject to talk with Clara about that neither of them would feel too uncomfortable with. "Please, miss, forgive me for asking, but may I inquire as to how you came to be bruised so badly in the first place? Miss Florence said it was because of a gentleman." She looked down at her feet as she asked Clara about her bruises. Perhaps this was too personal? What was she supposed to talk about as a lady's companion anyway? Was it like being friends and sharing secrets or was she expected to keep a more formal relationship with Clara. She didn't know, but whatever she was expected to talk about, she would do her best.

"Well, it is certainly true that I have sustained my bruising as a result of a gentleman's actions yes," she replied. Prudence tensed, fearing that perhaps Clara had been attacked. "But nothing as dramatic as Florence has made it all out to be." Clara shifted in the sheets, attempting to make her sore leg more comfortable. "You see," she continued. "Lawrence, Reverend Cavendish's son, entered the same room I was trying to exit and I fell as the door collided with my leg."

Prudence relaxed as she could see that the accident was genuine and there had been no foul play.

Clara sighed. "It was my fault really. I had wanted to help young Mr. Cavendish with his business venture and so I..." she trailed off. Should she tell Prudence? She hadn't meant to mention it at all but as she had come this far she decided that two heads must be better than one and so proceeded to tell Prudence of her entire plan.

"Can I trust you to keep my confidence in a matter most delicate?"

"Of course, mistress. I give you my oath that I shall take your truth to the grave unless you instruct me otherwise," Prudence nodded solemnly.

Clara looked into Prudence's honest eyes nodding, satisfied that she was making the right choice. However, the less Prudence knew, the less of a burden it would be to her.

"Lawrence is currently in the process of establishing a new business venture but is struggling to find capital and so I have decided to help." She sighed. Prudence leaned back on her stool, wondering why this was all such a big secret.

"That is very admirable of you, miss," she offered, hoping it was the correct response, but Clara brushed it away.

"No, no, that is of little importance. I have in my possession a cotton plantation and a mill on Concord Street, left to me in a trust by my father and it is my intention, or at least it had been until my recent incapacitation, to secretly earn a wage within one of the factories and learn about my late father's trade whilst anonymously donating my earnings to Lawrence's business," she finished.

Prudence gasped, a look of horror crossing her face. "Begging your pardon, mistress, but the risk is far too great. If you were to be caught it would cause a scandal and your late father's employees would feel betrayed by your underhanded approach."

Clara looked at Prudence closely, her eyes were darting this way and that. She was clearly very upset by the notion, but it couldn't simply be because of Clara's reputation surely, after all, she had known her less than a day. Clara was sure there was something else.

"Wise words indeed Prudence, but you are assuming I would be caught. I should disguise myself completely and travel from here and not my own residence." Clara looked smug as she believed she had thought of everything, but Prudence appeared even more distressed.

"Please mistress, I beg you to reconsider, these factories can be dangerous, they are not safe." Her hand briefly touched the scar on her cheek before she snapped it back down to her lap anxious not to draw attention to it, but Clara had already noticed.

"Oh, Prudence, you received your scar in a factory did you not?" Clara gasped as realization dawned.

Prudence nodded her head slowly, her eyes downcast. "Yes, mistress," she muttered.

"Please, may I inquire as to how you came to get it?" Clara asked kindly as Prudence shifted uncomfortably on her stool.

"It must be a month or so ago now," she started quietly, casting her mind back. "I was in the employ of 'Kettering's Cotton Works PLC'. I was transferring the sheets of raw cotton from the wash to the press, but the machine malfunctioned and started clogging up with sheet upon sheet of cotton. This led to a build-up of pressure as the steam couldn't be released correctly and the machine exploded."

Clara held her breath, horrified by what Prudence was telling her. Prudence pressed on.

"I caught the majority of the blast with my face as shards of metal rained down upon me. One large piece of jagged iron struck me square on the cheek, ripping into my face and causing my scar." She stopped, her fingers tracing the line down her cheek.

"Prudence that is dreadful. I am truly sorry that that has happened to you, it must have been terrifying and awfully painful." Clara's eyes were filling with tears at the thought of her in so much pain.

Prudence continued., "Mr. Kettering was on the factory floor at the time and I thank the good Lord that he was ma'am. He rushed me up to his office and sent a boy out for a doctor. He came back with Doctor Guiter who cleaned and stitched me." She looked down at her hands clasped in her lap.

"Mr. Kettering took me out of the factory and asked me to come and work for his family as a live-in housekeeper, which I readily accepted. Mr. and Mrs. Kettering have been very good to me." Prudence's eyes started to fill with tears as she did her best to keep control. "I shall probably never marry and I shall certainly never be as pretty as you ma'am, or indeed anyone, for although the redness will fade, I shall always have this scar." Prudence took a few moments to compose herself before continuing to make her point.

"The steam machines in these factories are all very well ma'am and I am certainly not insinuating that your father's factories, or indeed Mr. Kettering's factories, are unsafe, but please heed these words of the wise. Your injuries will heal and your scars will fade as Doctor Fletcher made them carefully with a clean, sharp-edged knife, not a great, dirty lump of jagged metal."

Prudence had given Clara a lot of food for thought, and she wondered if there could be a position for her that would allow her to earn a wage in a much safer environment.

Prudence regarded her mistress for a moment. "Would it be

correct of me to assume that you not only want to earn a wage but also to experience what it is like to work for someone else?" she asked.

Clara considered this. She hadn't really given it much thought but now that Prudence had suggested the notion Clara realized that she had indeed been excited by the idea of the experience. And it would be of great use to her in managing her father's, no, *her* cotton mill.

Chapter
Six

Clara winced as Prudence carefully peeled away the first layer of bandages to reveal her wounds to the open air. Prudence took them in as she prepared the rubbing alcohol in a basin. She had been administering the treatment exactly as Doctor Fletcher had instructed her, three times daily, for the past two days and from the look of the wounds they appeared to be healing well. She swabbed each line of stitches with alcohol, making Clara twitch her muscles as sore twinges of pain jolted through her leg each time the alcohol-soaked swabs touched her skin.

"My apologies ma'am, but I do believe your scars are improving," she commented as she continued to clean each wound as gently and thoroughly as she could. Clara looked at Prudence through blurred, tear-soaked vision.

"Thank you, Prudence." Clara clutched at her pillows as Prudence gently smoothed the thick green poultice given to her by Doctor Fletcher over Clara's hot, angry sores before winding clean, sterile white cotton bandages securely around the upper half of her leg. She was just helping her back into bed when a sharp knock sounded at the door.

"Would you ask whoever is there to kindly wait as I compose myself, Prudence dearest?" Clara asked.

Prudence nodded and deftly marched across the room. Upon opening the door, however, she was taken aback as standing before her was a lady whom she had not ever seen before.

"My mistress asks that you permit her a moment as I have just finished tending her wounds," she informed the newcomer politely.

"Of course, but please would you inform your mistress that Miss Orm is here to see her?"

On hearing the familiar sound of Amelia's voice, Clara called out in delight from her bed. "Oh, Amelia, how thoughtful of you to visit me." She pulled herself into a seated position and made herself as comfortable as she could as Amelia bustled in.

"Clara, dearest heart. I came as soon as word reached us," exclaimed Amelia as she rushed to Clara's bedside and clasped her hand. Prudence fetched another chair from the adjoining room before retiring.

"Please ring should you need me, ma'am," Prudence said and bowed her head slightly to Clara and Amelia.

"Thank you, Prudence. I am indebted to you once more." Clara smiled warmly and was delighted when Prudence returned in kind. She turned her attention to her new visitor as she made herself comfortable.

"I am most dreadfully sorry, Clara dear," Amelia burst out as she fished in her muff for her handkerchief. "Had I but known the extent of the damage young Mr. Cavendish had inflicted, I would, of course, have sent for a physician." She dabbed at her eyes delicately with her clean, white handkerchief.

"Please don't blame yourself, Amelia dearest." Clara was distressed to see her guardian in such a state. "I was at fault for not being honest. Mr. and Mrs. Kettering have been most kind and have ensured that I have had the utmost care and attention."

Amelia squeezed Clara's hand as a voice came from the other side of the door, accompanied by a polite tap.

"Clara my dear? May I come in?"

"Of course, Mrs. Kettering, do please," Clara replied as Ophelia pushed open the door and glided elegantly into the room. She immediately crossed to Amelia and clasped her hands.

"Amelia my dear, it is so good to see you." She smiled warmly as Amelia looked at her childhood friend with a mixture of gratitude and delight.

"Please accept my heartfelt gratitude Ophelia for the care and consideration you have shown Clara. Had I known just how injured she was, I would never have imposed upon you and your family."

Ophelia shook her head, brushing off Amelia's apology. "Not at all Amelia dear, Clara has been a delight and Joseph and I have been only too happy to have opened our house to her." She sighed. "My only wish would be that it was under more favorable circumstances." She seated herself on the edge of Clara's bed. "You will, of course, stay for luncheon? I have instructed Miss Parker to set an extra place. Clara of course, has been prescribed complete bed rest and as such dines up here with Prudence, but I should very much welcome your company."

Amelia smiled warmly at Ophelia, grateful for her offer of hospitality. "Thank you, Ophelia, dear. I am only too glad to accept your kind invitation. I would also like to extend my congratulations on young Florence's betrothal," she replied.

"Thank you, you are most kind. We are, of course, delighted with Mr. Baxter's proposal and are looking forward to Reverend Cavendish's service in earnest." She turned to Clara to inform her that lunch would be served directly and that she shall send for Prudence before briefly shifting her attention back to Amelia. "We shall expect you in the dining room whenever you are ready, Amelia dear." Then she took her leave, moving gracefully across the floor without so much as a rustle from her taffeta skirts.

Amelia, though reluctant to leave Clara until she had assured her that she would be fine, rose to her feet and followed Ophelia down to the Kettering's impressive dining room, stopping momentarily to remove her traveling clothes and bonnet by the front door. Joseph Kettering was already seated at the table but rose to his feet as Amelia entered the room.

"Miss Orm, wonderful to see you again," he greeted her.

"Please, have a seat." He pulled out a chair and waited for Amelia to seat herself.

"Please accept my humble apologies Mr. Kettering for any undue stress that Clara might have caused you and your household. Reverend Cavendish has expressed a wish to settle our debt with you with regard to the doctor's fee you so kindly paid for Clara's treatment," Amelia paused a moment as she lowered herself gracefully into the seat Joseph held out for her.

"If you would be so kind as to forward the bill," she continued. "Reverend Cavendish shall reimburse your expense."

Joseph, returning to his own seat, looked Amelia directly in the eye. "My dear Miss Orm, please do not give it another thought. The bill has been settled and I should deem it an honor that you let me remember the late Mr. Johnson in this manner as Willis was a dear friend of mine."

Amelia smiled. Suddenly, the door opened and in came Ophelia, accompanied by Florence. Joseph's face lit up as he rose to welcome his family into the room and busied himself seating his wife and daughter as Miss Parker set about serving luncheon. Joseph bowed his head as he led the gathering into grace.

"For what we are about to receive, may the good Lord make us truly thankful, Amen."

Raising her head, Amelia congratulated Florence on her engagement, thus setting the pace and theme for the conversation. Florence prattled happily away about her wedding preparations as Joseph sat looking on proudly. Eventually, though the subject returned to Clara and what was to be done about her immediate situation.

"Doctor Fletcher has prescribed at least three weeks complete bedrest," informed Ophelia as Amelia expressed a wish to take Clara home with her. "And, as I am sure you shall agree, dearest, I should not want the infection to return, as I am certain that it shall should we move Clara so soon after her operation."

Amelia nodded in agreement. Of course, any further infection should be avoided at all costs. "We are well aware of your preparations for Florence and Mr. Baxter's union, Ophelia my dear, and I should not wish to impose on you further by asking you to care for Clara also." Amelia reached for the jug of water and poured half a glassful before setting it back down carefully in the same spot. Ophelia regarded her friend thoughtfully, smiling to herself at how particular she was. She hadn't changed much at all.

"I have instructed my housemaid Prudence to act as Clara's companion and, thus far, I understand that she has been of great comfort and use to Clara," Joseph told Amelia as he placed his knife and fork down side by side across his plate. "Doctor Fletcher has educated her in the correct treatment of Clara's wounds and I feel that our best course of action is to leave Clara as she is: in our care. If you deem it necessary I shall, of course, hire a nursemaid." he paused slightly before continuing. "However, I have every faith in Prudence and Clara appears to have taken to her well."

Amelia nodded in agreement. "Thank you, Mr. Kettering, I concur, moving Clara in her current condition may cause more harm than good."

Joseph smiled warmly at Amelia in reassurance that her young ward would be well cared for.

"However," she continued. "Reverend Cavendish should very much like to extend an open invitation to you and your family should you ever need hospitality in the parish of St. Michael's. Especially with your upcoming wedding Florence dear."

Florence's cheeks flushed with excitement at the thought of Owen.

"Amelia, you are most kind and we accept your generous offer with gratitude," Joseph replied and rubbed his hands together as he spied Miss Parker coming in with their desert. "And with that agreed, can I interest anyone in Miss Parker's exceptionally excellent Boston cream pie?"

***

"Boston cream pie ma'am?" Prudence proffered the dish of desert towards Clara, who took it with enthusiasm. She popped the light, gooey pastry into her mouth, allowing herself to revel in each sugary sweet bite. Miss Parker really was an excellent cook. She looked across at Prudence who sat waiting for Clara to finish.

"I do wish you would dine with me Prudence, it is tiresome and lonely eating by oneself."

Prudence had observed the general rule of almost every household. The staff do not eat with their employers. But she was a lady's companion now, was her position the same, or did companions dine together with their charges? Unsure as to what was the appropriate protocol, Prudence had erred on the side of caution and opted for the former, but clearly, Clara felt differently.

"Thank you, mistress, I shall, of course, do as you ask." Prudence cleared away Clara's lunch things and rang for Miss Parker to come and take them back down to the kitchen.

Clara shifted uncomfortably in her bed as her thoughts returned to searching for a solution to her current problem. What to do about Lawrence's museum funding. She glanced at Prudence to find her parceling up her laundry ready to be sent out. She really needed an outside opinion and, seeing as Prudence was already aware of the situation, she seemed the most logical person to discuss it with. However, given how astonishingly candid Prudence had been and how much it had upset her to talk about the subject last time, Clara was unsure whether raising the topic again was a good idea.

As luck would have it, though she need not have worried, for it was Prudence who approached her. She finished tying up bundles of Clara's bandages and moved across to linger nervously at the foot of Clara's bed. Clara looked at her expectantly, but for a short time, she simply stood there, clearly wishing to speak but not seeming to find the words. Eventually, she plucked up enough courage to address her mistress.

"Ma'am?"

"Yes, Prudence?" Clara smiled warmly, encouraging her to say more. The girl took a step closer, wringing her hands anxiously.

"M-may I speak with you regarding the point you raised with me." She paused, her fingers unconsciously brushing her scar. "You remember when you asked me about my injury?" she finished, blushing.

Clara reached over and tapped her hand on the chair beside her. "Yes, Prudence dear, of course. Come and sit beside me."

Prudence, hesitant at first, but then appearing to make up her mind, marched up to the chair and threw herself down into it, indicating that she was strong in her resolve. Clara sat on the urge to laugh. This was clearly hard for Prudence and the last thing she wanted was for the child to clam up completely.

"I've been thinking ma'am and I must confess that I am fearful that you are still looking for a way to carry out your notion of working in the factory." The words came bursting forth, all tumbling over one another in an effort to get themselves out before Prudence changed her mind. Clara raised her eyebrows in surprise.

"You have?" Clara asked, her eyebrows raised in surprise. Prudence nodded solemnly. "Well, yes Prudence dear, I admit, you are right. My mind is made up and I feel I must find a more suitable position within the mill. Perhaps one that is not as dangerous as working a press," she mused thoughtfully as Prudence crossed, uncrossed, and re-crossed her fingers together nervously in her lap.

"Please mistress, won't you reconsider? I am afeared that you will do yourself greater harm and it is I who is responsible for your wellbeing and care." She stopped and looked at Clara, a pleading look upon her face. Clara smiled at her companion.

"My dear Prudence, I am sure that there are other jobs to be done in the factory that would not require me to be in such immediate danger. Perhaps in the offices or something of that nature." A quick look at Prudence's expression reminded her that she really had no clue about working life. She thumped her hand down onto her sheets making Prudence jump in surprise. "Well, no matter what I know I shall find a way. If it is the will of God, then there will be a way, and I shall just have to work a press as that is the only machine I have even heard of." She glanced at Prudence's fear-stricken face feeling a little guilty for dragging the poor girl into her situation in the first instance. She smiled at her warmly. "Don't worry Prudence dearest, I shall be sure to keep as safe as I know how."

Prudence fidgeted a little in her seat, dismayed that Clara was thinking of still going to the mill, after all, she had told her. By rights, she felt that she should inform Mrs. Kettering of what Clara had planned, but as she had given her oath that she would take Clara's secret to the grave, she felt there was little she could do. She bit her lip. What should she do for the best? She was certain that the machines were dangerous, she had the scarring to prove it, but without her help, the innocent Clara might fall victim to a similar injury—or worse.

After more lip biting and squirming she made up her mind. If Clara was going to go ahead with her notion, then she was going to need her help whether Prudence liked it or not. Having the deception of Mr. and Mrs. Kettering on her conscience was a little more preferable to having Clara's health, or worse, her life on there instead. After all, she was the closest thing to a friend she had ever had and she wanted very much to do well in her new role.

She leaned into Clara, fearful that what she was about to divulge would be overheard. She felt sure that it could cost her not only her job but her home too and, swallowing hard, she forced herself to speak. "I may have been a little too... over dramatic with my descriptions of the machines in the mill. Not all are so hazardous. Indeed, some are not as dangerous at all. When I started work in Mr. Kettering's factory I was what they called a 'spool girl'. That meant I spent my time attaching the long threads of cotton onto large wooden spools and setting them to spin. Then when they were full, I would swap them for fresh ones and the entire process would start again. Then once I had an entire crate full of completed spools, I would stop the machine and take them over to looms and sewing machines."

Clara interrupted her, stopping her flow of words as she cut in. "And you think it is a way that I could work and not be in any danger?" she asked excitedly.

Prudence nodded silently.

Clara sat back against her pillow, deep in thought for a moment, but then another stab of discomfort from her leg brought her crashing back into the present. It was a nasty realization that it simply didn't matter what she wanted; Clara was incapacitated and would be unable to go anywhere. She smiled weakly.

"Prudence, you are an absolute dear, but I am unable to leave the confines of my bed to bathe, how am I to attend a job?" She lowered her head and looked forlornly at the shape of her leg beneath the sheets.

Without thinking, Prudence reached out and placed her hand on Clara's. "Mistress, you have been instructed to rest for three weeks and you are well into the first of them. If you could be a little patient I have an idea that may work."

Clara looked at her companion, a little quiver of excitement sparked in her stomach. She took Prudence's hand in hers and gave it a little squeeze. "Thank you, Prudence, I owe you a huge debt of gratitude already." She smiled broadly as Prudence returned the squeeze.

Her plan was a simple one. They would both wait until Clara's stitches had been removed and her leg was stable. Then Clara should write to the mill searching for a position for her young ward. Clara could then arrive at the factory as Isabelle Crofton, Prudence's own sister, for whom Prudence had official documents to prove Clara's identification.

"But, won't this inconvenience your sister? Someone cannot be in two places at once, I would surely be discovered fairly swiftly should I not?" Clara frowned as Prudence shook her head sadly.

"Ma'am, my sister passed on some months before I took the position at Kettering's. The factory foremen are uninterested in verifying their worker's identities and are far more concerned with turning a profit, so I highly doubt you will be stopped." Prudence dropped her eyes. She felt incredibly guilty for her betrayal of the Ketterings trust. Prudence simply felt so moved by Clara's resolve that she wanted to help, besides she felt that Clara would have found a way to carry out her plans, even without her help. At least this way Prudence could ensure that Clara would be in a far less dangerous position.

Anyway, she thought to herself, *if Clara is ever to pull this off, she really is going to need my help.* Simply smudging her face and giving her Isabelle's old clothes and boots were not going to convince anyone of Clara's poverty. She needed to learn to act and speak the part too; that would take a little time and a lot of practice on Clara's part. With any luck, she may abandon the idea as too involved, but somehow Prudence knew that Clara was too headstrong to merely give up at the first hurdle.

Clara spoke, startling Prudence from her thoughts and bringing her back into the present. "I shall attempt it," she said, her steely resolve evident in her voice. "But I shall need your help Prudence dear."

Prudence nodded earnestly but stopped when she realized the full extent of what Clara had planned.

"I shall need you to pretend to be me and stand in as my

double when I am not here should anyone look in on me." Clara stopped as she saw the look of sheer horror on Prudence's face as she withdrew her hands from Clara's grasp.

"Begging your pardon ma'am but I cannot deceive Mr. and Mrs. Kettering in such a manner and, if you do not mind my saying so, it is unfair of you to ask me to." Her voice cracked with emotion as she began to panic.

Clara, realizing her costly mistake, offered her apologies to Prudence and tried to reassure her. "Yes, you are quite right Prudence dear, please accept my apologies. I would never dream of putting you in such a compromising position. We must think of another way."

"Mistress, I want to help you and I will of course but not if it means lying to Mr. and Mrs. Kettering."

Clara again took Prudence's hands in hers and, looking her squarely in the eye, then promised solemnly that they would do whatever was necessary not to deceive anyone, least of all Mr. and Mrs. Kettering. She had no idea why this had suddenly become so important to her.

Certainly, helping Lawrence and fulfilling her late father's wishes was the right thing to do, she was certain. However, at the same time, deep down, she could feel something beginning to grow like a new strength in her that she never knew was there. Was this God? Was this inner voice the divine guiding her towards the path he had chosen for her? Clara was unsure. What she knew for certain was that Prudence had been sent to her for a reason and she would do everything in her power to carry out God's will.

"Mistress?" Prudence spoke, interrupting Clara's thoughts. Clara smiled warmly at her look of concern. "Are you feeling unwell?"

Clara patted Prudence on the hand. "I can assure you, dearest, I'm fine, but what am I to do now? We are in agreement that no hurt or deception should come to the others through our actions, but how am I to be in two places at once?"

It was indeed a perplexing problem and one that would take a little more thought. A knock sounded as Ophelia's muffled voice came through Clara's bedroom door.

"Clara dear? Are you in a position to receive guests?"

Prudence raced to open the door to Ophelia as Clara called out her reply, "Of course, Mrs. Kettering, please do come in."

Prudence stepped back as Ophelia entered and crossed to Clara. "Thank you, Prudence, there is a fresh pot of coffee ready in the dining room, you may pour a cup for both Clara and yourself."

Prudence nodded. "Thank you, ma'am," she answered and then left Ophelia talking with Clara.

"How are you feeling my dear?" asked Ophelia kindly as she lowered herself into the chair Prudence had just left. "It has been decided that as you are in no fit state to travel that you are to remain here as our guest until you have made a complete recovery and are deemed well enough to leave your bed by Doctor Fletcher."

Clara smiled, her calm visage hiding the relief she felt. It had simply not occurred to neither herself nor Prudence that she might have been sent away, thus rendering their plans useless. "Thank you, Mrs. Kettering, I am forever indebted to you."

Ophelia smiled at her. It was hard to think that this was the same child that, only a few short years ago had been toasting bread with Florence and listening to Amelia's stories around the nursery fire.

"Also, my dear, you are to receive a visit from young Mr. Cavendish, so it will be necessary to move you briefly to the daybed in the parlor. Personally, I'm not at all certain that the excitement of the move nor from a meeting with Lawrence is entirely the right path to take. Both Amelia and Reverend Cavendish also hold these feelings." Ophelia smiled as she saw the crestfallen look on Clara's face. "However," she continued, "it is out of my hands as Mr. Cavendish insists on seeing you and I am told will not be put off."

Clara giggled as she thought of her hot-headed suitor. Normally this kind of passion would be reserved for something ancient that he had pulled from the ground. "Thank you, Mrs. Kettering," she replied.

"Not at all Ciara, I was young myself once, and I can remember how agonizing each long wait was between visits from Joseph." She smiled to herself as she allowed her mind to wander back to her youth.

Joseph had grabbed not only her attention but also her heart from an early age when her father had taken her to her first social outing. A birthday party for a colleague. She remembered the fresh-faced young man who had confidently sat and engaged her in delightful conversation, smiling at her broadly throughout their entire encounter. It was only a matter of weeks before she had heard from him again as he came to call upon her. A mere year later he had presented his credentials to her father and asked for her hand.

Clara watched the expression of pure love and admiration on Ophelia's face and she wondered if she looked the same when she thought of Lawrence. "Mrs. Kettering, may I ask when Lawrence shall be calling? I would like to be dressed to receive him."

Ophelia let out a little cry of laughter. "Oh, my dear, you have plenty of time to make yourself presentable to your beau. He is not due to arrive until the day after next." Still smiling, she crossed the room to the door, passing Prudence carrying a tray of fresh coffee and a plate of Miss Parker's homemade almond biscuits across to Clara. She stopped and turned back. "I wonder if you might spare Prudence for a short while as I need Florence's headdress collecting from Mrs. Bloomindale's milliners this afternoon and I have sent Miss Parker on an errand to the post office. Also, I have just received word that Mrs. Baxter is due to arrive shortly and I shall need to be in to receive her."

Clara looked at Ophelia with a mixture of awe and admiration. She wasn't sure that she would cope as well with a wedding to prepare for and a sick friend on an extended stay who herself was receiving visitors. Yet, Ophelia hadn't so

111

much as a hair out of place; never dropping her cool, calm exterior nor seamless grace for the merest second.

Clara smiled. "But of course, Mrs. Kettering, I only wish that I could be of some use in Florence's wedding planning, I was so looking forward to it too."

Ophelia knew that this was true. Clara and Florence had been inseparable growing up and it did seem a terrible shame that Clara would be unable to attend the wedding. Perhaps a blessing could be arranged or some such. She put it from her mind, determined to focus on the job at hand, after all, one wedding was enough to organize without the prospect of two.

Chapter
Seven

Alexander Cavendish arrived by cab at the home of his Uncle Anthony. He collected his luggage, paid the cabbie, and proceeded to walk up towards the house. He reached out to ring the bell, but just as he did so the door flew open and there stood his cousin Lawrence. Red in the face and out of breath. He stared at Alexander in complete surprise.

"Alexander dear fellow, what brings you here?" Lawrence asked as he beamed at his cousin.

"Uncle Anthony requires my help. He wrote to me and requested that I come to sta.," Alexander grinned. Lawrence picked up two of Alexander's bags and carried them inside.

"Come in sir and I shall inform Father of your arrival." He led the way to Anthony's study, still clutching Alexander's bags. He set them down outside the door and knocked.

"Come," called Anthony as Lawrence pushed open the door.

"Alexander has arrived Father," he said and beckoned Alexander to follow him inside.

Anthony immediately jumped up from his chair and crossed the room to greet his nephew. "My dear boy, you do look well. Your journey was uneventful I trust?" He clasped Alexander's hand and pumped it up and down as he walked him over to a large chair by the side of his desk. "Sit my boy, sit."

Alexander sank into the soft leather.

"And what news of my brother and his good lady wife, are they well?"

"Thank you, uncle. My journey was a pleasant one," Alexander leaned forward slightly, resting his hands on his knees. "Mother and Father both send their love. Yes, they are both well thank you. Business is good and father has said that he can spare me for as long as you need me." He smiled. "Although, I am somewhat intrigued. Your letter mentioned an obscure law?"

Anthony nodded. "Yes, yes, but we can get to that after supper. Lawrence, please make your cousin comfortable in the guest room and I shall inform Mrs. Dimbleby that there is a need for an extra place at the table."

Lawrence led Alexander out and off up the stairs to the room beside his own, collecting his bags along the way. He pushed open the door and placed Alexander's luggage down on the bed.

"I shall leave you to unpack and settle yourself. There is a small washstand behind the screen," he said as he indicated to a stand, already prepared with a jug of warm water, soap, and a clean towel. Alexander removed his coat and hat and threw them down beside his bags.

"Thank you," he replied as he turned to his cousin. "Word has reached me that you are involved with opening an unusual attraction. I must say, I am deeply curious."

Lawrence grinned as he launched himself into his favorite topic, his beloved museum vision. "And we intend to exhibit many artifacts from around the world."

Alexander gasped, clearly impressed by what Lawrence was proposing. "Fascinating. Where are you acquiring your artifacts and antiquities from? Are they voluntarily donated or will you need to purchase items with which to fill your museum?"

Lawrence sighed. "I do have a contact at the university who has access to many items which I plan to exhibit, and many of them will be on a permanent loan basis. However, there are a few items which the university can spare and I have many empty cases within my museum to fill. I have many sellers but limited funds."

Alexander pondered the problem. Lawrence suddenly clapped his hands together, startling Alexander back to the present.

"At any rate, we shall need to purchase a great many items before opening our doors, but we can discuss that at another juncture. I can see that you are road weary and probably more than a little hungry. I shall leave you to wash and change." Then he left Alexander to become familiar with his new surroundings.

Lawrence turned right past Clara's room. He slowed to a stop outside as he could hear voices within. Had she returned? Was she well enough now to travel? He knocked and waited for Clara's voice, but instead, Amelia called him in.

"Ah, Mr. Cavendish, good. Would you be so kind as so ascend this ladder to reach the hat box at the top of the wardrobe? I am afraid that I have no head for heights and Mrs. Dimbleby and I are unable to reach it." Amelia pointed to a large black hat box that had slid to the very back of the wardrobe roof.

"Of course, Miss Orm." He smiled. "Alexander has arrived, I have put him in the guest room beside mine."

Amelia clasped her hands together at the thought of seeing Alexander again. "Wonderful. I shall welcome him once we have finished here." She walked over to the ladder and held it, indicating that she was ready for Lawrence to climb it. He quickly retrieved the heavy hat box.

"Where would you like it, Miss Orm?" he asked politely.

Amelia pointed to the floor in front of the bed. "Just there if you would be so kind Mr. Cavendish thank you."

Lawrence nodded and placed the hat box at the foot of Clara's bed. He turned to go. "If you have no further use of me, I shall be in the library." He made for the door as Mrs. Dimbleby and Amelia wrenched the lid off the box, exposing its contents.

"Yes, thank you, Lawrence."

Mrs. Dimbleby turned to Amelia. "Is this the one Miss Orm?"

She nodded. "Yes, it is in need of a complete update. On the day of her accident, I believe Clara was planning on taking this to Mrs. Bloomindale's shop for repair." She reached in and pulled out a pretty white bonnet with a blue silken band. She could see that it had been well worn, for it was indeed looking tired.

"I do remember that one. Goodness, I believe she practically lived in it," Mrs. Dimbleby exclaimed as Amelia turned it over in her hands. "But yes, I believe you are right Miss Orm, it certainly is in need of a complete overhaul."

Amelia placed it carefully back within its box and refitted the lid. "Yes, I believe this should cheer her up nicely." Amelia smiled. She tapped the top of the large round box. "I shall take it with me when I go into town tomorrow morning and drop it in with Mrs. Bloomindale. Then I shall deliver it to Clara sometime the following week. That should give old Mrs. Bloomindale ample chance to work her magic." She picked up the box and carried it down to the hallway in a bid to remind her to take it with her the following morning.

As she turned to go back up the stairs, Alexander tapped her lightly on the elbow. "Good afternoon Miss Orm, you are looking well."

Amelia turned and beamed at him. "Alexander, how good it is to see you! You have settled in well I trust?"

Alexander nodded. "Yes, thank you."

"You have grown into a fine gentleman, it must be a good ten years since I saw you last." He certainly had grown, Amelia remembered a boy, small for his twelve years, but here he stood, towering above her.

"And what of the delightful Miss Johnson?" He grinned, but his face soon fell as he saw the expression on Amelia's face.

"I am afraid that Clara met with an unfortunate accident and has since been taken very ill. She is convalescing currently in the company of Miss Florence Kettering."

Alexander looked perplexed. "An accident you say? What has befallen her?" he asked, his face full of concern.

"She was knocked down."

Amelia was just explaining to Alexander what had happened when Lawrence came around the corner into the hallway. He rushed up. "Oh, it was all my fault, Alexander. I was such a clumsy ape. Crashing through the door, I knocked the wind right out of poor Clara and sent her sprawling. I feel truly awful about the whole affair." He dropped his head. "And when that letter arrived two weeks ago detailing an awful infection and an emergency operation to save Clara's leg, well. You can imagine." He sank down at the foot of the stairs, the epitome of sadness.

"Steady on there, old fellow. It sounds like an accident to me." Lawrence looked up, grateful that his cousin should be so kind about it. Alexander continued, "I should imagine it has been an awful ordeal for the poor girl, but you had no intention of hurting her. Give Isaiah a read, I think you might find great comfort in it." Alexander smiled.

"Thank you. I will," Lawrence replied as he pulled himself up off the stair. The gong sounded signaling that it was supper time. "Come along Alexander, I want you next to me, otherwise Father will have you discussing work throughout the duration of your meal," stated Lawrence.

Alexander chuckled as he followed his cousin to the dining room. Lawrence stopped and offered his arm to Amelia and they made their way to supper. As they entered the dining room, Anthony was already in there discussing with Mrs. Dimbleby the addition of Alexander for the foreseeable future.

"Very good sir. I shall automatically set a place for the young man unless instructed otherwise," Mrs. Dimbleby said.

Anthony smiled. "Thank you, Mrs. Dimbleby." He turned as his family came in and took their places for supper. "Ah, Alexander. I do need to see you after supper about an obscure law which prohibits work on Sundays. As you know, I fully appreciate that the Sabbath be recognized as a day of rest, but what exactly does this entail?" He paused for a breath. "For example, many of our parish meetings take place on Sundays, as does Sunday school and of course the summer fete. This is of particular concern to me as there is a law that states that it is unlawful to dance on Sundays but there's the children's dance to consider and, of course, dancing in general. There will also be the sale of refreshments and general goods at the fete. I should very much like to—"
But he didn't get to finish as Amelia interrupted him.

"Please reverend, let him at least eat first. I'm certain that there will be plenty of opportunities for you to discuss your legal concerns with young Mr. Cavendish over the coming weeks." She smiled at Anthony.

"Of course, my dear. I must apologize, Alexander, I have been in a great state of panic regarding the new legislation and I am incredibly confused. I should very much like to avoid breaking the law."

Alexander smiled. "I shall give you any assistance I can, Uncle Anthony."

Anthony smiled at his young nephew. Having one lawyer in the family was useful enough, but his brother was not always on hand to assist in these matters. However, now that his son had graduated with an impressive first, from Yale no less, it made these problems much easier to deal with. Anthony bowed his head in prayer, giving the others a few moments to follow suit before saying grace.

"Christ our Lord in heaven, we thank thee for thy bounteous gift, for Alexander's safe arrival, and for Clara's continued healing. Amen." He raised his head. "Speaking of Clara, have we had any word, Miss Orm?"

Amelia relayed parts of the letter she had received only that morning from Ophelia. "Mrs. Kettering tells me that Clara's wounds are healing well, but the stitches have yet to come out. However, she feels that if she continues at the current rate then she should be back home with us within a week or two."

Anthony beamed. "Excellent news." He looked around at his family, all seated before him. "I believe my prayers are being answered. All we need now is Clara home safe and well and I would feel truly blessed."

Mrs. Dimbleby brought in their supper. Anthony looked delighted as he lifted the large cloche and peeped beneath. "My word Mrs. Dimbleby, the Lord may provideth, but you certainly know how to bring out the best in his gift," Anthony praised her. "This poached fish looks and smells delicious."

Mrs. Dimbleby smiled at the compliment. "Thank you, sir, I know my way around a fish. Shall I serve the potatoes?" She held up a large silver serving dish.

"By all means Mrs. Dimbleby. We are all very much looking forward to your fare."

She nodded and ladled out a large spoonful of boiled potatoes on each plate. As their cook continued to serve their supper, Amelia turned to Alexander.

"I hear that you graduated with a first, that is an achievement that must make you and your family extremely proud."

Alexander smiled. "Thank you, Miss Orm. I feel though that my father is the one who should receive your praise. If it were not for him letting me shadow him in his work, I am truly certain I would not have achieved the same level of results."

Anthony swallowed a large mouthful of fish and reached for the jug of water to pour himself a glass. "Nonsense dear boy. It is your due diligence and hard work that has earned you your accolade. Certainly, your father should be recognized as the provider of the knowledge, but it is you who sought to do your best and you who should wear that honor with pride."

Lawrence smiled. He had been the recipient of a similar speech upon graduating last year. Alexander felt his cheeks flush with color as he looked down at his plate.

"Thank you for your kind words. I am looking forward to working alongside Father in the courtroom," Alexander replied. "Father told me only yesterday that as I have earned my right to be a lawyer I now have to learn to become an excellent one."

The assembled party nodded in agreement at such wise words.

"Your father is a good, honest and just man. I have no doubt that you shall thrive by taking his advice and following in his footsteps," Amelia added.

Alexander beamed with pride to think that his father was so highly thought of. "I am both flattered and humbled Miss Orm that you should remember my father so favorably." Alexander placed his knife and fork down neatly on his plate, feeling full, satisfied and happy.

"By the way Lawrence, I had the good fortune of running into your college professor this morning," Anthony began, "he has informed me that he has managed to obtain a great many artifacts which he believes would be of great interest to the general public from his connections with the Charleston

Library Society I believe. I have invited him to dine with us the day after tomorrow." He paused, helping himself to more sauce. "I wanted a chance to speak with the professor directly regarding how we are to store and care for the antiquities that you shall be the custodian of. Especially as they remain the legal property of the university archives. I should hate for anything to deteriorate due to negligence or mishandling on our part."

Lawrence smiled happily at the thought that his father supported his vision, especially in light of his recent strained discussions with him on the matter. But surely now that his father had offered the hand of friendship to Professor Baxter, it would make it easier for him to see how charming and delightful the Baxter family are and maybe then he would understand his feelings towards his beloved Sophie. Mrs. Dimbleby trundled in with her trolley to clear away the empty plates and to serve their desert.

"Mrs. Dimbleby you outdo yourself, my dear, this marmalade roll is outstanding," Anthony complimented as the others all nodded their agreement, their mouths full of the sticky, sweet treat. Mrs. Dimbleby's chest swelled with pride as she trundled her trolley back to the kitchen to start work on the washing up.

Amelia dabbed her mouth delicately with her napkin and addressed the room. "If you would all kindly excuse me, I have some correspondence I really must see to."

Anthony smiled, nodding as he, Alexander, and Lawrence raised themselves out of their chairs and Amelia left the room. Anthony also made his excuses and left, making his way back to his study for 'a moment of contemplation with God' as he called it.

Lawrence leaned across to Alexander to whisper in his ear, "Or, as us mere mortals prefer to call it, having a snooze."

Alexander choked back a chuckle as his uncle retired from the dining room, leaving him and Lawrence alone. Alexander turned to his cousin. "I hear that you are to be married," he said, his voice a little cool and distant.

Lawrence rolled his eyes. "Well father wishes me to marry Clara, but..." he trailed off, leaning forward and resting his head in his hands. "May I be frank with you dear fellow?" he asked letting out a weary sigh.

Alexander drained his glass and set it back on the table top. "Of course, sir, what's troubling you?"

"Father wishes me and Clara to wed, but my heart belongs to another. He has threatened to cut off funding for the museum if I refuse to take Clara as my wife." He looked up into his cousin's eyes, hoping to find an answer there. "But that matters not to me; I will not hurt my darling Sophie."

Alexander leaned forward and placed his elbows on the table, sympathizing with Lawrence's plight. "But have you tried telling Uncle Anthony that you have no interest in Clara that way? Perhaps he—"

"It is of little good Alexander. I have told him that I will not marry Clara and that I intend to marry Sophie Baxter, but that was when he threatened to thwart my vision." He dropped his eyes down to look at his hands. "What do you think I should do?" As Lawrence spoke, he glanced up to catch a strange look on Alexander's face.

"Where did you say that Clara was convalescing?" he asked.

"The Kettering family are tending to her in Morning View House on East Battery down by the quayside, why?" He looked at his cousin suspiciously. *What does he have in mind?*

"I hear that there is a fine seafood restaurant on East Battery, I think I may treat myself to some oysters during my stay," he said cryptically. Lawrence looked at him a moment longer before changing the subject.

"I must say that it was a stroke of good fortune father inviting Professor Baxter to luncheon as I would so like you to meet him, Alexander. He is a fascinating gentleman who has been of great support to me." Lawrence then led the way out of the dining room and down towards the library where he planned to show Alexander some of the many interesting antiquities he had already accumulated.

"I look forward to meeting him, he sounds charming," Alexander replied as he followed Lawrence into the library, closing the door behind them. Lawrence crossed to a large wooden table on the far side of the room. It was laden with many interesting looking objects, each tagged with a name and a number. It was clear that Lawrence had been researching each piece and cataloging it as it came in. Alexander looked over towards the bookshelves where three large tea chests stood, indicating that the items on show where only a fraction of Lawrence's steadily growing collection.

He pointed to a large stone figurine, intricately carved with ancient pictograms running along its base. "I say, what is this interesting looking piece?"

Lawrence looked up from one of the books he had been flicking through. "Hmm? Which one?" He looked in the direction Alexander was pointing. "Ah, that is an early stone representation of our Lord Jesus Christ. Fascinating to think isn't it? That was found in Georgia believe it or not."

Alexander leaned in to get a closer look. "Georgia? It looks African to me."

Lawrence nodded his head. "Yes, that's what is so fascinating about archeology. You are right, it is African, but what would a statue of Christ be doing there? And how did it make its way to Georgia to lay in the dirt for centuries before being unearthed by a man digging foundations for his house?" He picked it up, turning it over gently in his hands. "Each piece holds a mystery and it is my job to unlock as much of it as I can and inform others so that they can truly appreciate its value and significance."

Alexander regarded his cousin in awe. It was clear that Lawrence was a born historian. He had always been this way. Alexander remembered when they were children. He would be skinning his knees and ripping his Sunday best climbing the large tree that stood at the bottom of the vicarage garden, meanwhile, Lawrence would be sitting on the lawn flicking through his books on ancient civilizations. He smiled fondly at the memory. They were happy days.

"So," Lawrence startled him out of his daydream. "What do you think?"

Alexander took a deep breath in, releasing it slowly, and letting it whistle past his front teeth. "I think it is an incredible feat Lawrence and I commend you for even having the courage to attempt it. I also feel that it shall be a tremendous success once you have everything correctly researched and displayed. Do you have a building in mind?"

Lawrence nodded. "Yes, I have already put in an offer to lease the large empty property on Meeting Street."

Alexander's eyes grew wide. "That is quite a substantial property, the lease alone would surely cost more than the museum would earn in profit in a month?"

Lawrence grinned at his cousin. "Normally, I believe that you are quite right, it would. However, Professor Baxter has managed to negotiate a rather sizable discount on the understanding that the museum will be an extended storage facility for the college archives."

Alexander beamed at him. "Well, that is clever sir. I should very much like to see inside."

Lawrence's face fell. "Yes, as would I, but my application has not yet been approved."

Alexander looked again at the large tea chests full of artifacts still to be cataloged. "Lawrence, forgive me, but how is it that you are able to fund this great endeavor?"

Lawrence sank down into a chair and indicated to Alexander to do the same. "With a large amount of increasing difficulty. Father has agreed to help with some of the funding, and there is a distant relative who has shown quite an interest in becoming a dormant partner for a small share of the profits, but there are still a great many things that shall require financial backing to complete before I am able to open the doors to the general public." He leaned forwards. "I do have limited funds myself, and I have taken on a number of paid research projects with the college archive department, but I still have a long journey ahead."

Alexander thought about this for a moment, mulling over in his mind the enormity of what Lawrence was trying to achieve. He put his hand on his cousin's shoulder. "Permit me to help you, dear cousin, if I am able. I should very much like to be a part of your great museum." He smiled as Lawrence clasped his hand, beaming.

"I had hoped that you would sir, I had dearly hoped that you would."

A knock sounded as Mrs. Dimbleby called through the door. "Coffee gentlemen?" Alexander rushed to open the door. He stood back to allow Mrs. Dimbleby access. "Thank you kindly, sir." She placed the tray on a clear table and retired back to the kitchen to prepare a second tray for Anthony and Amelia. Lawrence held out a steaming cup of coffee to Alexander who took it gratefully.

"Thank you, Lawrence." He took a sip. "So, what would you say would be the best way to proceed?" he asked as he stood carefully drinking his hot beverage while Lawrence leaned back into his chair, coffee cup in hand.

"In all honesty, I am unsure, however, now that I have another man onboard, I am certain that Professor Baxter will be in a position to advise us."

Alexander drained his cup and placed it back on the tray. He was sure that there was something he could do. Perhaps he knew of someone who would offer to put their financial weight behind the project. After some thought, he came upon an idea. "Lawrence, have you given any thought to sponsorship?" he asked.

Lawrence looked up, his eyes wide. "Do you know I hadn't? Alexander, you are truly a blessing sent by God himself. That sir is a capital idea."

Alexander beamed, glad that he had already been of some help. Now it was just a matter of approaching the right people in the right manner. He looked at his cousin for a moment, watching as he carefully wrapped a small pot in a sheet of cotton before laying it down in a box. *So,* he thought to himself, *Lawrence doesn't have feelings for Clara after all.* He smiled to himself as he felt a flicker of emotion deep in his chest at the thought of what a trip to East Battery might bring.

Chapter
Eight

"Mrs. Baxter how delightful to see you. Please do come in. Miss Parker would you be so kind as to brew a fresh pot of tea?" Ophelia asked as she ushered her guest in.

Miss Parker closed the front door and, with a slight nod of her head, dashed off towards the kitchen, eager to deliver Mrs. Kettering's request. On reaching the kitchen door, however, she stopped. Her large frame resting against the wall for a moment as a wash of weariness came over her. *That's funny,* she thought, she could hear voices. With a shock, she realized that she could clearly hear the conversation between Mrs. Kettering and Mrs. Baxter.

Now, Miss Parker was not a nosey woman nor would she condone the practice of eavesdropping, but as she stood there, waiting to catch her breath, she rather enjoyed overhearing the conversation. Who knows, she might even learn the intended recipient was of the beautiful bridesmaid gown she had seen hanging in the guest bedroom.

"Now Mrs. Kettering, I am to understand that Florence's bridesmaid is unwell?"

Miss Parker leaned a little closer to the wall, hoping to catch a name.

"What on earth are you doing Miss Parker, are you ill?" Florence placed her arm through the crook of Miss Parker's before walking her into the kitchen. "I realize it is all so exciting and you must be run ragged without Prudence's help." She paused and looked at the old cook, her face plastered with concern. "Shall I ask Father to appoint more help?" she asked as Miss Parker smiled warmly at her.

"Miss Kettering, I must admit that I am feeling a little weary of late what with all the wedding preparations and young Miss Johnson, but I assure you that I am fine. I am just letting the excitement overwhelm me a little that's all." She reached over and squeezed Florence's arm. She raised herself up from the chair where Florence had kindly seated her. "And now I must prepare some tea for your mother's guest." She sighed as she set the kettle to boil and prepared a tray laden with tea things and sweet treats. She marched back to the parlor and knocked smartly.

"Come," Ophelia called brightly as Miss Parker pushed open the door and entered the parlor, just in time to hear the end of the conversation. "Ah, very good Miss Parker just set it down here thank you. Don't worry about pouring, I shall serve Mrs. Baxter, however, please take a tray up to Miss Johnson."

Miss Parker nodded her acknowledgment as she turned to leave the room. Ophelia turned to Mrs. Baxter.

"Milk and sugar Caroline?" she asked.

Mrs. Caroline Baxter shook her head slightly. "Just milk Ophelia dear please."

Miss Parker allowed herself a second or two longer than usual to close the door, still hoping that she would catch a little more of the conversation.

"I believe that the dress may need to be altered to fit. Sophie has a much shorter stature than the Miss Johnson you describe." Caroline took the cup offered to her by Ophelia. "Thank you, dear."

"Would your niece be free to attend a formal fitting this coming week do you think? I should like to give the seamstress time for any alternations you deem necessary."

Miss Parker grinned to herself as the door clicked closed behind her. *So, it was to be Mrs. Baxter's niece, eh?*

***

"Please, allow me." Joseph carefully scooped Clara up in his strong arms and carried her back down to the parlor, where she was to receive her guest. He placed her gingerly on the daybed as Prudence fussed about her. Covering her injured leg and carefully arranging her skirts.

"Thank you, Mr. Kettering." She smiled brightly. "I must confess that it is nice to be sitting in your cozy parlor." Clara looked up at kind Joseph as he adjusted his shirt sleeves.

"Yes, as they say, my dear, a change is as good a rest." He smiled as he made his way to his private study. He stopped by the door and turned to his wife. "I shall be unavailable for the best part of the day my dear."

Ophelia gave him a sympathetic smile before addressing Clara. "Now Clara dear, if you feel at all unwell I wish for you to inform Prudence at once, even if young Mr. Cavendish has not yet left, is that understood?" Ophelia's voice was firm but kind as she was anxious to prevent another infection. Clara nodded.

"Of course, Mrs. Kettering, I shall alert Prudence if I feel the tiniest of twinges." She smiled broadly at Prudence as the bell rang out from the hallway, signaling the arrival of Lawrence.

"Mr. Cavendish for you ma'am." Prudence carefully showed Clara's visitor into the parlor. Clara looked up in surprise. Instead of the scruffy, dark-haired, gangly youth she expected, she found herself looking up into the clear, deep blue eyes of a very smart young man. His sandy colored hair was cropped short, neatly cut around his ears and his face clean shaven to show off his slightly squared jaw.

A large grin spread across Clara's face as her heart soared with delight. "Alexander! What a pleasant surprise!" she exclaimed as he knelt down beside her.

"Clara my dear, when I heard from Miss Orm what had happened I had to come and see you for myself. My, you have grown into a handsome young woman," Alexander complimented as he gazed at her, taking in her golden curls and soft pink lips. He remembered the days when he would sit beside her at the feet of Amelia as she read them stories in front of the nursery fire before bedtime. He blushed slightly

133

as he remembered, he used to gaze at her longingly then too.

"Please, do sit. It has been far too long," Clara replied and smiled again, making Alexander chuckle at the way her pretty little cheekbones lifted as she spoke.

"Thank you." He sat down in the chair opposite as Clara turned to Prudence who was looking thoroughly confused.

"Oh, I'm so sorry dearest! Let me explain. This isn't Lawrence." She looked at her companion happily. Prudence frowned.

"Begging your pardon sir, but you did give your name as Mr. Cavendish, did you not?" she asked, worried that she had made a mistake. Would the real Mr. Cavendish arrive at any moment, perplexed and annoyed to find another gentleman calling upon his betrothed?

Alexander beamed at her as he nodded enthusiastically. "That's right, miss. I am Alexander Cavendish, Lawrence Cavendish's cousin. I grew up with Miss Johnson. We are old friends and I thought I might cheer her up by surprising her." At this, he produced a posy of wildflowers from behind his back and offered them to Clara.

"Oh, Alexander, they are lovely. How thoughtful of you!" she cried, delighted with his gift. She passed them to Prudence. "Would you put these in water for me, Prudence dear?"

Prudence rose to her feet, nodding. "Of course, mistress," she replied, hurrying away with the small bouquet.

Clara turned to Alexander. "How long have you been in town? Did you have a long journey? My, it has lifted my spirits seeing you again." She giggled excitedly, hardly able to contain herself.

Alexander beamed at her, delighted that his visit should bring her as much joy as it did him. He sat back in the chair, admiring Clara. "I arrived at the vicarage yesterday and when I learned that Lawrence was planning a visit, well..." He dropped his eyes, slightly embarrassed by his confession. "I wanted to get my visit in first," he finished weakly. It sounded so preposterous now he had actually said it. Clara looked at the cheeky expression on Alexander's face and her heart quickened slightly. Was this merely delight at having an old friend surprise her? Or was it something more? She couldn't tell, but at that moment, she hardly cared. It would be wonderful spending time with Alexander again.

"How long do you plan on staying in Charleston? You are not planning on returning too soon I hope?" she asked. She felt suddenly crestfallen at the merest suggestion that he may have to leave soon. He grinned at her, instantly restoring her delight.

"Father has given me an extended leave of absence from the office. Everything is in hand and he still has old Mr. Potsworth to assist him as he has a good few months before his retirement," he replied, reveling in Clara's little giggles and smiles.

"And what of Lawrence? Is he well?" she asked. "He did feel terrible about my accident and I would hate to think of him sitting at home feeling as dejected and remorseful as he was when I left." Prudence bustled in with a pot of coffee. Alexander's face fell for a moment, but he quickly recovered.

"Do not worry yourself, my dear. My cousin is burying himself in his work and has taken heart from news of your rapid recovery." He smiled as Prudence offered him a steaming cup.

"Cream, sir?" she asked as she prepared a second cup for Clara.

Alexander shook his head. "Thank you no, I prefer a stronger taste." He sipped his drink as he watched Prudence creaming and sugaring Clara's coffee. "Forgive me, but are you the same Prudence who has so diligently cared for my dear Clara?"

Prudence looked up at Alexander, his familiarity with Clara had not gone unnoticed. She nodded. "Yes, sir. I am Miss Johnson's companion," she dropped her head a little, embarrassed for Alexander to see her scar. But he had either not seen it, or it was of little interest to him, as he simply smiled at her.

"Prudence has been an absolute dear. I honestly believe that if it were not for her care, my recovery would have been a lot slower and much more painful." Clara nodded earnestly as she praised her maid.

"Then for that, dear lady, I am forever in your debt," he took another sip of his drink as he continued talking with Clara. In fact, it was another three hours before he finally rose to his feet. He crossed to Clara and knelt down beside her once more.

"It has been the most enjoyable afternoon my dear and I really do wish you a complete and speedy recovery." He kissed Clara's hand gently making her blush and giggle with delight. "I shall be staying with Uncle Anthony a while longer and shall look forward to your return home." He got to his feet and turned to Prudence. "Thank you, again dear Prudence, for the thoughtful and thorough care you have shown to my darling Clara." He paused as Prudence raised her eyebrows slightly at his use of such a familiar pet name. He continued, "and I look forward to hearing news of her rapidly improving health." He smiled at her warmly as she bowed her head slightly.

"Thank you, sir," she said, embarrassed for being praised so highly for simply caring for a friend. "Would you be able to tell us when we should expect Mr. Lawrence Cavendish?" she asked innocently. Alexander glanced across to Clara, seemingly watching for her reaction, but all he could see was a slight grimace as she shifted her sore leg to a more comfortable position. He turned his attention back to Prudence.

"I shall inform Lawrence that he is still expected. I should imagine he shall wish to call upon Clara within the next day or two." He donned his hat. "Good day dear lady." He tipped his hat lightly to Prudence before allowing himself one last glance back at Clara before stepping out into the cool evening breeze.

***

Professor Baxter leaned back, his stomach full and his heart warm. He looked across at his daughter Sophie, engaged in conversation with Lawrence at the far end of the table. He turned to Anthony. "My dear sir, that was an exceptional meal and I thank you heartily for the opportunity to discuss with you young Lawrence's ideas." He glanced up as Mrs. Dimbleby collected his empty plate. "Thank you, my dear, I thoroughly enjoyed your delicious repast."

Mrs. Dimbleby smiled as she trundled her trolley away into the kitchen. Anthony followed the professor's gaze down to where Lawrence was entertaining Sophie. For the first time ever, he began to question if an arranged marriage was the best thing for both Clara and Lawrence. He had never seen his son this animatedly involved with anyone before; his excitement was usually restricted to anything that hadn't been pulled from the depths of someone's backyard.

"Wonderful isn't it? Some of those items have been kept in the library societies archive for decades. Imagine the delight of parents and governesses nationwide as they actively engage their young wards in natural history by actually showing them examples of the very things they are studying. Thank you, dear lady," Professor Baxter said as he took his coffee from Mrs. Dimbleby.

Anthony nodded. "Indeed sir. I am very much looking forward to perusing some of the antiquities myself, but tell me—" he paused to take a sip from his cup before setting it back down on its saucer. "Are there any special measures to caring for such items? I should very much wish to avoid any damage," he finished, draining the remnants of his coffee and setting the cup down on the table.

Professor Baxter smiled. "I shouldn't worry about that, sir. All the artifacts are being handled by Lawrence and he has had intense instruction during his studies." He laughed. "I feel that he probably knows far better than I do." He looked down at the table expecting Lawrence to react to the compliment, but instead, he was still deep in conversation with Sophie. He smiled warmly as he turned his attention back to Anthony. "They seem truly enamored of each other do you not agree, reverend?" he asked as Anthony continued to watch his son.

"Indeed." He glanced across at Amelia. "Please excuse us, Miss Orm as I wish to introduce Professor Baxter to Alexander." He nodded towards the window where Alexander could be seen walking up the path towards the front door.

"Of course, reverend." She smiled as Anthony lead the professor out of the dining room and through to intercept Alexander. She turned her attention back to, what she referred to as 'keeping an eye' on Sophie and Lawrence.

"It is so lovely to see you again, Miss Baxter my dear," Lawrence began cheerily. "I have been so involved with my work that I feel that I have neglected to call upon you quite as often as I had intended." He smiled, clearly captivated by the young woman sitting beside him. Sophie giggled, brushing a strand of her shoulder length, light brown curls back into place.

Some would've called Sophie plain with very little in the way of physical charm, but Lawrence adored her. From her upturned nose to the freckles across her smooth, plump cheeks, every feature seemed to be charming to him. She turned her light hazel eyes to meet his.

"Dear Mr. Cavendish, I understand that your work is important and I lay no blame on you for your indulgence of it. You need not apologize to me." She smiled showing off a row of beautifully even teeth. Lawrence beamed at her.

"Ah, just the fellow," Anthony said as he re-entered the room. "Dreadfully sorry to interrupt miss, but Lawrence is needed in the library." Anthony smiled warmly at Sophie before turning his attention to Lawrence. "We are at a loss as to how to use your filing and labeling system," he admitted as Lawrence excused himself from his conversation and followed his father from the room.

Anthony stopped before they entered the library and turned to his son. "Do you feel it fair of you to continue to woo Miss Baxter when you are already promised to Clara in the eyes of God?" he asked.

Lawrence looked into his father's eyes with all the grit and determination he could muster. "Father I have told you. I am in love with Sophie Baxter and I fully intend to marry her. Besides..." he trailed off for a moment. "There is another for Clara." He smiled at his father's perplexed expression and proceeded to open the library door.

"Lawrence dear fellow, good of you to join us," Alexander called to his cousin. "I have tried to explain to the professor here, however, I believe I am getting into an awful muddle. Tell me, was it date first and then item number followed by the department or item number, date, department?" Alexander asked, a confused expression plastered across his face.

Lawrence smiled at his father as he took the label from Alexander. He pointed to the numbers clearly marked. "Date first, then item number. It is very simple," he explained.

Anthony looked from Lawrence to Alexander. Could he be who Lawrence had meant? Could he have interpreted God's will incorrectly? He decided that it needed more thought but filed it away to discuss with both Lawrence and Amelia another time.

***

Anthony poured out two cups of tea and handed one to Amelia before settling himself down into his favorite armchair. He stirred his drink absentmindedly as he pondered on the problem of Lawrence and Clara. Setting the teaspoon down on the side of the saucer he turned to Amelia. "Miss Orm," he began. "I wish to engage your wisdom, if I may, on a matter pertaining to Clara and Lawrence's betrothal." He leaned forward slightly in his chair. Amelia calmly took a sip of her tea.

"Of course, Reverend. I shall assist in any way I can," she replied. Anthony sighed and set his teacup down on the arm of his chair.

"May I inquire as to the nature of Clara's feelings towards Lawrence?"

Amelia looked at him for a moment deciding how best to respond. "I believe that she cares for him, and wishes to honor both yours and the late Mr. Johnson's wishes," she replied cautiously, unsure as to where Anthony was taking this train of thought.

"But you do not believe that she is against such a union?" he asked, remembering clearly the looks of admiration Lawrence had given Sophie. He wondered if knowing how much attention Lawrence had been giving Miss Baxter would have upset Clara.

Amelia regarded the question carefully. "I would say that she is accepting of it, for she believes that it is the will of God that she is to be joined to Lawrence." She took another sip of her tea as she glanced at Anthony.

"I am fearful to say that Lawrence is less than keen to wed Clara and has seen fit to give his heart to another." He sighed.

"Miss Baxter?" she asked, although she already knew.

Anthony nodded. "Indeed," he replied. "And I am at a loss as to what to do. Lawrence seems to believe that Alexander may have intentions towards Clara, though I have not seen evidence myself of such a notion." He paused and looked at Amelia thoughtfully. "Although," he added slowly, "a union with Alexander would still be a connection between our two families, would you not agree, Miss Orm?" He grinned at Amelia as she continued to sip her tea.

"It is as you say, reverend." She paused as she mulled the thought over in her mind. "However, it does all depend on Alexander and Clara's feelings on the matter," she finished.

"Of course," Anthony nodded.

Chapter
Nine

Clara found herself, for the second time that week, sitting on the little day bed in the Kettering's parlor awaiting the arrival of Lawrence. She smiled to herself as she remembered the last time she had sat there. She started guiltily as she realized, with some surprise, that she was disappointed that her caller was to be Lawrence and not Alexander. She shifted her weight awkwardly to make herself a little more comfortable as Lawrence's voice drifted in from the hallway.

"I believe I am expected. Lawrence Cavendish. I am here to see Miss Johnson." Prudence showed him into the parlor before being sent for a pot of hot coffee. Lawrence seated himself on the sofa across from Clara, a look of concern and remorse upon his face. His glasses were pushed up onto his head and hidden in his messy mop of thick dark hair.

"Clara, I cannot apologize enough," he said as he presented Clara with a small posy of flowers. "Please, can you ever forgive me. I have not once thought of anything but your discomfort since Mrs. Kettering's letter reached us."

Clara smiled, pleased with his gift. "Thank you, Lawrence, they are lovely and please, do not think for one minute that I lay any blame on you for my misfortune. If I had been more truthful with Amelia, this would not have happened."

Lawrence smiled, visibly relieved that Clara was still friendly towards him, but the fact remained that he was ultimately responsible for Clara's condition. Clara looked at him and tried to assess her feelings. She felt sorry for the sensitive creature he was, certainly, and she did indeed care deeply for him, but she was still unsure that it was love. She recalled how Florence's face illuminated with happiness every time she thought of Owen Baxter, and the looks of admiration and adoration Mr. Kettering lavished on his wife. But here, now in this room, although she was glad of Lawrence's company, she could hardly call herself giddy with euphoria— unlike Alexander's visit a mere two days before. She put it to the back of her mind. After all, it was God's will, was it not? If so, then she must do her best.

"Tell me of your museum Lawrence, how is it progressing?" She expected the familiar light to come on in his eyes and the usual enthusiasm that comes to him when he has the chance to talk about his passion. Instead, he merely shrugged.

"Until I find financial backing, I am afraid that it is nothing more than a series of empty rooms." He sighed. "Professor Baxter has been instrumental in finding leads for artifacts and exhibits, but unless I have the means to purchase them, I am nothing more than a man with a list of items for sale."

Seeing Lawrence so disillusioned with the dream that he had endlessly talked of since they were children was heartbreaking. It highlighted to Clara that it was more important than ever for her to find a way to implement her plan. If not to help the man she loved, at the very least to help her brother.

"How are you feeling now? Is your leg any better?" Lawrence continued. "Miss Orm says that you are not well enough to make the journey home, I am most frightfully sorry Clara." He smiled weakly as he tried his best to convey his feelings of remorse. Clara smiled at him.

"Oh, it isn't as bad as all that Lawrence, I assure you. I have a wonderful companion in Prudence, whom I owe my very leg to so I'm told. My only regret is that I can no longer be a bridesmaid for Florence." Clara paused as Prudence bustled in with their refreshments. She set the tray down on the table and, as her mistress was not able to serve her guest, she poured out two cups of coffee.

"Cream, Mr. Cavendish?" she asked politely, ignoring Lawrence's momentary look of horror as he noticed her scar. Well, she thought, she had better get used to that as it will probably happen quite often.

Prudence had mused often over the past month that, rather than a terrible curse, perhaps her accident had been a blessing in disguise. After all, does the good Lord not work in mysterious ways? It had brought her the one thing she needed most in her life: a friend. Lawrence looked away, embarrassed that he had been staring.

"Just a little please," he replied.

"Very good sir," Prudence said and added a small drop of cream to Lawrence's cup, then handed it to him. She then set about preparing one for Clara.

"It is an awful blow that you cannot attend Florence's wedding Clara, it is that I feel the worst for," he looked down into his coffee. "And I shall be attending in your place, it hardly seems fair." He sighed. Clara looked up in surprise. What did he just say? Surely, he did not mean that he was taking her place as Florence's bridesmaid.

"I'm terribly sorry Lawrence, but you have me at a loss. How are you able to take my place?" she asked.

Lawrence took one look at Clara's innocent, confused face and let out a burst of laughter. "I see what you mean though," he said through tears of laughter. "No, I have been invited as Miss Sophie Baxter's escort. Owen Baxter is a cousin of hers. She shall be the one in the dress, not me."

Clara smiled weakly. So, she had been right, Sophie and the professor were related to Owen and now the girl whom Lawrence had lavished with attention on the afternoon of her birthday party was to take her place at the side of one of her dearest friends. It was very nearly too much to bear.

"Clara, what's wrong? Do you feel unwell?" Lawrence stood in panic and raced over to Clara as she felt the blood leave her face. Lawrence was not the only one to have noticed and Prudence darted across the room to attend to her.

"Mistress please speak to us. Do you feel any pain?" Prudence could feel the panic rising in her stomach as she observed Clara's pale, expressionless face. After what felt like an absolute age, Clara spoke.

"I'm sorry to have worried you both. I am fine really, just a little tired," she said, and she gave Lawrence a weak, thin-lipped smile.

Relieved once more, Lawrence sank back into his seat, but he was not to remain there for long. Prudence, sensing that something was not right, had gone to alert Ophelia, who came gliding in.

"It looks as though we have attempted too much too soon," she said to Clara, smiling at her kindly as she checked her forehead. "Two callers in as many days seems to have taken its toll far more than I had expected." She turned to Lawrence. "I am afraid that your visit has drained Clara and I think it best that we return her to bed. My apologies Mr. Cavendish, but I feel that it would be wise for you to take your leave now and allow Clara to rest." Ophelia's reservations regarding moving Clara a second time were proving to be well founded. She called for Joseph to come and transfer Clara back upstairs to her room.

Lawrence stood. "I am truly sorry. I had no idea my sister was in such fragile health."

Ophelia noticed his use of the word sister. *Interesting*.

"I shall indeed take my leave, but may I be allowed back at a later date to check up on her?" he asked earnestly.

"Of course. You are always more than welcome here, Mr. Cavendish, and you shall be kept abreast of Clara's condition," Ophelia replied before she swept out of the room, following her husband upstairs as he carried a very lethargic

Clara.

Lawrence spotted Prudence as she set off after Ophelia intending to settle Clara into bed. He stopped and caught her by the elbow. "Excuse me miss but am I to assume that you are my sister's companion, Prudence?"

Prudence nodded silently. She had picked up on the use of sister also and she felt sure that it was his fault that Clara had suffered a relapse. "I am Miss Johnson's companion sir, yes," she replied as politely as she could as she looked down at where Lawrence was grasping her elbow. He released her, embarrassed.

"May I inquire as to the exact nature of my sister's injuries? I have been told that she was involved in an operation but I have not been given more specific information than this."

Prudence quickly explained what had happened from her vantage point atop the chair during Doctor Fletcher's visit. All the color drained from Lawrence's face as the extent of Clara's plight dawned on him. Prudence, eager to make sure that her mistress was comfortable, rang for Miss Parker to see Mr. Cavendish out.

"Forgive me, sir but I fear I may be needed to attend my mistress. Miss Parker shall show you out." She darted upstairs, eager to reassure herself that Clara was alright. She knocked at Clara's bedroom door and waited to be admitted.

Ophelia's voice sounded from within. "Prudence? Is that you?"

Prudence answered immediately. "Yes ma'am"

"Wait there I should like a brief word with you. I have nearly finished settling Clara."

Prudence waited patiently for Ophelia to emerge. Before long she did indeed glide out of the door, calling back to Clara over her shoulder."Try to get some rest, my dear. The excitement of seeing Lawrence coupled with the move has tired you." She closed the door softly and, beckoning to Prudence to join her in the parlor, led the way downstairs. She swept into the room and indicated for Prudence to close the door behind her.

"I am not the sort of person to pry, Prudence dear and I would not expect you to break a confidence, but I must confess to having concerns regarding Clara and Mr. Cavendish's relationship." Prudence nodded, she had felt the same. Ophelia continued, "And to that end, I wish to ask if Clara has mentioned how it is that they are to be married when young Mr. Cavendish seems to regard her as his sibling." She paused, this was clearly a difficult question to ask, but one she felt she must. "Forgive me, but is this betrothal perhaps entirely fabricated within Clara's imagination?"

Prudence shook her head slowly. "No, ma'am. As I understand it, the late Mr. Johnson and the Reverend Cavendish agreed that Miss Johnson would be married to young Mr. Cavendish as soon as it was financially viable to do so."

"I see." Ophelia nodded her head as she began to

understand the situation a little more. "Was anything said to have affected Clara in this manner triggering a relapse?"

Prudence cast her mind back to the conversation, trying to pinpoint where it was that Clara had first taken ill. She couldn't be sure but she felt that it was sometime around the discussion of the bridesmaid, what was her name again? She couldn't quite remember as she was trying her best not to listen.

"I cannot be certain ma'am, but I first noticed Miss Johnson's pallor during a discussion about the replacement bridesmaid, but I must confess to not being able to remember the young lady's name." Prudence could see that Ophelia was putting the pieces together and was not entirely happy with the result.

"One last question if I may, is Mr. Cavendish intending on attending the wedding as Miss Baxter's escort?" Prudence nodded. Ophelia's fears were confirmed. Clara was not just bedridden with an injured leg, but she suspected that Clara was in bed suffering a broken heart. She decided that the best course of action would be to write to Amelia at once and ask for her advice and guidance on the matter.

"Thank you, Prudence dear, you have been most helpful. I shall not ask you to break your mistress' confidence again. However, I feel that Clara has set her sights on a suitor who has his heart elsewhere."

Prudence frowned, unsure if her employer had understood the entire situation correctly. "Begging your pardon ma'am, but I feel that it may be a little more complex." She looked up at Ophelia who gestured for her to continue. "Two days prior to Mr. Cavendish's visit, Clara received another caller, a Mr. Alexander Cavendish. He stayed for the entire afternoon ma'am and both he and Miss Johnson seemed very familiar." She dropped her eyes. "He appeared captivated by her ma'am," she finished.

Ophelia's eyes widened as the penny started to drop. "And you feel that Clara is, not only disappointed that she cannot attend Florence's wedding, but also confused by her feelings for both Lawrence and Alexander Cavendish?" She asked. Prudence nodded.

"Miss Johnson tells me that the Reverend Cavendish foretold her betrothal in a vision from God," she said. Ophelia nodded gravely.

"I see. By accepting her feelings for Alexander, she would be, not just betraying her father and the good reverend, but also her faith in God." She sucked her cheeks in as she pondered the problem. "Thank you, Prudence, I shall give it some more thought."

Prudence proceeded to tidy away the coffee things and carried the tray through to the kitchen, a look of worry etched across her face.

"Penny for your thoughts," Miss Parker asked and smiled. Although unmarried and having no children of her own, she had always been a mother hen and felt that she was akin to a matriarchal figure for the younger staff under her. Prudence sighed.

"I think Clara's faith is being tested by our good Lord and I don't think I know how to help her." She sighed. Miss Parker nodded as she clattered and clanked pot lids and kettles, busily preparing supper.

"And we know that for those who love God all things work together, for good, for those who are called according to His purpose," she called over her shoulder as she stirred a large pot of bubbling broth. "Romans 8:28," she reminded Prudence who smiled and nodded, already feeling a little better. "I shall have Clara's supper things ready shortly my dear. Young Florence was in here earlier asking after her health and saying she might pop her head round later," she, added, glancing at Prudence who looked a little taken aback.

Although she had the greatest of respect and cared for Florence dearly, she feared that in Clara's current state, a visit from a flighty friend might not be the best idea. Especially as that flighty friend is in the middle of preparing for a wedding that Clara was clearly not going to get.

"But Clara was taken ill earlier, so Mr. Cavendish had to leave. She was put back to bed. I shall have a word with Mrs. Kettering and see how she feels about it." Prudence finished washing out the coffee pot and stood it on the drainer to dry before heading off to find Ophelia and to check in on Clara.

When Prudence approached Clara's door, however, she could already hear the good-natured Florence chattering away about the preparations for the wedding and how romantic it was that Lawrence had brought her flowers knowing that she was so ill. Prudence cringed as she knew that hearing those words would be upsetting for Clara.

However, until the supper was ready, she really didn't have a legitimate reason for interrupting, so instead, she headed back down to the kitchen to see if Miss Parker needed any help with the evening meal, leaving Clara and Florence to their girl talk.

"Back again so soon? I thought you would be needed upstairs." Miss Parker looked over at Prudence, surprised to find her standing in the doorway offering her help with the supper things.

"Clara has a visitor currently. Shall I set out the table, cook?"

Miss Parker nodded, pleased at having Prudence back. There wasn't another like Prudence. Not only was she a hard, honest, and diligent worker, she was also good company and had raised her spirits on many cold mornings over the past month or so. She allowed herself a moment to watch the girl as she moved about the kitchen, almost dancing around as she collected the things that she would need for the dining room, placing each item carefully onto the trolley before wheeling it into the dining room, stopping to collect some clean linens from the closet at the side of the stove. *A well-oiled machine,* she thought to herself proudly as she went back to her apple pie.

As Prudence returned to the kitchen, Miss Parker held out Clara's supper tray, ready for Prudence to deliver it. As per Clara's request, Prudence's own supper was also included and so, Prudence found herself once more outside Clara's door. She set the tray down as she tapped on the door. She received no answer. She knocked again, a little louder this time, but again, when no answer came, she began to feel anxious.

"Miss Johnson? Miss Johnson, It's Prudence. I have our supper here. May I come in?" As Prudence listened a small, weak, muffled voice came from inside the room. Worried that Clara may have been seriously ill, Prudence pushed on the door and entered, carrying the supper tray in with her. She set it down on the low dresser as she approached Clara's bed.

"Miss Johnson? Are you feeling unwell? Should I send for Doctor Fletcher?"

Clara was lying on her side, curled into as much of a ball as her sore leg would allow her to be. Her shoulders were moving and trembling. Prudence could see that she was clearly upset. Clara was sobbing into her pillow. Overcome with feelings of sorrow and dismay at seeing her friend and beloved mistress in such distress, Prudence reached her hand over and clasped Clara's shoulder. Gingerly, she pulled her close and held her as the full force of Clara's tears took hold. Her body quivered as sob after sob shook her delicate frame. Prudence stroked her hair, allowing Clara to muffle the sound of her tears into her apron.

"Miss Johnson, don't take on so. What on earth is the matter? What can be done to bring a smile back to your pretty face?"

Clara pulled herself up as best she could to sit and look at her companion. Her face was streaked with tears and her eyes were red and puffed, it was clear that she had been crying for a good while. She took several deep breaths as she tried to steady herself enough to speak. Eventually, the sobs began to subside and she felt able enough to convey to Prudence the nature of her sadness.

"I know you will think me a wicked, wicked friend and I have never been a jealous person, not ever, but..." she trailed off as she fought to keep her sobs under control. "But, it is my belief that Lawrence's friend Miss Sophie Baxter means far more to him than simply an acquaintance. The mere thought that she shall be paraded through the church wearing the dress meant for me, on Lawrence's arm, on my dearest friend's wedding day is all just too much." Clara's eyes again filled with tears as she buried her face in her hands to sob anew.

Prudence crossed to the dresser and pulled out a clean white lace handkerchief and handed it to Clara. She took it and dabbed delicately at her eyes. "Come now," she soothed kindly. "We have no guarantee of that. Miss Baxter is a cousin of the bridegroom and has been asked to step in at the last minute. I should imagine if you had been a bridesmaid, as was intended, then you should have been on the arm of Mr. Cavendish." She put her hand on Clara's and smiled at her reassuringly. Then a thought struck her. "Forgive me mistress but I couldn't help noticing the way Alexander was looking at you." She paused, worried that she may have said too much.

Clara smiled through her tears. "Dear Alexander. I must admit Prudence he and I have always felt close." She looked at her companion. "Oh Prudence, you are a dear, you really are. Please accept my apologies for causing such a scene." She looked down at the handkerchief she had clutched in her

155

hand. "Florence is positively euphoric in regards to marrying her beau. She tells me that Sophie is a darling creature who seems incredibly grateful to have been thought of and asked to be a bridesmaid."

Prudence could see that Clara was a kind-hearted girl by nature and that she wanted to like Sophie. She crossed to the table to retrieve the supper tray. "Would you try a bite ma'am? I am quite certain that you should feel better for it." She set the tray in front of Clara who eyed the food with little interest. However, not wanting the food to spoil nor to offend her hosts, she pulled the tray nearer to her.

The delicious smell of Miss Parker's hearty supper quickly made her change her mind as she took a spoonful of hot chicken broth. She swished the tasty soup around her tongue, cooling the liquid a little before swallowing, and found that she was indeed hungry and would go on to finish the entire bowl.

Chapter
Ten

Clara stared at the underside of the pretty blue canopy as the fresh dawn sunlight streamed in at the window, bathing the room in dim light. She let her mind return to the subject that had prevented her from sleeping all night long: Lawrence Cavendish. She suspected that his feelings for Sophie stretched far beyond his feelings for her, but it didn't really change anything. Their union was the will of God, her guardian, and her late father. And so, that being the case, she must do her utmost to fund her future husband's museum. If that meant pretending to be Isabelle Crofton then that is exactly what she must do, for as long as it takes.

Her face set in steely resolve, she attempted to pull herself up into a seated position. She winced as hot twinges ran up and down her sore leg. She moved to try and get into a more comfortable position. *Blast this leg,* she thought. She would have to wait until she had healed before she could do anything, but this was now her second week. The week her stitches were due to come out and also, the week of Florence's wedding to Mr. Baxter. A knock sounded at the adjoining door between her room and Prudence's.

"Come in Prudence, I'm awake," she called. Prudence

pushed open the door and entered, carrying clean bandages, rubbing alcohol and the thick green substance that she had smeared onto Clara's scars three times every day for the past week.

"Good morning ma'am, did you sleep well?" she asked. Clara sighed a heavy sigh as Prudence pulled back the sheets to expose Clara's bandaged appendage.

"In all honestly Prudence, I did not, but I have made a decision."

Prudence stopped what she was doing to look her mistress square in the eye, anticipating what was to come next.

"I have decided that I wish to continue with my original plan to raise money for Lawrence's museum venture and take a job as a spool girl in my late father's mill."

Prudence looked down at Clara's leg as she unwound yesterday's bandages. She was certain that Clara would have given up on the notion once she had discovered that Lawrence had given his heart to another, but it seemed that she still felt duty bound to honor the wishes of her father.

"I shall support you in any decision you wish to make, mistress. However, I feel that a change of identity and clothing will not be enough to allow you to step into factory life." Prudence glanced up at Clara as she spoke. Clara looked confused.

"I'm unsure as to what you mean. Surely I should not actually need to be impoverished in order to secure myself a position?"

Prudence shook her head. "No ma'am, but your manner and use of language will reveal your identity as soon as you engage with someone in conversation," Prudence explained. Clara gave her a puzzled look.

"But you speak beautifully Prudence and you were employed within the factory, were you not?"

Prudence nodded, this was true, her level of speech matched her position as housekeeper and allowed her to engage in polite conversation with callers and occasionally business associates of Mr. Kettering's.

"I have taken extensive lessons in the art of elocution ma'am, at the behest of Mr. Kettering, in order for me to practice my role within his household."

Clara nodded slowly. Of course, it would not do at all for a gentleman of Mr. Kettering's standing to have ill-educated, rude domestic staff. "I see, but how am I to conduct myself appropriately if I am unable to speak?" She sighed.

Prudence wiped her greasy hands, thick with Clara's medicinal lotion, before proceeding to dress the wounds with fresh bandages. "You shall speak, for if you are certain that you wish to proceed with your original notion, then I shall educate you in the art of informal speech," she replied. Clara smiled at her as she counted herself lucky to be blessed with such a thoughtful and caring friend. "Are you certain that this is something you need to do mistress?" Prudence placed Clara's leg gently back onto the bed and adjusted the sheets. Clara nodded firmly.

"Prudence, the Reverend Cavendish told me himself that my marriage to Lawrence is the wish of God." She dropped her eyes, unsure of what she was about to say next. "Even if I may care for Alexander," she added quietly. Prudence placed the alcohol, bandages, and poultice on the dresser.

"Very well ma'am. If it pleases, we shall start after breakfast for I believe we may not have much longer than two weeks for you to learn and practice until you are able to confidently converse with another factory worker."

Although this was true, Prudence felt that Doctor Fletcher may still advise Clara to keep off her leg for a further week once the stitches have been removed. Even so, the wounds were clean and healthy and had already begun to heal nicely. If Clara did need to walk with a limp for a while, this may add to the character that they were trying to portray, thus making her story of impoverished orphan all the more believable. Once Prudence was quite convinced that Clara was comfortable, she made her way down to the kitchen to collect her breakfast tray.

"Here we are dear, eggs, bacon, toast, coffee, and orange juice. I have included your bowl of oatmeal also."

Prudence smiled as Miss Parker winked at her. Oatmeal and a weak coffee had been Prudence's breakfast of choice ever since the first morning Mr. Kettering had brought her home from the factory.

"Thank you, cook. I shall return the tray once Clara has finished," she replied. Leaving the kitchen, Prudence met Ophelia heading for the stairs, clutching a letter in her hand.

"Ah, Prudence. I shall be unavailable today as I have a number of appointments with Florence, would you be so kind as to inform Miss Parker that Mr. Kettering shall be dining alone at luncheon?"

Prudence nodded in response as Ophelia continued up to her private room at the top of the house. Prudence tapped on Clara's door.

"Come in," Clara called. She felt much brighter now that a firm decision had been made, and she was quite looking forward to working in the factory. Although she had not a clue what factory life entailed, she felt certain that she would do her best and earn enough money to buy enough artifacts that Lawrence could open his museum. Her face fell, just a little, as she thought of Lawrence and Sophie, but she pushed the thought firmly from her mind. This was no time for self-pity.

Prudence placed Clara's breakfast down in front of her and she tucked in hungrily, the crispy bacon snapping and crackling as she pushed it onto her fork. Just the way she liked it. Wiping the remains of the deep golden egg yolk off her plate, she popped the forkful of bacon into her mouth, savoring the salty flavor. Prudence sat beside her to eat her bowl of hot oatmeal.

"How shall we proceed today, Prudence? I have been thinking and we may need strategies in place should Mrs. Kettering or Florence call upon me."

Prudence placed her empty bowl back onto the tray and picked up her steaming cup of fresh coffee. "We shan't need to concern ourselves with that today, mistress. Mrs. Kettering is running errands with Miss Kettering all day and shall not be back until supper."

Clara smiled, relieved. It was going to be hard enough keeping her 'anti-elocution' lessons well hidden from the Ketterings for the remaining two weeks. She had no idea whatsoever how she was to keep her physically leaving the house once a day, every day to attend work a secret.

A sharp knock sounded, followed by the voice of Ophelia. "Clara dear, may I step inside for a moment, I need to speak with you," she called, her hand resting on the door handle.

"But of course, Mrs. Kettering."

Ophelia gracefully entered the room and crossed over to Clara. "I have received word that Doctor Fletcher shall arrive today to remove your stitches and to give his final assessment of your injuries."

Clara, surprise registering on her face, looked up at Ophelia, a little distressed to find her with a frown upon her usually placid face. "So soon? That is excellent news is it not?" she asked.

Ophelia appeared to recover as she answered Clara. "Yes, yes, excellent news. However, I am more than a little irked that both Joseph and I shall not be home when he comes to call." She turned to Prudence. "Prudence my dear, please take careful note as to what Doctor Fletcher has to say on Clara's scarring and how much longer she is to remain in bed." She stopped to think for a moment. She continued, clearly making up her mind, "Ask him to forward his bill to Mr. Kettering and we shall settle our account upon receipt."

Prudence nodded. "Yes ma'am," she replied. "When shall we expect your return ma'am?" Prudence enquired of her employer as Ophelia headed for the door.

"I should expect to have finished no later than supper." She turned to Clara. "I am truly sorry that I cannot be here for Doctor Fletcher's visit my dear, but with Florence's wedding in three days' time I really do need to keep these appointments."

Clara smiled warmly. "I fully understand Mrs. Kettering, have a good day."

Ophelia then removed herself from the room, leaving Prudence and Clara to proceed with the first of Clara's lessons. Things started well as Prudence explained the many differences between their worlds and backgrounds.

"For example, we were both orphaned at an early age. My parents, however, were of the working class. My father worked on the great cotton plantations to feed myself and my sister. We were unable to afford doctor's fees and so when my mother contracted malaria there was little we could do but to watch her die."

Clara clasped her hand to her mouth, as she listened to Prudence's sad story of the death of her family.

"I was six when I had to start working in the cotton fields. I was picking all day to support my ailing father and my younger sister. I was forced to continue to work due to my

163

father's poor background and as such, when my father died, Isabelle and I continued to work at the plantations until I was moved to the new factory."

Clara looked at Prudence as though she was seeing her for the first time. The shy, retiring wallflower that she had assumed her to be when she first arrived had turned out to be an intelligent and strong individual indeed.

"And my background is starkly different from yours: a privileged child raised in an upper-class family. When my parents were killed in a house fire, Mr. Cavendish took me and my governess in and raised me as his adopted daughter. My father's mills and money held in trust for me until the day that I should marry." It hardly seemed fair to Clara. She had not worked a single day in her life, and yet she had wealth waiting for her. Prudence, on the other hand, had worked her entire life and, unless Mr. and Mrs. Kettering remember her in their wills, she shall have nothing.

Prudence continued, "So many of the people you will be working alongside will have come from a similar background to me, only they wouldn't have been so fortunate to have had a large piece of metal lodged in their faces."

Clara's face dropped. Fortunate, how on earth could Prudence consider that fortunate?

"What on earth made you say that?" she asked.

Prudence smiled, clearly amused by Clara's question. "If God had not let my accident befall me when he did, I should not have acquired the role of housekeeper to the Kettering family, and I certainly would never have met you. Would you not call that fortunate?"

A big smile slowly spread across Clara's face. "I would indeed, my dear Prudence, I would indeed."

The lesson went on for perhaps another hour until a knock at the door interrupted Clara's practice with a, particularly difficult concept. The art of hiding her education.

"Many of your fellow workers, if not all, will not have had any formal education and will certainly have no knowledge of many things outside of their own basic needs, and the needs of their families. If you are to succeed in your mission, you must have them believe that you are as ill-educated as they," Prudence had said.

Now, Clara was trying to think up ways of hiding her eighteen years of knowledge, breeding and privileged upbringing. At that moment, there was a knock at her bedroom door followed by Miss Parker telling her that Clara had a visitor.

"Come in," Clara called and Prudence showed the doctor in.

"Prudence my dear, a delight to see you again." The young doctor beamed at her. Prudence could feel her cheeks flush with color as she cast her eyes down to her feet.

"Thank you, doctor," she mumbled, clearly embarrassed. Doctor Fletcher smiled to himself as he turned his attention to Clara.

"Ah, Miss Johnson. And how are you feeling this morning?" He took off his coat and rolled up his sleeves, ready to set about the task of removing Clara's stitches.

"I have been healing well, doctor. Please accept my sincerest appreciation for your intervention during my infection. I really am most awfully grateful."

Doctor Fletcher brushed this away with a small shake of his head. "Nonsense, my dear. I heal the sick and the needy. I was more than glad to have treated your malady. Now, have you experienced any pain over the past two weeks?" he asked as Prudence helped Clara into a comfortable position for the doctor to examine her leg.

"Twinges mostly, doctor, but they have been easing recently," she replied.

Prudence undid the clean bandages to expose Clara's stitches for the doctor to inspect.

"My dear girl, these are healing excellently. It is clear that you have diligently attended to your mistress. I am most impressed."

Again, Clara noticed Prudence blush.

"Thank you, doctor, I shall fetch hot water and clean towels for you," she said as she dashed from the room. Clara made a mental note to casually mention the doctor again to test her theory. However, it really was quite obvious that Prudence liked Doctor Fletcher.

"Right, Miss Johnson. Today I shall be removing the

stitches, nothing more. I am glad to see that the swelling has completely subsided." He turned Clara's leg carefully this way and that, checking for any anomalies that would need further treatment. "And the bruising has started to fade. Good, good." He replaced her leg and reached down for his bag to check that he had everything he would need.

"Tell me, have you kept to your bed as I bid you?"

Clara nodded diligently.

"Yes, doctor. I was carried downstairs on no more than two occasions by Mr. Kettering to receive guests, but I have not used my leg and it has been elevated the entire time I assure you," she replied.

The doctor pushed his blonde hair back from his emerald green eyes as he retrieved a pair of magnification spectacles from his bag and pulled them over his head.

"Excellent, Miss Johnson. I should say that another week of rest and this leg shall be fine."

A short rap on the door interrupted him as Prudence arrived with the towels and soap.

"I have instructed cook for a kettle of water, sir." She placed the towels on the end of Clara's bed before running to the shared bathroom to draw a basin of cold water. She carried it in and placed it on Clara's dresser.

"Wonderful, Prudence my dear, thank you."

Prudence again blushed and smiled, dropping her head in

embarrassment.

"Miss Johnson, may I enter?" Miss Parker's muffled voice came from behind Clara's closed bedroom door. "It's Miss Parker, I have the water you requested."

Prudence ran to open the door for the cook to bring the kettle in.

"Good afternoon, Doctor Fletcher, where would you like this, sir?" She held up the hot water.

"Excellent. Just there on the dresser if you please," he indicated to a space beside the basin on top of Clara's dresser.

Miss Parker set the kettle down, smiled at Clara, winked at Prudence and left to go back downstairs to see to luncheon. Prudence also turned to leave but Clara called her back.

"Oh, please stay, Prudence. I feel certain that I shall need you here." Clara smiled at Prudence as she came back in and seated herself beside Clara. "Thank you, dearest, I am most nervous and I shall be glad of your company."

Prudence smiled warmly at Clara and took her hand in her own and gave it a squeeze to let her know that she was happy to support her friend in her time of need.

"Now then Miss, you may feel a slight pinch as I cut each set away, but other than that, the procedure is quite painless. Are you ready for me to begin?"

Clara nodded as the doctor pulled the glasses down over

his eyes and bent his head low over Clara's leg as he cut the first set of stitches. Clara winced and tightened her grip on Prudence's hand.

"Nearly there now, just two more sets to go. You have been most brave Miss Johnson."

Doctor Fletcher snipped the last set of stitches away as Clara relaxed her leg.

"There now. Prudence, my dear, if you would be so kind as to clean and dress the leg, I shall clean my hands and tools."

Prudence nodded. As she rose and moved towards the dresser, she brushed past Doctor Fletcher, causing a little color to her cheeks. Remembering Ophelia's earlier words, Prudence asked the doctor how long Clara was to remain in bed and how he felt her scars were healing.

"Oh, you have taken such excellent care of your mistresses wounds that the scars are healing nicely. Now that the stitches have been removed they shall start to gradually fade. As for the bed rest, I should give another week of rest to ensure that none of the wounds reopen. After which, Miss Johnson should take short lengths of gentle to moderate exercise and rest often." He smiled broadly at Prudence showing off his high cheekbones. Prudence pretended not to notice.

"My employer, Mrs. Kettering, would like me to express her apologies at being unable to attend Miss Johnson's appointment with you today. She has asked that you forward your bill and it shall be settled upon receipt," Prudence, who had delivered the entire speech to the bedroom carpet, started as the doctor put his fingers softly under her chin and gently raised her face up to meet his.

"That's better. I am certain that the carpet would welcome my fee. However, if I am to eat this week, I should prefer it if it was I who receives payment." He grinned at Prudence as she gazed up into his face, unsure as to what to say.

Eventually, she found her voice. "Y-yes of course. Thank you, doctor," she stammered. Clara stifled a giggle as she thought how pleasant and witty the young doctor was, and how poor Prudence was having to hide her feelings.

"I shall see myself out. Be sure to call upon my services if you feel any pain or swelling, Miss Johnson. Otherwise, I should expect you up and about again in another week." With that he took his leave, closing the door softly behind him.

Prudence returned to cleaning and dressing Clara's leg as Clara broached the subject of Prudence's feelings towards Doctor Fletcher. "The doctor is very bright and cheerful, isn't he?" she asked innocently. She looked at Prudence who pretended to be far too busy concentrating on wrapping her leg.

"Yes, Mistress, I expect he was pleased to see how well you have healed." Prudence hoped very much that this was, at least in part, to how well she had cleaned and treated Clara's scars. She changed the subject, eager to get off the topic of Doctor Fletcher as she didn't want to answer any embarrassing questions from Clara.

"Do you wish to continue our earlier lesson?" She asked. Clara nodded.

"I should think so, Prudence, I thought I was rather starting to improve."

This was true, Prudence was impressed as to how quickly Clara was taking to slang terms and the concepts that she had been raising.

Doctor Fletcher had given them a week to work with, and at the rate, Clara was going, Prudence felt that a week may just be enough to get Clara well versed in the art of slang and to help her to fit in with the other factory workers.

"Ah ain't layte yit sahr," crooned Clara, exaggerating her southern accent. "Heyer y'all are."

At this point Clara stopped and clasped her hand to her stomach as the loudest sound she had heard in a long time, emanated from it, indicating her hunger.

"I do beg your pardon, Prudence."

Clara's horrified expression indicated to Prudence that they had become so engrossed in Clara's studies that they had very nearly worked through their afternoon meal.

"I believe that it is time for luncheon, ma'am. With your leave, I shall go and fetch the tray."

Clara nodded as Prudence rose from her chair and made her way towards the door.

"And I shall continue to practice until your return," Clara

called after her.

Prudence sped down the stairs and through to the kitchen where the most delicious smells were wafting through to her nose, reminding her stomach that she hadn't eaten since breakfast.

She pushed open the door to find Miss Parker just plating up two meals and placing them under a stainless-steel cloche. She caught sight of Prudence by the door.

"Your young doctor still here, Pru?" she asked, gently teasing Prudence sending her red again.

"I am at a loss as to what you might mean, Miss Parker." Prudence allowed herself a little smile as she thought of Doctor Fletcher, but she set her expression back quickly as she caught sight of Miss Parker's knowing smile. "If you are referring to Doctor Fletcher and enquiring as to whether he is still tending to Miss Johnson, then I am afraid the answer is no, he is not. He left well over an hour ago, which I suspect you already knew."

Miss Parker grinned.

"And what news of Clara's leg?" she asked, hoping that it would be good news.

Prudence proceeded to fill her in as Miss Parker placed two helpings of cherry pie onto the tray complete with a jug of thick, yellow custard.

"That is good news. Please tell young Clara that we are all looking forward to seeing her up and about." She picked up a second tray laden with Mr. Kettering's meal and followed Prudence out of the kitchen, but turned off towards Joseph's private study as Prudence climbed the stairs back up to Clara's room.

As she entered Clara called out to her. "That smells maighty fane there. Ah'm so hangry ah could eat a caw." She beamed at Prudence as she brought the tray in and set it down.

"How was that?" she asked proudly. Prudence giggled.

"Very good ma'am." She smiled. Clara really seemed to be enjoying herself. But it was important to remember why she was learning in the first place. "However, I hardly feel that there will ever be a need to say such a thing."

Clara nodded, pushing herself up on her pillows. Prudence was right, of course, but then she had only said it to amuse.

Clara looked at her maid. She really seemed to have come out of herself since they had started working on her speech lessons. She cast her mind back to the shy, slightly sad little maid she had met when she first arrived. Getting a smile from her then was almost impossible, and now here she was giggling with her.

Maybe God had sent her malady just at the right time as he had inflicted Prudence with hers. She smiled to herself as Prudence placed the tray carefully across her lap and removed the steel cloche.

Chapter
Eleven

"And I dun seen anythin' like that a'fore mayam, an I din't do nothin' no how." Clara looked at Prudence. "Am I any better?"

It had been three days since Clara and Prudence had finalized their arrangements and Clara had started her lessons. Prudence nodded with satisfaction.

"I believe so mistress. Indeed, it appears that you may be nearing the next stage of becoming my sister," she replied. Clara giggled. She quite liked the idea of becoming Prudence's sister. She could see them attending Church together, shopping together, chattering together and exchanging presents at Christmas time.

She stopped to think about this. Surely though that would be almost everything that they do now? The only difference being that Clara was still bedridden and was forbidden to leave the house, even to attend Church on Sunday. So maybe friends would be better than sisters after all.

"So, what must be done next if I am to truly be a member of the factory workforce?" she asked, eager to move forward.

Prudence surveyed her companion thoughtfully.

"We must dress you appropriately mistress," she said at last.

Clara clapped her hands together in delight, thoroughly enjoying herself.

"Could we do that now do you think?" Clara asked, anxious to see what she would've looked like as Isabelle Crofton. But Prudence shook her head firmly.

"I am afraid that it would be far too risky, ma'am. Miss Kettering and Mrs. Kettering are currently in the parlor being attended to by the seamstress. This will be Miss Kettering's final fitting before her vows tomorrow morning."

Clara's face fell as she thought again of Lawrence walking with Sophie on his arm, and of her beautiful Florence dressed in her wedding finery. Handsome Joseph walking her to the altar to hand her to Mr. Baxter. She blinked back tears. It all hurt so much. Prudence reached over and gave Clara's hand a squeeze.

"Mistress?"

Clara looked up into Prudence's friendly eyes.

"The Lord himself goes before you and will be with you; he will never leave you nor forsake you. Do not be afraid; do not be discouraged."

Clara smiled at the familiar passage in Deuteronomy. She nodded. Prudence was, of course, right. It was necessary for it to be this way, after all, if she had been heavily involved with the wedding, she would not have managed to prepare, nor execute her plan. No, God had other work for her tomorrow and she needed to put her heart and faith in that instead.

"Thank you, Prudence. I believe I needed to hear that," she sighed. Prudence smiled warmly as Clara dabbed her eyes dry with her handkerchief.

"Now, I do believe—" she was interrupted by a tapping at the door.

"Clara, dearest heart? Are you awake? It's Florence, may I come in?"

Clara smiled as Prudence made her way across the room to open the door.

"Of course, dearest."

Prudence opened the door wide as Florence stepped in, dressed from head to toe in beautiful white silk. Her headdress of flowers and veil pushed back for Clara to see her face. Her white, long-sleeved gown billowed out in a long train which Prudence set about draping carefully out over the carpet behind Florence so that Clara could see the entire dress.

"Oh Florence, my beautiful Florence." Tears formed in Clara's eyes as she looked at her friend. But this time they were tears of pure joy as she gazed upon her childhood friend's blissful expression. "You look absolutely perfect." She dabbed her eyes again with her handkerchief as Ophelia stepped into the room behind her daughter.

"Oh, Mrs. Kettering, Florence looks an absolute dream. I am so happy for you dearest."

Florence smiled at Clara.

"Are you happy to wear your gown now, Florence? Now that Clara has been the first to see you in it?" Ophelia smiled warmly as she witnessed the closeness between the two girls.

"Oh, Clara, I had to show you first. You simply had to be the first to see. Do you think it will do?"

Clara fought back tears as she looked from Florence to Ophelia.

"I believe that Mr. Baxter is the luckiest man to have ever walked God's earth," she whispered to her friend. Tears welled up in Florence's eyes as she moved across to close her arms around her bedridden friend.

"Thank you sweetest," she whispered into Clara's ear. "I'm sure that you will be next, my love." She walked back to where her mother was watching, a proud smile plastered on her face.

"I think it would be best if you were to remove the gown now, Florence dear, we should not want anything unfortunate to happen to it the eve before the wedding."

Florence's face turned to horror at the thought of what she would do in such a situation.

"Oh, that would be horrid. Clara, I must change."

Prudence helped her to gather her train and Florence carefully made her way back down to the parlor to change back into her day dress. Ophelia stayed behind anxious to talk with Clara.

"Clara dear, I know that you are more than a little disappointed that you cannot be a bridesmaid to Florence tomorrow, but please rest assured that Florence has talked of nothing but your exclusion and how she would change the situation if it was within her power to do so."

Clara smiled.

"Mrs. Kettering, Florence has always been and continues to be my oldest and dearest friend. I believe that she would argue with God in his heaven if she thought that it would do any good for me," she replied sincerely.

Ophelia smiled. "It is true, I am deeply disappointed that I shall not be there on Florence's special day, but please try to make her understand that I am happy for her to enjoy her day and that I love her very much."

Ophelia crossed the room and planted a kiss on Clara's head.

"I am certain that Florence shall be in once she has changed. She has much to tell you I imagine." Ophelia turned to find Miss Parker standing at the door holding the late morning's post on a silver tray.

"Thank you, Miss Parker, please place it in my room and I shall read it once the dress is safely packed away within its sheath."

Miss Parker bowed her head slightly.

"Very good, ma'am."

Ophelia made her way back down to the parlor where Prudence had assisted Florence out of her dress and into her day wear. She was now covering Florence's gown with its protective cover.

"Thank you, Prudence. I shall take the gown with me as I am on my way to my room, I shall hang it in there to protect it for tomorrow."

Prudence nodded and handed the dress carefully to Ophelia. A knock came at the parlor door.

"My dears, there is a messenger arrived from Finchley's. The flowers shall be ready for delivery by eight. Is this correct, Ophelia dear?" Joseph waited for his wife to answer. Instead, she appeared at the door, ready to take charge of the situation.

"Thank you, Joseph." She turned her attention to the messenger. "Thank you, kindly. Please inform Mrs. Carter that eight will be excellent, however, please make sure that they arrive promptly as the carriage shall not wait. Also, whilst you are here miss, may I ask you to just remind your employer that a box of buttonholes and corsages are to be delivered simultaneously to Mr. and Mrs. Baxter's residence in Legare Street."

The messenger girl nodded.

"Yes, ma'am," she said and she ran back to Mrs. Carter's

flower shop to convey the message.

Ophelia closed the front door.

Prudence looked on with admiration as Ophelia confidently and calmly handled each situation as it arose without so much as a sigh. She wondered how she would cope in a similar situation, but doubted that she would.

She climbed the stairs once again up to Clara's room. Clara was waiting, sitting on the bed with her legs dangling over the side.

"Mistress!" Prudence squealed in distress as Clara attempted to stand on her damaged leg. "Please, I implore you, return to bed at once!"

But Clara ignored her. She pulled herself up shakily, placing her foot on the floor, wincing a little as her tight, cramped muscles complained heavily under the strain. She took a few tentative steps, easing and gently stretching her leg as she moved over towards her dresser.

Prudence ran towards her, but Clara put up her hand to stop her. She continued to walk over to the wardrobe, building up a little speed as she moved. Eventually turning at the far end of the room by the door connecting her room to Prudence's.

"Please mistress, you should not want to reopen your wounds!" Prudence screamed out in horror as Clara turned too quickly and tangled her legs in her nightgown. Down she came, crashing into her dressing stool and trapping her injured leg beneath her, she landed on a jagged piece of wooden floorboard and let out a howl of pain.

Prudence raced downstairs to inform Mrs. Kettering. But, seeing that Ophelia was so busy dealing with Florence's wedding preparations and could not be disturbed, she ran to hammer on Mr. Kettering's study. Joseph emerged looking flustered.

"Prudence! Why are you pounding on my door in such a manner?" Joseph took one look at the expression on her face and guessed what might have happened.

"Please sir, Miss Johnson has had a fall, sir!"

Joseph flew up the stairs to find Clara, fully conscious, crying out in pain, her tangled nightgown cutting into her scarred leg.

Without any thought to her garment, Joseph tore into it to release her leg, droplets of blood were visible on her bandage. Joseph scooped her up and once again laid her down on her bed.

"Prudence, fetch Ophelia to me at once. Tell her that Joseph has insisted."

Prudence ran downstairs to find Ophelia busily directing two men maneuvering a large box from the kitchen to a waiting carriage. Florence's wedding cake.

"Mrs. Kettering! Mrs. Kettering!" Prudence called as she sprinted down the hallway. Ophelia turned.

"I am afraid I am unable to assist Prudence, can the matter

be dealt with by Joseph." She turned back to the two cake handlers.

"But Mrs. Kettering, Mr. Kettering as told me that you are to attend him at once. Clara's bandages are blood-soaked."

Ophelia's eyes grew wide as she abandoned the two men carrying the cake. She turned her attention to Prudence.

"Where are they, Prudence?"

A loud scream followed by the sound of ruined cake hitting the ground reached their ears as Florence, who had been coming around the corner and had not known about the cake removal, stood with her hands clasped over her mouth, her eyes wide with the horror of her cake smashed across the tiled hall floor. Ophelia put one hand to her head as she turned to Prudence.

"I have not the time, this shall have to wait. Take Florence into the kitchen and calm her with a warm milk and a tot of hot brandy. Then ask Cook to clean up the ruined cake. Once Florence has been delivered to Miss Parker, you run to Doctor Fletcher and tell him what has happened," she said as she darted up the stairs.

She glided swiftly into Clara's room to find Joseph cradling her on the edge of her bed, her bandage now dripping with blood.

"I have sent for Doctor Fletcher," she said as she took in Clara's ripped nightgown. "What happened?"

"I am not sure of the details. I was alerted by Prudence

hammering on my study door. I arrived to find Clara tangled in her night things on the other side of the room screaming in pain."

Ophelia sat down on the edge of the bed indicating to Joseph to lean Clara against her.

"Oh Mrs. Kettering, I cannot apologize enough. I am a silly, silly girl," Clara sobbed as Ophelia tried to calm her.

"Before you get to that," she turned to her husband, "Joseph there has been a rather unfortunate accident with Miss Parker's cake. I shall need a replacement. Are you able to take a cab to Mr. Smithers and see what he is able to cater for us at such short notice?" Joseph nodded.

"Yes, my dear, I shall go straight away."

Ophelia turned her attention back to Clara.

"Now, Clara dear, explain to me exactly what happened."

Clara sniffed, choking on her sobs. "Oh, Mrs. Kettering, what an ungrateful, wicked girl I am to put you all to so much trouble, and at such an important time for Florence." She sniffed. "I was so determined that my leg was healed and I wanted nothing more than to see Florence be married that I thought that I would try out my damaged leg. But I caught my foot in my nightgown and now I have ruined not only all of Prudence's hard work but poor Florence's cake too. I am a wicked, wicked child."

Ophelia cradled Clara's head in her arms.

"No, my child, you are not. Impatient, yes, reckless, it would seem so, but wicked? No." She sighed. "Although it is true that Florence's cake is laying in ruins outside the kitchen door, it is not something that cannot be fixed. Smithers is an excellent craftsman and I am confident that he will have something for us."

Prudence came dashing in, Doctor Fletcher close behind her. He took one look at Clara's torn gown and bandages and removed his coat. He unwound the dressing to see the extent of the damage.

"Miss Johnson, I must say I am impressed. Many of my patients wait until I have given them a clean bill of health before they attempt to dance." He smiled up at Clara as he looked at her bloodied leg. "I shall need alcohol and swabs, Prudence dear, please."

But he need not have asked, for Prudence was already standing holding the bottle of rubbing alcohol and four swabs. He took them from her grinning.

"Right, this may sting a little, but I need to clean away the blood to have a proper look." He doused a swab with alcohol and proceeded to clean Clara's skin. She winced in pain.

"I can see what has happened." He pointed to a fresh gash on the side of Clara's leg. "You haven't opened a previous wound, my dear, you have created a new one." He looked again, trying to decide whether stitches would be needed.

"Shall she need suturing, Doctor Fletcher?" Ophelia asked calmly as the doctor squinted into the wound.

"Hmm, it is a little deeper than I would have ideally liked. However, I don't think that we need put Miss Johnson through any more unpleasantness as there is not enough flesh either side of the wound to anchor the stitches to without disturbing one of the healing scars." He looked at the surrounding skin once more before making up his mind. "Yes, I think that we can clean and dress it sufficiently enough without the need to suture."

He reached again for the bottle of alcohol and cleaned gently around the wound before tightly winding a clean bandage back around Clara's leg.

"The green poultice, doctor? Is that needed?" asked Prudence as she crossed to the dresser to retrieve the pot. But Doctor Fletcher shook his head.

"Not now I'm afraid, Prudence. It cannot be used on an open wound. We shall have to settle for rubbing alcohol and bandages henceforth." He got to his feet, using the alcohol to clean and sterilize his bloodied fingers.

"I am truly sorry, doctor. I am a silly, silly girl." Clara looked so remorseful that the doctor knelt down to look her in the eye.

"Miss Johnson, remember this. We are all part of God's divine plan. Sometimes we may feel that we are cheated, or deprived of the things that matter most to us, but know this, God has far larger plans than we are aware of. You may find that one day you will look back on the times in your life when you thought that all was lost and realize that without those times you would not be where you are." He rose to his full height.

"God works in mysterious ways, and it is not for us to judge them, but to have faith in the Divine."

Prudence looked at the doctor, a strange mix of pride and admiration mixed with another feeling she couldn't quite understand washed over her. She smiled, unaware that she had been gazing at him for well over a minute. She started guiltily and averted her eyes.

"I shall take my leave then, Mrs. Kettering. I shall not charge for this treatment. Consider it a wedding gift."

Ophelia smiled gratefully as he turned to leave.

"Thank you for your kind generosity, Doctor Fletcher."

He bowed slightly to Ophelia before turning to Prudence. "Delightful to see you again Prudence."

Prudence blushed furiously as she tried to thank the doctor. "T-t-thank you, Doctor." She turned and busied herself collecting up the blood-stained bandages and dirty swabs. Doctor Fletcher donned his hat and coat and took his leave.

"How very kind of the dear doctor not to charge for my silly mistake," Clara berated herself again.

Ophelia squeezed her hand as Prudence fetched a fresh nightgown from the dresser drawer. She watched her thoughtfully. The glances she had given the good doctor and the beaming smiles he had given her had not gone unnoticed.

She smiled to herself, maybe the Divine was at work today too.

And maybe she needed to get downstairs and settle Florence before anything else should happen. Leaving Clara in Prudence's more than capable hands, she made her way to the door. She stopped and turned back to look at Clara.

"I do hope you heed the doctor's wise words this time, Clara. You were lucky not to have reopened the deeper wounds. Being sutured is a long and deeply painful affair. You were lucky to have been spared." She smiled as Clara nodded.

"Of course, Mrs. Kettering, you have all been most terribly kind," she muttered as she dropped her head in shame.

Ophelia flew down the stairs and into the kitchen where Miss Parker was cuddling a sobbing Florence.

"I'm afraid she is inconsolable, Mrs. Kettering." Miss Parker informed her employer as, on seeing her mother, Florence again burst into floods of tears.

"The cake, Mother, the cake."

Her mother took her in her arms and stroked her hair. "Yes, but it is not something that cannot be fixed. At this very moment, your father is placing an urgent order with Mr. Smithers, the baker. We shall see what he can do for us. You shall have a cake, Florence, it is not the end of the world."

Florence stopped sobbing long enough to look up at her mother. Ophelia smiled at her warmly. Poor child. She knew that this wasn't just a silly tantrum over a smashed cake, this was wedding day nerves.

She chuckled to herself as she remembered the night before her own wedding. Her mother had invited her Aunt and Uncle to stay in readiness for the ceremony the following afternoon.

Her Aunt, unbeknown to everyone but her, had used what she had thought was an old cotton rag to clean and polish her Uncle's shoes, not realizing that it was Ophelia's 'something old' and was, in fact, a small square of the muslin her mother had swaddled her in as a baby. It seemed to her a terrible crime at the time and she remembered being devastated. But her mother came down shortly afterward with an identical square of muslin, cut from the same piece of cloth.

"I'm so sorry about your lovely cake, Miss Parker," sniffled Florence. "I'm certain that it would have been heavenly."

Miss Parker shrugged and smiled.

"These things happen to the best of us, Miss Kettering, especially when emotions are running high."

Chapter
Twelve

Prudence hovered in and out of Clara's bedroom door, anxious that she should be the first to take delivery of the mail that morning. Poking her head out for the tenth time in as many minutes, she was rewarded by the ringing of the doorbell. She flew down the stairs and threw open the door.

The mailman stood, a little alarmed at the breathless, red-faced little maid that greeted him.

"Howdy there, lil' ma'am. A large handful this mornin'." He handed a large wad of letters to Prudence, winking at her as he did so. "Weddin' cards I shouldn't wonder," he added as he tipped his cap and made his way back down to the front gate.

Prudence closed the door and quickly leafed through the letters. It appeared that the mailman was likely to be right, a large number of the correspondence was addressed to Florence. She stopped and quickly slipped a small brown envelop into the pocket of her apron before depositing the remainder of the mail in neat little-named piles on the hall table.

"I thought you were busy seeing to Clara, Pru."

Prudence spun around guiltily to come face to face with Miss Parker.

"I happened to be passing the door and I thought that you would be too busy with wedding preparations." Prudence smiled uneasily as Miss Parker narrowed her eyes, clearly suspicious.

"I shouldn't have thought though that whatever you were doing to make you rush quite so quickly would have allowed for you to stop and collect the mail." Miss, Parker squinted into Prudence's eyes, certain that she was hiding something. "But if you say that's what you were doin', then that's what you were doin'."

She stood looking at Prudence for a moment more before turning and walking back down the way she had come, leaving Prudence to race back up the stairs. She threw herself into Clara's room, closing the door firmly behind her. She stood composing herself for a moment, her back pressed up against the inside of the door as she took a deep breath to calm her nerves.

"Was it there, Prudence dear?" Clara asked as Prudence, composure regained, walked as calmly as she could across to the bed. Pulling the envelope from her pocket as she went.

"Yes, Mistress. However, Miss Parker very nearly caught me. It is my belief that I would have been ordered to leave had I been discovered."

Clara's eyes grew wide as she thought about the ramifications should either of them be discovered in their execution of Clara's plan.

She took the letter from Prudence's outstretched hand, swallowing hard. She looked down.

Miss D Cooke,

Hallswood Home for Wayward Girls, East Battery, Charleston.

Nervously, Clara ripped open the top and pulled out a small, neatly folded letter from within. She opened it up and began to read.

Dear Miss Cooke,

We thank you for your correspondence expressing a wish for a position of spool girl within our establishment for your eldest ward Isabelle Crofton. If Miss Crofton could attend tomorrow morning at the hour of Nine O'clock with the relevant work documents, we shall add her to the company payroll.

In kindest regards,

Mr. R Griffiths

Manager

Clara refolded the letter and placed it back inside the envelope before turning to face Prudence.

"Isabelle has been offered the position," Clara spoke with barely a whisper. "I am to arrive tomorrow morning at Nine."

Prudence looked at her young companion, her fair skin, her pretty golden curls and, perhaps most striking of all, her expression. She had expected Clara to have been nervous, scared even of her endeavor, and quite rightly so. However, the sparkle of excitement in Clara's eyes was plainly seen. Clara smoothed down the bedclothes.

"Are we now to move on to stage two?" she asked. Prudence nodded slowly as she disappeared into her own room and came back carrying a plain, simple, unlaundered dress and boots. Items were taken from Isabelle's old chest that had been delivered to her on the eve of her sister's passing.

Clara eyed the grimy dress dimly. What had poor Isabelle been subjected to that her clothing was in such a state?

A sharp knock sounded at Clara's door. Moving swiftly, Prudence swept both the dress and boots beneath Clara's bed and pulled the sheets down low.

"Come in," called Clara, as Prudence quickly picked up Clara's hairbrush and pretended to be actively involved in styling her hair. Ophelia pushed open the door and glided silently into the room.

"Clara, dear, Joseph has returned and a new cake shall be delivered to Mr. and Mrs. Baxter tomorrow morning in time for the celebrations to begin. I felt that you might like to be made aware."

A wide smile of relief spread across Clara's face. "Oh Mrs. Kettering, I cannot express my relief at such good news. I admit to having been greatly concerned that a suitable replacement might not have been found in time."

Ophelia smiled at her guest before turning to leave. "I shall be detained for the remainder of the day my dear as I have a fair amount to oversee before tomorrow's ceremony."

"Of course, Mrs. Kettering." Clara smiled, thankful that she should have a, largely undisturbed afternoon in which to prepare for the next stage of her plan.

"I shall look in on you again upon my return." Ophelia leaned forward and planted a kiss on the top of Clara's head. "Although I implore you, Clara, do not attempt to run before you are ready to walk." At this, she floated across the room, passing through the doorway and letting the door click softly behind her.

Prudence let out a loud sigh. Almost as though she had been holding her breath the entire time Ophelia had been in the room. She pulled the dress and boots from their makeshift hiding place and safely secreted them away back in their chest under her own bed. She crossed back into Clara's room and collected the rubbing alcohol and bandages from the low dresser. Clara pulled back the sheets to observe her leg.

As Prudence swabbed and treated the fresh wound Clara had sustained that morning, she could already see that it was healing well.

"I do hope I shall be in an appropriate state to walk tomorrow Prudence." Clara examined the red wound, which looked a lot less angry than it had done a few hours before. Prudence pursed her lips as she scrutinized the cut.

"It is regrettable that your appointment is not for a date a week from now ma'am, for I would feel far more comfortable allowing you to walk if your wound had had greater time to heal." She sighed. "However, it is unavoidable."

She knew this to be true. If work was turned down, the factories simply employed someone else. Jobs were few and far between and so to have actually been offered a position was an achievement in its own right.

Clara nodded, understanding at once that with everyone distracted by the wedding, and with the current economic market, tomorrow really was the perfect time. It could not be deferred to a later date.

"In any case, surely a limp would help to improve my character, would it not?"

Prudence thought about this. A child with a malady of some sort had certainly become far more the norm than a healthy child within the factories and plantations. Especially with medicine and medical care being beyond the reach of many impoverished families. Her hand flew to her face as she absentmindedly stroked her scar. Indeed, even she could be considered amongst the marred.

"I believe it would, ma'am."

Clara smiled.

"The good Lord really does work in mysterious ways." Clara

stole a glance at Prudence, smiling to herself as she remembered Doctor Fletcher's words. Prudence's cheeks turned crimson with embarrassment.

"It would seem so, mistress, it would seem so," she answered with a little sigh.

***

"Mrs. Kettering, ma'am, the flowers are here." Miss Parker stood outside Florence's room holding a large box of buttonholes and corsages.

The door flew open and Ophelia ushered her in before climbing back beneath Florence's gown to continue adjusting her underskirt and bustle.

"Excellent. Would you make certain that Joseph equips all the gentlemen with a buttonhole dear?" Ophelia turned her attention back to her daughter as Miss Parker gasped.

"Oh, Miss Kettering, in all my born days I have never seen a bride look as lovely." She wiped a tear from her eye as Florence beamed at her.

"Kind cook, I do so hope that you get a good seat in the church."

Florence turned to survey herself in her full-length mirror. Her gown flowed down to the floor, covering her white, satin and lace boots. The train of white silk flowed out behind her as Ophelia fastened her veil to her headdress.

"You look beautiful, Florence. You are sure to reduce your

father to tears." Ophelia smiled. She leaned forward and kissed her daughter on the cheek before standing back to admire her again.

A polite knock at the door sounded. Miss Parker opened it to find Prudence there supporting Clara.

"Miss Johnson I really do feel that you should be..." but Clara held up her hand in protest.

"Miss Parker, Florence and I have been together from the very moment we were brought into this world, and if I am unable to see her be married, I at least want to see her off. And I am adamant in this regard."

Clara set her jaw in a determined pose as Prudence held her elbow so that she wouldn't appear to place too much weight on her leg. After all, she would need a convincing alibi, and if everyone were to believe that her ability to walk was not as well established as it actually was, then it would be assumed that she was still bedridden.

Prudence shuddered a little as she tried to convince herself that what they were doing was not technically a lie as they had not spoken of the extent of Clara's injuries. Nor was it out and out deception as they were merely allowing people to come to their own conclusions, but it still felt deceitful to her and she would be immensely relieved when it was all over.

"Clara, you dear, sweet, silly thing," cried Florence as she crossed to the doorway to help her friend to a chair. "If you continue to act so recklessly I swear I shan't enjoy my wedding one bit," Florence gave Clara one of her best pouts, sending the pair into fits of giggles.

"That will do girls. Clara, if you have your heart set on this decision I shall not try to stop you. However, if Prudence and Miss Parker would be good enough to escort you to the landing where I should be grateful if one of you were to fetch Joseph's brother Charles to carry Clara down the staircase, I shall be presenting Florence to her father in the hallway."

"Very good, ma'am."

And between them, cook and Prudence held an arm each and carefully supported Clara to the top of the Kettering's sweeping staircase to wait in the grand entrance hall. Miss Parker then trotted down to find Joseph's younger brother to come and fetch Clara, remembering to pass the box of buttonholes to Joseph as she did so.

Clara stood at the head of the stairs watching all the suited gentlemen and the ladies in their fine Sunday hats all milling around awaiting Florence to make her entrance. Charles came bounding up the stairs.

"Forgive, Miss Johnson." He bowed low to Clara, who giggled as he swept her up in his strong arms. He was the image of his older brother. Indeed, Clara felt that other than the shock of brown hair, the two could quite easily have been twins.

He set her down gently on the guest chair in the hallway where she would have a good view of Florence's descent and subsequent departure. He bowed once again and returned to escort his own wife out to the waiting carriage once Florence and Joseph had left.

Suddenly, a round of applause started as Florence and Ophelia descended the steps, Ophelia gliding elegantly behind her daughter, holding out her train.

Clara pictured what it would be like to stand at the top of the stairs with Amelia and be presented to Uncle Anthony before being whisked off to the church where Alexander would be waiting. She gasped in surprise to think that she should picture, tall, strong, handsome Alexander and not shy, scholarly Lawrence. The pangs of guilt twisted awkwardly in her stomach making her feel a little sick. She tried to put it to the back of her mind. This was Florence's big moment.

And anyway, in just under an hours' time, she would be making her way to 'Daylight Cottons PLC' to start her double life as Isabelle Crofton the spool girl and she had no use for guilty daydreams.

"Florence, my dear, you are a sight to behold. Never have I been prouder nor humbler to be your father." Joseph's voice cracked as he choked back the tears that threatened to take hold. He took his daughter by the elbow and escorted her out to the waiting carriage.

Clara blew kisses and waved until the last of Florence's beautiful silken train was out of the doorway and safely on its way to St Michael's.

As Ophelia prepared to leave alongside her sister-in-law, an anxious knock sounded at the door. Prudence rushed to answer, thinking that perhaps Florence had forgotten something important, but when she opened the door she didn't find a flustered looking Joseph standing on the doorstep, but a flustered looking Lawrence instead.

"I must speak with Mrs. Kettering on a matter most urgent," he garbled as Prudence stepped back to allow him inside.

"Mr. Cavendish, I would have expected you to be at the church at this time with Miss Baxter."

At the very words, Clara began to feel light headed and motioned to Prudence to help her back upstairs.

"And indeed, I would've been, ma'am, but the cake did not arrive. I have, not ten minutes ago been at Mr. Smithers' bakery only to find that it had already been delivered here."

"Oh!"

Ophelia spun round to look at her kindly sister-in-law who, in all the excitement had completely forgotten to tell her that the cake had arrived.

"I unboxed it and set it out in the kitchen, Ophelia. I believed I was helping, I am terribly sorry. Was that wrong?"

"No, my dear, you had no way of knowing it had arrived at the wrong address." She turned to signal to Miss Parker, but she was already darting into the kitchen. Ophelia dashed after her, calling to Lawrence over her shoulder.

"Mr. Cavendish, if you would be so kind as to transport the

cake back with you and ask the Baxter's staff to erect it and then head towards your father's church as quickly as you are able."

Lawrence swiftly followed Ophelia.

"Of course, ma'am," he said as Ophelia burst through the kitchen door and helped her cook to collapse the large 4-tiered cake back into its boxes. Lawrence carried the cake out and into the waiting cab as the remaining guests all filed out of the Kettering's home and sped off to the church.

Prudence watched them leave from her vantage point at the top of the staircase. Quickly, she turned and darted back into Clara's room.

"Everyone is now safely on their way ma'am," she said as Clara adjusted Isabelle's dull, itchy dress. It was everything that Clara's dress was not. Itchy, ill-fitting and shapeless. Clara surveyed herself in the mirror. She hardly looked like herself at all.

Prudence had spent the best part of the last ten minutes brushing a dull powder into her golden hair to dull the shine. She had also insisted that Clara cake some of the same under her fingernails and smudged her face. Her hair she pinned back into as tight a bun as she could manage.

"Goodbye, Clara Johnson, heiress to the Daylight Cotton empire and Good day to Isabelle Crofton, spool girl and honest factory worker," she said as she swallowed hard against a sudden bought of nerves.

Prudence wrinkled her nose and squinted. It was almost as

though Isabelle were still here. She tried not to dwell on the thought as she pushed Isabelle's papers into Clara's hand.

"It is not too late mistress. If you feel that you do not wish to take your notion any further..." she trailed off as she caught sight of the look in Clara's eyes.

"Prudence, dearest heart, this is something I feel I must do. For if it is God's wish that Lawrence and I be joined, then so be it." She pulled herself to her full height and, refusing Prudence's arm for support, hobbled towards the door. Her damaged, weak leg dragging slightly behind her.

Prudence opened the door to let Clara through, and they were just making their way back downstairs when a knock sounded. Prudence initially thought to ignore it, the family were all out at the wedding anyway. But the knock sounded again and again signaling that whomever it was desperately wished to gain admittance.

Crossing the hall, she threw open the front door. Clara gasped in dismay as Lawrence quickly dashed in without waiting to be invited. She tried to hide her face, but it was too late, he had seen her, and mistaking her for a servant girl dashed up to her. She froze as she felt the panic rising within her. What should she do? She prayed to God to keep her secret safe.

"Miss, pardon me but please would you run to the kitchen and fetch the stand for the cake? Mrs. Kettering, in her rush to attend her daughter's ceremony, appears to have forgotten to package it with the rest of the wedding cake boxes."

Prudence sprang down the corridor to the kitchen leaving Clara alone in the hallway with Lawrence. Clara begged under her breath for Prudence to come back soon. She could feel her heart in her mouth as she tried to answer Lawrence. Would he recognize her? Would her cover be completely blown before she had even had a chance to set foot inside the factory?

"Did you hear me, Miss?" Lawrence bent his face down to her's, trying to get her attention.

"Ah'm so sorry sir, ah'm none too clever. My sister Prudence tells me ah'm slow," she mumbled in the same southern drawl that Prudence had spent the last two weeks teaching her.

"I do beg your pardon." Lawrence stepped back a little from this strange girl who directed the entire conversation to her feet.

Clara continued, starting to enjoy herself, despite her heart wanting to burst from her chest. Clearly, Lawrence hadn't a clue who she really was.

"Ah'm startin' my new job t'day sir," she drawled slowly.

But Lawrence didn't have a chance to answer as Prudence came bounding out of the kitchen carrying the box containing the stand for the cake.

Darting across the hallway in one leap, Lawrence grabbed the box from Prudence and wished her and her sister a good day as he threw himself back into the cab and sped off.

Clara beamed at Prudence as she felt a new confidence and independence she had not ever felt before.

"Goodbye, ma'am, please stay safe," Prudence bid her young companion. Clara smiled warmly at her.

"Goodbye. Ah'll be seein' y'all real soon," and with that she walked out of the front gate and off down the road towards the large wrought iron factory gates of Daylight Cottons PLC, to take her place alongside her workforce. Not as their employer, but rather as their equal.

Chapter
Thirteen

It was an excruciatingly long and difficult walk on muscles that were not used to exercise and Clara found that what one would've been a very pleasant wall along the seafront was, in fact, a pain-filled nightmare. She shuffled along beside the bright colored buildings, stopping frequently to catch her breath. She eased her weight to her right, letting her sore leg hang weightlessly for a minute or two before pressing on.

As she continued down East Bay Street, slowly edging her way to Concord Street and her father's cotton mill. As she passed the end of Tradd Street, she heard the familiar bells of the old church clock chiming out. Almost eight-thirty she thought in alarm as she tried to quicken her pace. She looked down at her wrist, expecting to see her usual pretty, silver bracelet watch, but instead was greeted with her own sooty flesh. She shook her head as she remembered that Prudence had advised her to remove her jewelry and trinkets.

"The poor would have little use for such fine items and would have sold them long before. They certainly would not dream of wearing such things to work." She guessed Prudence was right. "And anyway, ma'am, a bracelet could get snagged on a machine and cause you great injury."

And so, Clara's watch had been confiscated, along with the locket of her mother's. She absently moved her hand about her chest, wishing to feel it's comforting shape. She moved on, anxious to get there on time.

As she turned out of Adgers Wharf, she saw it. The large, brick-built block, supported by a latticework of heavy wooden joists jutting from the walls of the building and burying themselves into the ground on either side of the ugly, red building made for an unsightly blot on an otherwise bright and cheery landscape.

Clara shivered as she looked up at it. She limped up to the large wooden double doors of the factory, rang the bell and waited. She could feel the panic starting to take her as she wondered just what lay in store for her behind the huge wooden gates.

As in many times such as these, Clara found herself mouthing the words to one of her favorite verses, Philippians 4:13. This one had brought her comfort through many times of great stress or worry.

"I can do all things through Christ which strengthened me." She smiled feeling a little better as she continued to wait. After a short while a man, about six feet tall and looking as though he was wearing a child's shirt and braces opened the door. He eyed Clara suspiciously. She swallowed hard, trying to gulp down her fear and anxiety. She took a deep breath and continued to introduce herself, or rather, Isabelle.

"Mah name is Isabelle sir and Ah'm to start on the spoolin' t'day. Mistress Cooke told me to ask for the foreman," she drawled in the thick southern accent.

The man flicked his eyes over her, taking her in as he slowly moved his jaw up and down. Clara guessed he was chewing tobacco.

"Lemme see yer papers," he growled. Clara produced the documents and the letter addressed to 'Mrs. Cooke' offering her the position. The man leaned to one side and spat. He snatched the papers from Clara's hand and squinted at them before grunting and opening the side door to let her in. Clara limped through the open door which the unpleasant man promptly slammed behind her.

Suddenly, the calm, light spring breeze was gone as she was immediately plunged into the hot, humid confines of the grimy mill. She could feel waves of nausea churning up her stomach and threatening to empty it. She took a few deep breaths as she did her best to keep up with the tobacco chewing man, her damaged leg burning as she dragged it along behind her.

She looked around her in awe as, although Prudence had warned her what to expect, she never dreamed that it would be anything like this. The overwhelming heat and noise threatened to swallow her whole as the man led her through billowing clouds of steam and across thin metal walkways.

Far below on the factory floor, she could see the workers stationed at their machines. Row after row of large metal frames all thundering as they spewed out reel upon reel of cotton threads.

Now she understood why Prudence had been so worried when she had first mentioned her idea, some of the huge metal beasts loomed above their tiny masters, looking for all the world as though they were just waiting for a chance to devour them. Clara shuddered.

After another short walk along yet another suspended walkway, the unpleasant man stopped.

"You wait here," he barked at Clara as he disappeared through a door.

She leaned over the thin metal railings a little to get a better view of the factory floor. Directly below her, she could see a strange mechanical construction of iron and timber, clattering and clanking as large cogwheels turned a mighty leather band. A child, who could be no older than ten was balancing on the thin edge of a raised platform as he tossed handfuls of fluffy raw cotton into a huge hopper. He swung himself expertly back and forth as he emptied a large basket of fluff into the machine.

Clara gasped in horror as the child, his basket empty, swung himself up into the hopper and packed the fluff down into the belly of the huge metal beast. She continued to watch as she wondered what on earth she thought she was doing. But before she could pick herself up and flee, the tobacco chewer suddenly reappeared and beckoned for Clara to follow him through.

On the other side of the doorway, Clara found that she was standing in a dingy makeshift office. Papers were strewn over every available surface and another surly looking man was sitting in a tattered wood-backed chair in front of a grimy window stained yellow with years of neglect.

The tobacco chewing man stomped off without so much as an introduction to Clara as to whom the seated man was. Clara supposed that this was, in fact, the factory foreman.

He looked up, appearing to notice her for the first time. He gave her a sickly smile showing off what few tawny, yellowing teeth he had left.

"Miss Crofton, I presume?" his partially whispered tones crept through Clara like a cold draught of air. She instantly disliked him.

"That's right," she drawled. He glanced down at the papers that the gateman had dumped in front of him.

"I see you are our new spool girl." That smile again. Clara had to stop herself from shuddering at the disgusting state of his mouth.

"That's right, sir," she repeated. He stood up and walked towards the door, and, motioning to Clara to follow he led her back down the way they had come and out onto the factory floor.

The oily, greasy smell hit her nostrils making her gag. She reached for her handkerchief and was momentarily surprised to find that it wasn't where she usually kept it, pinned to the inside of her waistband. With no pocket lace to cover her sensitive nose, Clara realized that it was yet another of the factory's sensory assaults that she would just have to learn to endure.

The foreman took Clara through a maze of machines, each more fearsome looking than the last. Until eventually they came to a stop beside a long, iron framework of spikes. Clara guessed that this must be a spooling machine. She could already see a girl about her age if not younger, working the machine with her nimble fingers.

The nameless foreman breathed in Clara's face, his putrid breath making her, already churned stomach beg for mercy.

"Y'all gonna be workin' with Mary here." His voice almost inaudible amongst the machines as Clara strained to hear him. He turned to go.

"Please, sir, how am I to work this..." Clara remembered herself just in time, switching back to her slow, southern slang.

"Ah've not done this here contraption before, an ah ain't never seen one like it neither," she corrected herself. The foreman narrowed his eyes suspiciously as Clara tried her best to look innocent and ill-educated.

After some thought, he appeared to reach a decision and started to walk off, calling back to Clara over his shoulder.

"Mary'll show yer."

Clara approached the skinny, dark-skinned girl that the foreman had introduced as Mary.

"Ah'm Isabelle, an I ain't got no clue how t'use this here machine," Clara felt a little more confident with the slang as the more she was able to use it, the better at it she became.

Even so, her new companion looked at her strangely.

"You ain't from around these parts?" she asked, a confused and slightly suspicious look crossing her face. Clara looked at her, taken aback. What could she say? If she told her the truth and her accent was indeed a little off then Mary might suspect that something was amiss, but if she pretended to be from elsewhere then she may pick completely the wrong region to match her strange dialect.

As she pondered, Mary appeared to mistake her indecisive pause as a reluctance to answer.

"S'okay, we all got secrets we don't wan' people a'knowin'." She smiled at Clara, her soft brown eyes reassuring her that this girl was no threat. She held out her hand.

"Mary-Anne Tyler," she rattled off. Just as Clara was about to take the proffered hand, Mary fell about in fits of giggles.

"At least, that's what mah daddy dun called me," she cried in between bouts of infectious laughter. "But everyone just calls me Mary," she finished. Clara beamed at her new friend as she looked down at Clara's booted feet.

"Y'all gonna be sweatin' in those. They ain't no use to yer here," she cried.

Clara looked down at Mary's bare feet, filthy and calloused from working on the dirty factory floor. As she had no intention of taking off her boots, no matter how hot her feet became, she decided to ignore Mary's point and instead turned her attention back to the spooling machine.

"Mah sister tells me ah'm slow, but ah learn fast," Clara indicated to the machine in front of them. The spools of cotton on one side were spinning away happily. The spikes on Clara's side, however, remained stationary and empty. Mary glanced at the large iron spikes.

"Ah'll start 'em up for you. Then it's up to you ter move 'em and swap 'em. It ain't hard once you got 'em spinnin'." With that, she expertly threaded the spools with the start of the cotton thread and gave them a spin. As the machine clicked into life, Clara quickly saw the spool reels fill with threads of cotton. Mary tugged at the full spools sending them clattering into a basket at her feet before quickly loading up another two empty bobbins and setting them spinning.

Clara watched, eagle-eyed until it came to her turn. Although considerably slower than Mary, Clara found that the work was easy and strangely satisfying. Before long, her basket was full. She turned again to Mary.

"Excuse me, I do beg your pardon, however..." Clara's hand flew to her mouth at the horrible realization that she had given herself away. How could she be so careless! She continued to berate herself under her breath as Mary turned to her.

"Sorry Izzy, you say somethin'? Ah can't hear you above the din," she yelled. Clara breathed a sigh of relief as she thought how ironic it was that the very noise she had detested when she had arrived that morning had actually worked in her favor. She raised her voice and tried again.

"What do ah do with the full basket a'spools?" she shouted

over the drone of clanks and whirrs of the many spooling machines on this side of the mill. To say nothing of the roars and hisses coming from the looms and presses on the other side of the room. Mary picked up her own overflowing basket.

"Yer follow me." She winked at Clara as she marched off across the factory carrying the fruits of her labor. Clara limped slowly behind Mary, struggling to keep up with the girl's pace. Mary stopped and looked round to see if Clara was indeed following her.

"Ah says ter follow me," she called. But her expression changed from one of mild annoyance to one of concern as she saw Clara struggling to move her stiff, sore leg. "What yer dun there?" she asked when Clara had eventually caught up with her.

Clara looked down at her leg. She certainly didn't wish to lie to Mary, not after she had been so kind. Instead, she opted for a half-truth.

"Ah got mah leg infected. It bleeds sometimes an it hurts real bad." Clara looked up at Mary, expecting her to start asking probing questions as to the nature of her infection. But instead, she just nodded as though the entire fact that Clara had a disfigurement was very matter of fact and wouldn't be of much interest to pursue. She turned and continued on, albeit a little slower this time, occasionally looking back to make sure that Clara was keeping up.

Eventually, she stopped in front of a large loom. She loaded the bobbins on the top, pulled the thread down and threaded it into a heavy wooden shuttle which sat at the end of a spring-loaded iron arm. Mary cranked a handle and pushed the shuttle to get it going. Suddenly, the machine sprang into life as the motion of the shuttle caught hold and the pressure was allowed to release in a jet of hot steam. She gestured to Clara to set her basket down on the floor and handed her another empty one from the pile beside the loom.

Clara stared at the metal monstrosity, her eyes wide with a mixture of fear and awe as it thundered and clattered, occasionally billowing out huge puffs of steam like a gigantic, mechanical dragon.

"Beautiful ain't it?" Mary looked up at the iron beast with an air of pride. "Ah've been workin' her 'bout ten years now. Ever since..." she trailed off suddenly clamping her jaw tight shut. Clara looked at her in surprise.

"Since when?" she drawled, trying hard not to sound eager, but rather slow and uninterested.

"Since never you mind. Like ah said, we all gots secrets, Miss Isabelle."

Hurt and a little alarmed by Mary's sudden change of character, Clara picked up her empty basket and made her way back to the spooling machine. She had just finished filling the second basket when a loud klaxon sounded. She looked around horrified. Was there a fire?

Mary stomped up behind her and threw her empty basket down beside Clara's full one. She stretched out her arms, crunching and clicking her shoulders.

"And not before time neither," she said as she walked off.

Clara stood and stared at her, thoroughly confused. Was she supposed to stay and work or should she follow? Mary turned to look at her.

"What you doin' just standin there for? Ain't yer hungry?" She gave Clara a puzzled look as Clara carefully limped her way up towards where Mary was standing waiting for her. She winced with each step, her leg tired and sore but she tried hard not to let Mary see.

"Ah, sure am." She smiled at Mary.

"Lord O' Lord, you're a strange one and no mistakin'." Mary raised her hands to the ceiling in exasperation as though calling on God himself to unlock Clara's secrets and help her to understand. "Eats're this way," she called as she marched off in the direction of the dining hall.

Clara's stomach groaned at the thought of a good hot meal. She hadn't realized just how hungry she was until Mary had mentioned it. She sidled through the heavy wooden door that Mary had held open for her and found a room filled with people all jostling for a place at the long wooden tables. Mary pushed for a seat and pulled Clara down with her.

"Yer gotta git in an' git a spot otherwise y'all gonna be standin' at the back." She motioned with her thumb to a line of workers all standing with their backs pressed up against the wall of the dining hall waiting for a table to become free.

Clara reached for the large metal jug of water and poured herself and Mary a cup. Mary drank it down in one gulp.

Holding the glass up to the light, Clara inspected the

murky looking water and, deciding better of it, carefully placed her drink back down on the table. She swept her eyes around the cramped dining hall with its uncomfortable wooden benches and dirty straw-lined floor, Clara began to feel nauseous all over again.

A wooden platter of what looked like bread was banged down into the center of the table as a large woman pushing a trolley dealt out the workers luncheon. The entire table immediately fell upon the platter, pushing and shoving for their share.

Mary sat back holding two lumps of bread, triumphantly in the air.

"To the victor go the spoils," she quipped as she tossed one of the chunks onto Clara's plate. A little while later a small bowl of a semi-warm, grey colored liquid arrived in front of Clara. She regarded it suspiciously.

"You better be likin' mushroom soup Izzy," beamed Mary as the foreman appeared and banged his spoon against a large pot for silence. The entire room bowed their heads in prayer as the foreman led them all in grace.

After the last echoes of the muttered 'amen' had died away, the room again erupted in chatter as the entire workforce tucked into lunch.

Clara dipped her spoon into her bowl daintily, lifting the congealed grey substance to her mouth. She closed her eyes as she tipped it down, shuddering as the cold, slimy, tasteless liquid slid down her throat. She opened her eyes and was astonished to find the entire table looking at her, their mouths open wide.

"Why're y'all starin' at me?" she muttered as many of her co-workers got back to the task of shoveling the last of their soup into their mouths. Clara turned to Mary. "Why're they all lookin' at me?"

Mary plunged her spoon into her bowl to take a large mouthful of soup-soaked bread.

"Y'all be eatin' strange," she mumbled into her bowl, her mouth full of bread mush. Clara's cheeks burned with shame as she realized that yet again, she had given away her upbringing. She looked at the others and tried her best to copy what they were doing.

"What you doin', girl? You gotta dunk the bread to soften it up." Mary broke off small pieces of hard bread and dropped them into Clara's bowl. "Ain't you never had bread a'for?" Mary wiped the bottom of her own bowl with the remainder of her crust and washed it all down with a second glass of water.

Clara fished out a blob of grey bread, her refined pallet fighting against her will as she raised the spoon to her mouth. Without trying to think about what she was about to do, she opened her mouth wide and chomped down on the spoon. She swallowed the disgusting lump whole as she tried to imagine that it was one of Mrs. Dimbleby's exquisite dumplings.

"Mistress Cooke was always strict with us. She always

said, sit up straight Miss Crofton and eat your soup right and one day you might just be eatin' with the King of Nowhereland." Clara glanced at Mary, hoping that her excuse for her differing table manners was a good one. Mary threw her head back as her body rocked with laughter.

"Ah knew you was gonna be good company, Isabelle." She grinned. Clara smiled at her. She had managed to get away with it this time, but she really must try harder to make sure that there were no more mistakes in her behavior.

Mary pushed her empty bowl away as a second klaxon sounded indicating the end of the lunch break. Clara raised herself from the wooden bench, her leg burning with the pain of having to sit so long in such cramped conditions. As she turned to leave she looked back over her shoulder, just in time to see one of her fellow workers tip the remainder of Clara's soup quickly into her mouth before she dashed off back to her station. She clutched at her still empty stomach as she began to realize some of the problems that had been going unnoticed in her family's absence for far too long.

"How long've you bin a worker here?" she asked Mary as they walked back to the spooling machine.

"When ah was just a tot, mah daddy brought me over on a huge boat. But when we got here, he was caught and sold off as a slave." She sighed. Clara gasped as Mary continued with her tale. "Ah was sent to the plantation fields to pick cotton. Ah kinda liked it. But ah missed mah ma and mah daddy." Mary gazed into the distance, remembering a life once lived. She shook herself back to the present.

"Anyhow. One day, a man came an told me he needed workers in his factory an so here ah am. That were about ten years ago ah reckon, but ah'm not too good with numbers." Mary grabbed an empty spool and loaded it onto the spooling machine. Clara followed suit and soon the two girls were lost in their work once more.

Suddenly, Clara felt an overwhelming presence behind her and, turning around, she could see the whispering foreman watching her. He gave her another sickening grin.

"Mary," he wheezed in Mary's ear making her spin round in surprise. "Loom eighteen is jammed again. Go clean it. You," he said turning to Clara, "Keep this machine moving while she's gone." With that he slunk off, his long, bandy legs causing him to lollop away across the factory floor. Mary and Clara watched him until he was out of sight before Mary tugged the last two spools off her machine and tumbled them into the waiting basket.

"Ah gotta go clean eighteen ah guess," she called over her shoulder as she marched off in the direction of the defective machine leaving Clara alone with the spooling and her private thoughts.

She set another two spools spinning as she pondered upon what she had seen so far. The dirty environment, the lack of adequate food and seating in the dining hall, and she didn't even want to think about the strange, whispering foreman. But it all led her to the same, perplexing question. If her father was not in charge of the factory anymore, then who was?

A sudden ear-piercing scream filled the factory making Clara jump in surprise. She pulled off the two full spools and dropped them into her basket. She stopped the machine, listening out for...

A second scream came clanging across the room followed by a desperate plea for help.

"Mah arm! Mah arm! I can feel it breakin'!"

With a shudder of horror, Clara recognized the voice. She took off across the factory in the direction of the screams of agony, moving as fast as she dared on her crippled leg.

She rounded a corner and came face to face with the biggest loom she had ever seen. Its huge, black wrought iron arms were swinging down as the shuttle passed from side to side. And each time the iron swung, Mary screamed out in pain as the mechanical giant chomped down on her arm.

Clara glanced around, horrified that no one was coming to Mary's aide. In fact, no one had even turned from their work. She could feel anger start to boil inside her stomach. The foreman slunk up behind Clara.

"Stupid girl," he spat at Mary.

"Please, Mr. Griffiths, git me out!" pleaded Mary between her panic laced screams as the machine crunched down repeatedly on her arm.

"And lose half a day's production because you were stupid enough to put your arm in a moving loom?" He let out a low laugh as he turned to leave. Clara grabbed his sleeve as he walked by her.

"Sir, you have to let her out!" she cried, almost forgetting her accent in the heat of the moment. Mary screamed as another blow struck her arm. Tears streamed down her face as she begged the foreman for mercy.

"Ah dun wanna end up like poor Katie. Please! Mah arm! Ah'm gonna lose mah arm!" she screamed anew as the machine continued to swing down on her arm, blood was now soaking through the sleeve of her dress. Mr. Griffiths tugged his own arm from Clara's grasp.

"I dun recall askin' you your opinion. Git back to your station," he growled as he tried a second time to leave. Clara limped after him as fast as she could. She overtook him and stood in front of him, pulling herself up to her full height and completely abandoning any attempt at her southern dialect.

"I demand you release that child!" she screamed in his face. He stopped.

"Oh, you do, do you?" He snarled, his face inches from Clara's as the foul stench of his breath encircled her threateningly.

"I do, sir. Release her or, as the good Lord God is my witness, I shall not spin another spool for you, today or any day," she stuck out her chin in defiance.

Mr. Griffiths' face contorted into a wicked grin and without warning the back of his hand came smashing into the side of Clara's face knocking her off her feet. She crashed to the ground, landing on her wounded leg. She screamed out as

220

Mr. Griffiths leaned down to whisper in her face.

"I dun care who yer think y'are little missy, but in here you do as ah say. y'hear?" He straightened up and turned back to where Mary was still screaming in agony, kicking Clara hard in her back as he did so.

"Git back ter work." He crossed over to the machine, the unforgiving iron bar, now spattered with Mary's blood, smashed down yet again causing a sickening crunch. He banged his fist on the side valve of the machine, knocking it off, cruelly smirking as it painfully wound down, each blow to Mary's arm lasting twice as long as it had, causing her to writhe in agony.

Eventually, the iron bar lifted and Mary dropped to the floor, clutching her bloodied arm. Mr. Griffiths leaned over her.

"Git up yer useless maggot. Y'of no use ter me if yer can't work. Find somethin' ter stop the blood and git back ter work." He spat in her face before turning and lolloping back up to his office, furious that all this time had been wasted.

Mary dashed over to Clara who was still lying winded on the floor, struggling to breathe through her sobs. Her bandage was once again stained with blood, the fall having opened her youngest wound.

"Are y'hurt real bad?" she asked, still trembling and clutching her ruined arm.

Clara, gingerly rolled onto her back, looking up at Mary, her eyes wide with fright. She had no idea that her Father's factories were like this. She let her eyes fall to Mary's tattered arm, the guilt of her privileged upbringing burned in her chest. She closed her eyes as two large tears ran down her cheeks.

"I'm so sorry," she whispered. Mary pulled her to her feet.

"Sorry? Sorry!?! You saved mah arm! He was gonna let me die in there, but even though you ain't got nothin' outta it but a busted leg an a blow t'yer head, you spoke out for me." She pulled Clara closer to her. Her head spun as she swooned. And, trailing blood and supporting each other, the two friends made their way to the factory infirmary.

***

Prudence threw up her hands in horror as Clara fell through the front door and into her arms.

"Mistress!" she cried in dismay. Clara looked up at her, her eyes weary and tear stained.

"Prudence, dearest, it was far more awful than I had imagined it to be," she managed as Prudence supported her up the stairs to her room.

"Ma'am, will you not reconsider?" Prudence carefully leaned Clara back into her bedside chair as she removed her boots. She looked at the fresh bandage on Clara's leg, tutting in disgust at the uneven way it had been loosely wound around her wounds rendering it practically useless. She removed the offending article and cleaned Clara's leg with alcohol before applying a fresh bandage.

Clara allowed Prudence to pull off the dirty, scratchy dress of Isabelle's. As Clara leaned forward Prudence gave a little squeal of horror at the large boot-shaped bruise that had blossomed on Clara's back. She raced to the bathroom cabinet to fetch a bottle of witch hazel. She gently daubed the bruise with the solution, tears forming in her eyes.

"Mistress, I have failed you. I take full blame for the injuries you have sustained. I should not have allowed you to even contemplate working in a factory, let alone actively encouraged it," she cried sadly as Clara placed her hand tenderly on Prudence's shoulder.

"Dearest heart. I can be as stubborn as a mule when I wish it. It was my decision and mine alone, I hold you accountable for nothing and am forever in your debt." She raised her head as Prudence let out another gasp followed by a sob of deep despair. Clara's cheek bore an angry red and blue swelling in the spot where the foreman had struck her. She dabbed and fussed over the mark until Clara eventually called for her nightdress.

Prudence helped Clara into clean undergarments and night things before brushing the powder from her hair, allowing some of the golden sheen to shine through once more. She helped her into bed, just in time as a gentle knock sounded on her door.

"Come in," Clara called, as brightly as she could. Ophelia glided into the room as Prudence plumped and straightened Clara's pillows.

"Clara my dear... Good heavens!" she exclaimed as she

caught sight of Clara's face. "What on God's green earth has happened?"

Clara looked at her, desperate not to lie but how could she tell her the truth?

"I-I struck my face on the footstool after my fall," she stuttered. It wasn't a complete lie, she had knocked her face a little. Ophelia tilted her head up to get a better look at the disfiguration to her cheek.

"Clara dear, I must offer my most sincere apologies. Had I not been so preoccupied with Florence's vows I feel certain I would've noticed this far sooner." She turned to Prudence. "Has Doctor Fletcher seen to this?"

Prudence shot a glance at Clara before shaking her head.

"No, ma'am, the mark appeared after the good doctor had already left. I have been treating the area with witch hazel rub," she replied as honestly as she could. Ophelia seemed unconvinced and was about to ask a further question when Clara changed the subject.

"Please, Mrs. Kettering, tell me about Florence's beautiful wedding. I have been thinking about it all day," she begged.

Ophelia smiled kindly. "It was a beautiful day, Mr. Baxter made a handsome groom and Florence has lots to tell you herself I am certain. But you look tired my dear. Please try and get some rest before supper." She kissed Clara's head tenderly as she rose to leave the room. She stopped by the doorway and indicated to Prudence to follow her. Outside Clara's room Ophelia asked Prudence more awkward questions regarding Clara's facial bruising.

"Do forgive me, Prudence. However, it is clear to anyone with an ounce of common medical knowledge. That wound was made today," she said. Prudence hung her head in shame as she was forced to admit that the bruise was fresh.

"I shall ask you an honest, straightforward question Prudence and I expect an honest answer, do I make myself clear?"

Prudence nodded.

"Now, I do not hold you responsible and I have no doubt of your loyalty to Clara, which is only right and proper. However, when one's health is in jeopardy it is sometimes necessary to betray a trust. Do you understand what I am asking of you?"

Again, Prudence nodded.

"Yes ma'am," she whispered, dreading the next question.

"Very well then. Prudence, has Clara been walking on her damaged leg today, even though she has been expressly forbidden by Doctor Fletcher to do so?"

Prudence looked up at her employer with dismay, tears forming in her eyes.

"Oh, yes, ma'am." She quivered. Ophelia nodded, she could see how hard this was for poor Prudence and she admired her honesty and integrity in the matter.

"I see. And tell me, has Clara had another fall that Mr.

Kettering and myself have not been made aware of?"

Prudence nodded sadly.

"Yes ma'am," she replied. She hated betraying Clara, but she could not lie to Ophelia, not after all the kindness the family had shown to her. Ophelia took Prudence's hand in hers.

"I realize how hard this has been for you, my dear, and that keeping the confidence of two can sometimes seem an impossible task, but the good Lord only gives to us that which we are able to maintain." She paused as she looked into Prudence's watery eyes, red and puffed from crying.

"You are strong, Prudence, and it is my belief that God has chosen you as the one most suitable to the task of caring for Clara. I trust in Him as I trust in you." Releasing Prudence's hand with a reassuring smile, she turned and descended the stairs to inform Joseph of Clara's exploits.

Chapter
Fourteen

Alexander slid the knife into the gap and dragged it across. A jagged tear ripped the paper apart allowing him to read the letter therein. A big smile spread across his face as he rose from his chair. This was something Lawrence needed to hear.

He crossed the library and made his way towards Lawrence's private room, but just as he was passing the parlor he heard someone moving about. Thinking that it may have been Lawrence, he knocked politely.

"Come," called Amelia brightly. Alexander pushed the door open and entered the room.

"Pardon me, Miss Orm, but have you by chance seen Lawrence this morning?" he asked.

Amelia who was still busy admiring the exquisite work that Mrs. Bloomindale had done, looked up and beamed at Alexander.

"Ah, young Mr. Cavendish. I believe that he mentioned he would be calling on Professor Baxter today and would not be back before supper," she replied with a smile.

Alexander caught sight of the mended hat Amelia was holding.

"I say, that is a very pretty bonnet, Miss Orm." He smiled pleasantly, imagining how lovely Clara would look in such a charming garment. Amelia's eyes lit up. It was certainly money well spent if the hat was getting compliments even before it was upon Clara's golden curls. She sighed.

"Isn't it lovely? Mrs. Bloomindale has worked wonders with Clara's tattered old bonnet. This is to be a gift to aid in her recovery."

"A fine present. I am certain that dear Clara shall be well received of it, Miss Orm." Alexander nodded, pleased that Clara was the intended recipient after all.

"I shall be traveling to see her this afternoon, with a hope of bringing her home within a few days." Amelia beamed.

Alexander matched her smile, his eyes twinkling as he thought of his beloved Clara. He stopped to think about how lovely she had looked, even sitting in discomfort as she had been. It would be wonderful to see her again.

"Please remember me to Clara and pass on my warmest wishes, it will certainly be a pleasure to spend time in her company." He smiled again as Amelia nodded.

"Thank you for your kind words, Mr. Cavendish, I shall, of course, convey your message, although I hardly believe Clara would've forgotten you, nor some of the mischief that seemed to follow in your wake." She winked at Alexander, teasing him gently.

"Ma'am I believe you have me there." Alexander chuckled as he remembered some of the downright ridiculously idiotic antics he used to get up to, all in the hope of making Clara laugh. Yes, it would be good to spend time with her again.

***

"Good morning, I'm here to see Miss Baxter." Lawrence smiled at the Baxter's elderly housekeeper from behind a small bouquet of white roses. She smiled. Mr. Cavendish had clearly done his homework. Miss Sophie was an avid botanist and had a keen interest in floriography. The small, white rosebuds were a perfect depiction of the start of a love for a pure and innocent young maiden such as Miss Sophie.

"Very good, Mr. Cavendish. Miss Sophie is currently reading in the parlor, I shall let her know you're here." She stepped back to let Lawrence enter.

"Lawrence, my dear boy, delighted to see you. Come on in do," Professor Baxter boomed from the parlor doorway as his housekeeper closed the front door and took Lawrence's hat and gloves.

"Wonderful news! I have in my possession a magnificent vase, thought to be of the Ming Dynasty, which I have strict instructions to donate to your museum. Come and see it, sir, it is a wonder to behold." He grinned at Lawrence as he held his gift behind his back.

"Excellent, sir! That is, as you say, magnificent news." He turned his attention to Sophie. "Good morning Miss Baxter, I hope you are well?" He smiled as he gingerly took a seat, gazing at her adoringly. Professor Baxter smiled to himself as he watched the young man who was clearly infatuated with his daughter.

"I shall ring for some tea. Unless you would prefer coffee?" He looked at Lawrence.

"Tea shall be most welcome Professor, thank you," he said as he presented the roses to Sophie. "For you dear lady."

Sophie beamed, delighted with her unexpected present. And, more than a little, impressed that Lawrence had chosen the correct flowers for the occasion.

"Oh, Mr. Cavendish, how thoughtful! Thank you, they're lovely," she gushed as she clutched them excitedly. Lawrence smiled as he thought back to the first time he had met her.

It had been a dark, gloomy morning in late January, and as he stood outside the Horseshoe building, waiting for Professor Baxter, he had noticed a young lady walking quietly across the gardens, her nose stuck in a book. Without warning, the clouds burst as God opened the floodgates to his heavens and let the rain clatter down in large droplets, forcing the lovely young thing to close her book and dash for shelter.

He had at once darted forward and offered her his umbrella. And that was how he had learned that she was the professor's daughter and was herself interested in the science of nature. Indeed, the book she had been so engrossed in was that of the study of flora and fauna.

Lawrence smiled to himself as he thought about all the

visits he had made to see the professor after that first meeting. And how heartbroken he was to have been moving back to Charleston upon graduation. And how elated he had been at the news that the professor had taken a position at the esteemed Charleston College, which meant a move for the Baxter family, and him being a mere ten-minute cab ride from his darling Sophie.

"Tea, sir?" asked their aging housekeeper politely, bringing Lawrence back to the present. He started guiltily as he realized he had been staring at Sophie for perhaps a little too long.

"O-oh thank you," he stammered, taking the cup offered to him and sitting back in his chair. "Tell me of your studies, my dear. Did you manage to obtain a specimen of the elusive 'brush root'?" he asked, reveling in Sophie's delight as her face lit up. He settled himself comfortably to listen as his beloved talked animatedly about her hobby.

Professor Baxter smiled, the Ming vase could wait a little while longer. And on that thought, he quietly left the two in the company of his housekeeper, who had volunteered to act as chaperone, and made his way to his study.

Clara pushed open the heavy, wooden gate as she wearily joined the back of a queue of workers, all signing in at the front desk. After several minutes Clara reached a bored looking woman dressed in cap and apron.

"Name?" She barked as she scanned the list of employees in front of her.

"Cl... err... Isabelle Crofton," Clara muttered, hoping that the woman would consider her a little slow and not notice her slip up. She needn't have worried however as the woman waved her inside and turned to the next in line.

Clara limped off to find the machine she had been working the day before. As she passed the other workers all preparing for the day ahead, her thoughts turned to Prudence and how a nasty injury had led her to work for the lovely Kettering family and, in turn, meeting Clara. God had clearly seen that she would be needed elsewhere. She wondered what God had in store for poor Mary.

"G'mornin' Izzy," Mary greeted her. Clara looked up startled as Mary broke her train of thought. She laughed weakly. "Didn't mean ter scare you.'

Clara smiled as she took in the terrible bandage job that the half-hearted nurse had done on Mary's arm. Blood was still seeping through and with no splint, Clara feared that it would set crooked and Mary would be crippled for life.

Mary looked sickly and pale. Her smooth chocolate complexion had taken on a yellow hue and her clammy skin glistened with sweat at the exertion of standing and straining at the spooling machine. She staggered a little as she tried to lift up an empty spool reel, giving Clara the chance to see the full extent of her injuries, her bandaged arm still covered in fresh blood. It was clear that Mary was losing armfuls of blood. Clara marveled at her even being upright, to say nothing of working a machine.

"G'mornin', Mary. Did yer sleep well?" she asked, gesturing

to Mary's strapped up arm. Mary shrugged as though it didn't matter to her or anyone else, it simply was the way it was. Perhaps she was just happy to still have a job. But the dark circles and sunken eyes gave her away. It was clear to anyone that looked at her, Mary was in a lot of pain.

As Clara was about to insist that she must see a doctor and that she would cover her shift for her, a loud voice bellowed across the factory.

"Floor meetin'."

Clara looked in the direction of the noise and saw that the gateman was standing on top of a wooden crate in the center of the factory floor. Mr. Griffiths beside him. When he was certain that he had everyone's attention, the two men swapped their positions.

"Due ter yesterday's delays, y'all be workin' through lunch ter make up for it. An' yer can all thank Isabelle for that. Oh, and Miss Crofton and Miss Tyler?" He paused for dramatic effect, a cruel grin spreading across his sallow face. "Ah'll be stoppin' yer a week's wages ter cover the bandages and medical aide."

With that he stepped down off the crate, his ungainly limbs flailing clumsily as he clattered off to his office.

The workers turned to look at Clara, all whispering amongst themselves as they got back to their machines. Clara looked down at her feet, tears forming in her eyes.

"Ah'm dreadfully sorry y'all. Ah was only tryin' ter save Mary's arm," she called after them, but it was too late, the resentment had already begun to spread.

She limped back to her spools feeling utterly dejected. A week? She had planned to have enough money for Lawrence to open his museum within a month. But her pay had been stopped for an entire week? She turned to look at Mary beside her, struggling to reach the spools, her mangled, bloodied arm hanging uselessly in its sling.

"I'm so sorry, Mary." Clara burst into tears, again groping for the handkerchief that wasn't there. Mary turned and looked at her, clearly unsure as to what to do to comfort her.

"It's not your fault, Izzy. Ah swear that foreman is the spawn of Lucifer himself." She spat on the floor at the mention of the devil's name. Clara wiped her eyes on the cuff of her dress, feeling sure that Isabelle would've done the same.

"Who bosses Mr. Griffiths?" she asked. Mary looked at her, surprised.

"Y'don't know? His orders come directly from *her*," Mary spat on the floor a second time.

"Who's *Her*?" asked Clara, a puzzled expression crossing her bruised face. Mary's eyes narrowed.

"The old hag in charge a this place. She owns it. Sittin' there on a pile o'money that ah've bin slavin' ter make. Makes me sick to mah stomach." She spat a third time before turning back to struggle with the spools.

Horrified at the thought of some old witch claiming that

she owned her factories, Clara limped off to find the foreman. Seeing a girl carrying a basket full of raw cotton, Clara dragged her aching body over to tap the girl on the shoulder.

"Err, howdy Flora, d'you know where ah can find Mr. Griffiths?" she asked pleasantly. Flora turned her back on Clara.

Disgusted to have received such treatment for standing up for a colleague, Clara approached a young boy working on a press.

"Ah need the foreman, d'you know where ah can find him, please?"

The boy's eyes narrowed at Clara and again, he turned his back. She could see that talking to anyone here now was a waste of time. Losing her temper and forgetting herself, she got her face close to the child.

"Would you really have let Mary die for the sake of half a bowl of cold, lumpy soup? I find that far more deplorable than losing someone their luncheon break." And with that, she spun on her heel and hobbled off to find Mr. Griffiths.

The boy watched her go, a look of pure astonishment on his face. He hadn't understood a word of what she had just said.

Turning a corner, Clara stopped suddenly as there, peering into the side of a machine was Mr. Griffiths.

"Sir," she started. He spun round to glare at Clara.

"Ah never change mah mind, so ah wouldn't bother tryin' if ah was you," he growled, an unlit cigarette hung from his lips.

"Who's in charge here?" she asked. Raising herself up to her full height.

"Ah am," Mr. Griffiths leaned against a machine to light his cigarette.

"No, ah mean who gives the orders?" she tried again. Mr. Griffiths took a long drag.

"Ah do." He released a puff of smoke from the side of his mouth, his lips still clinging to the cigarette to keep it from falling. He took another drag.

"No, yer still don't..." she trailed off in surprise as he whipped the cigarette from his mouth, thrusting his face menacingly into Clara's.

"Ah don't know who yer are or who yer think yer are, but if yer've got a problem with me and mah orders, yer better take it up with old Miss Johnson. But ah warn yer, she won't listen ter the likes a you."

Clara stared at him, her mouth wide with horror. How dare he use her name!

"Sir," she said, her eyes growing cold and angry, this had gone far enough. "I can assure you that Miss Johnson would be appalled at the abhorrent conditions in which you keep your staff and I shall offer you this fair warning *Sir*. If you are not removed from this building by the end of the week, Miss

Johnson's family shall come and remove you themselves."

At this, Mr. Griffiths threw his head back, a low loud laugh escaping his nicotine-stained lips.

"Ah don't know where you learned ter speak, but the Johnson's are dead an' their spoiled brat of a kid dun care who yer are so long as the money dun run out." He flicked his cigarette butt away as he turned to face Clara head on.

"An' if yer dun git back ter yer station, ah'll take that bust up leg from under yer."

"You have had fair warning Mr. Griffiths. And you can expect a letter from Miss Johnson's lawyer. I can assure you of that fact." Hurt, red-faced and shaking with anger, Clara turned, dignity forcing her to walk upright and as smoothly as she could, gritting her teeth all the way back to the spooling machine.

As she sidled down between two huge presses, she smashed into a large arm stretching across her path. She looked up. A tall man in ill-fitting clothes was looking down at her.

"Let me pass," she hissed through her still gritted teeth. Without warning, he gave Clara a heavy shove sending her flailing backward. A hot sharp pain shot across her eyes as she smacked her head hard on the iron giant beside her. He turned and walked off without a word, leaving Clara clutching her throbbing head.

Clara dragged her poor, aching body out from behind the machine and, groping around for something to steady her, wobbled gingerly back to the spooling station. As she neared the machine, she could feel a black haze clouding her vision, her legs, suddenly buckling beneath her as she succumbed to the pain in her head.

Down she went as an alarmed Mary tried in vain to catch her.

"Izzy! What happened to yer?" Mary shook Clara, trying desperately to wake her. After a few minutes, Clara came to. She looked up into Mary's worried face.

"I cannot stay here another minute," she sobbed as she tried to stand. She fell back against her friend as her head spun causing waves of nausea to wash through her system.

"Ah'll help yer Izzy, hold on," Mary shouldered Clara up to her feet, grinding her teeth to the pain as she took Clara's weight on her bad arm, using the able one to grab hold of Clara's dress.

The two girls half limped, half stumbled towards the gate. The gateman blocked their path.

"Where d'you think your goin'?" He growled. Mary froze, still supporting Clara.

"She needs fresh air. Ah dropped a basket a'spools on her head. She just needs a minute."

The gateman shifted his gaze from Mary to Clara, recoiling in alarm at her sickly complexion.

"A minute then," he grunted as he opened the gate allowing

the two girls to pass through. He slammed it shut again behind them.

"Ah dun know where yer live, but ah can only guess it's close to mah place. All the workers live on site. But come to think on it, ah haven't seen you around a'fore."

Clara looked at her friend gratefully. She wanted to get back to Prudence, she wanted, more than anything, her clean soft bed and some of Miss Parker's hot beef broth. But she couldn't risk Mary taking her back to the Ketterings, but she couldn't make it under her own steam. Without thinking she turned to Mary.

"Thank you, dearest, if you would be so kind as to put me in a cab, my companion shall assist me further."

Mary gently pulled Clara towards a small, run down looking shack, built up against the side of one of the factory outhouses.

"Willard musta hit yer real hard, ah dun think yer knows who yer are." She kicked the door open and dragged Clara into a small room with three cots covered in blankets. She placed her down gently, resting her head back on the cushion before collapsing onto the cot beside her.

Clara looked at Mary, she was breathing hard, her wound still leaking blood.

"You need to be seen by a doctor," she wheezed. Mary let out a scornful laugh.

"Yeah, o'course, ah got money enough fer that." She

panted. Clara pulled herself into a seated position, her head beginning to clear as she saw the full extent of Mary's injuries. She needed a physician and quickly.

Making up her mind, Clara pulled herself off the bed.

"Stay here. Ah'm goin' ter git the nurse," she told her. Mary grunted, her breathing coming in hard gasps at the exertion of helping Clara.

Clutching the wall for support, Clara dragged herself as quickly as she was able out of the cabin and along the factory wall to the Adger Wharf. She staggered along onto East Bay Street. Clutching onto fences and garden walls for support.

Counting the houses, she eventually came to the one she was looking for. She rang the bell and waited, holding on to the front gate for dear life. The door suddenly flew open as Clara collapsed at the feet of Doctor Fletcher.

"Miss Johnson!" he exclaimed as he scooped her up and carried her inside.

"I must apologize for my appearance Doctor and I shall explain, but first there is a girl in dire need of assistance. I fear she may be dying," she breathed. Doctor Fletcher rested Clara on the surgery sofa and grabbed his bag.

"Where is this lady to be found?"

Clara looked up at the good doctor, her eyes full of gratitude.

"Daylight Cottons' outbuildings in a little shack against the far wall. Please hurry, I fear we may be too late already."

Doctor Fletcher grabbed his hat from its hook by the door.

"Mrs. Carson! Bring Miss Johnson a glass of hot milk and brandy and sit with her until my return. I shall have another patient shortly," he raced through the door leaving Clara in the capable hands of his motherly housekeeper.

Hailing a cab, Doctor Fletcher threw himself into the back.

"Daylight Cottons and I shall pay you an extra ten cents if you drive your horse flat out sir!" he instructed the driver.

The wheels of the cab clattered across the cobbles as the good doctor raced to get to Mary. As the factory came into view, he didn't wait for the cab to stop, he jumped out and dashed around the side of the outbuildings to find the little shack Clara had described.

"Wait as I have an emergency!' he called back to the cabbie. Pushing on the door, he found Mary, barely conscious, her breathing shallow. Scooping her up in his arms he carried her back to the waiting cab.

"My surgery and hurry man, this child's life is hanging in the balance!" Doctor Fletcher looked down at the frail creature in his arms, assessing the extent of her injuries.

The cab came to an abrupt stop. Swiftly he carried Mary's limp body up towards his surgery.

"Mrs. Carson, take a dollar bill from my dresser drawer, the cab driver will need paying," he called as he dashed past her. Mrs. Carson nodded and bustled out the door with the money as Doctor Fletcher carefully lay Mary out on the hard wooden table in the center of the room.

"I shall expect a full explanation, Miss Johnson, once I am satisfied that you are both out of harm's way," he pulled the blood-soaked bandages from Mary's crushed arm. "Mrs. Carson! Hot water and towels!" he ordered as he dashed about his surgery gathering the items he would need.

Mrs. Carson shuffled in with towels and water, assisting the doctor where she could as he worked on Mary.

"She has lost a lot of blood. If I were in the university hospital I might've attempted a transfusion, but I fear it to be too much of a risk. We may lose the child to infection or blood loss," he muttered to his housekeeper as she did her best to keep up with the doctor.

Clara lay on the sofa, her vision hazy, drifting in and out of consciousness, willing herself to stay awake for Mary's sake.

At last, Doctor Fletcher stepped back, his hands and apron covered in Mary's blood.

"She will need complete rest if she is to make it through the night, but she is weak. Her fate is in the hands of the good Lord now, we must have faith in the Divine." He stood back to observe his handiwork.

"When you've done everything you can do, that's when God will step in and do what you can't do," he smiled to himself as the words of 2 Corinthians 12:18 clanged around his head reminding him of his time in the university hospital.

Leaving Mary still lying on the table, he tore off his apron and scrubbed his hands before turning his attention to Clara.

"Mrs. Carson, I shall need alcohol and fresh bandages." He looked into Clara's eyes.

"The bruising on your face is superficial, Miss Johnson, and I feel certain that your wounds are merely aggravated, however I am concerned for your head. May I inquire as to how you came to be in your present state?"

As Clara explained the events of the last two days, the doctor cleaned and dressed her leg. When she had finished, he leaned back, regarding his young patient in awe.

"My dear, Miss Johnson, I am unable to neither condone nor condemn your brave and selfless actions. You truly are a marvel, my dear."

Clara looked across at Mary, her breathing still shallow and labored as she lay on the table.

"But now that my secret is out, what am I to do?" she asked.

***

"I have an urgent appointment at the Exchange and Provost, would you mind awfully if I share your cab, Miss Orm?" Anthony looked across at Amelia, although it was clear that she had her mind on other things.

Amelia sighed as it occurred to her that once Clara was married, the strange, loneliness that she had felt this past month would be her constant companion. Perhaps it was time to give some thought as to what the future may bring for Miss Amelia Orm.

Seeing her downcast expression Anthony sidled across to her and took her arm in his.

"Amelia, my dear, we shall soon have her back with us. She has been well looked after and I feel that your little visit today shall lift her spirits no end," he said. Amelia smiled. Suddenly feeling a little silly for her selfish indulgence.

"That's better." He smiled at her warmly before turning and reciting Jeremiah 17:7, feeling that it might help Amelia feel a little better. After all, a small reminder that the Lord always has your best interests at the heart of everything He does has always helped himself.

"Blessed is the man who trusts in the Lord, and whose hope is the Lord," he recited softly. Amelia turned to the cook.

"I shall be back before supper Mrs. Dimbleby," she said as she adjusted her best travel bonnet.

"Very good ma'am. I shall have a piping hot meal for you ready." She smiled.

"I for one shall look forward to it Mrs. Dimbleby, I shall honestly." Carrying the hat box, Anthony helped Amelia into the waiting cab and they set off for Morning View House.

"Mr. Kettering tells me that although Clara tried to do a little too much too soon, she has not damaged herself too badly and has been cared for beautifully by her companion

Prudence," she said. Anthony nodded as the cab trundled along towards the Kettering's grand quayside house.

"My only concern my dear is that Clara shall not wish to leave Prudence behind. Do you think she will pine for her? It may cause a relapse," Anthony held onto the side of the cab as the cabbie took the corner a little too sharply.

Amelia considered this. Guiltily she realized that her concerns had mainly been for her own feelings on the matter and not Clara's. But the Reverend may have made a very good point. Clara and Prudence have been together for over a month and Clara had relied upon Prudence very heavily, the bond that will have developed might be too strong for Clara to bear breaking.

She wondered if the Kettering's would miss their housekeeper. She shook her head, berating herself for such a silly notion. She could hardly expect Ophelia to give her maid to Clara, no more than she could expect Anthony to take her in. Clara would just have to accept the situation.

"Just here sir if you would be so kind," called Anthony as they pulled up alongside the Exchange building. Amelia watched as the Reverend got down from the cab and climbed the steps up to the main building, clutching his bible. She shook her head thinking or the soul that he had hopefully gone to comfort sitting down in the depths of the Provost.

"Morning View, ma'am," called the cab driver as they pulled up outside the familiar frontage of the Kettering's, startling Amelia out of her deep thoughts.

She paid the fare and bustled up to the front door. She rang the bell. The door was opened by Miss Parker.

"May I help you, ma'am?" she enquired politely as Amelia gave her name and the reason for their impromptu visit. Miss Parker stepped back allowing them to enter.

"I shall inform Mrs. Kettering of your arrival, if you would like to seat yourselves in the parlor she shan't be a moment." She turned in the direction of the conservatory where she knew Ophelia was busily tending to her plants. But as she rounded the corner she bumped into Prudence, carrying a tray of coffee and crackers up to Clara's room.

"Clara's guardian is here Pru. You might need two extra cups." She smiled. Prudence froze. Clara was not yet back from the factory. What would she tell Amelia?

"You feelin' ok, Pru? You've gone an awful shade o'white." Miss Parker gave her a puzzled look. Prudence started, annoyed that her expression had given her away.

"Sorry. Yes, I'm fine. I just remembered Clara's leg must be redressed before anyone sees her. And she may want a clean nightdress before receiving visitors." She dashed off, still carrying the tray.

Miss Parker stared after her, still a little confused as to what had just happened. She put it down to Prudence feeling perhaps a little lost now that Clara was starting to heal enough to be able to go back home. She decided to cross that bridge when she came to it, after all, there was plenty of work downstairs to keep Pru busy. She continued on to inform

Ophelia of her visitors.

She eventually found Ophelia, or rather her employer's boots, as the rest of Ophelia appeared to have been swallowed by a large Rhododendron bush. She coughed politely.

Ophelia pulled her head from inside the bush and fished bits of broken stem and petals from her hair.

"Yes, Miss Parker, what is it?" She sighed as she placed her secateurs down on the low wall which circled the room.

"Miss Orm is here, ma'am, I have seated her in the parlor," she replied. Ophelia smiled warmly as she stood and brushed the dirt from her hands.

"Very good, we shall require tea and cakes to be served in the garden if you would be so kind, Miss Parker, please."

"Yes, ma'am." She smiled as she headed to the kitchen. Ophelia meanwhile, made her way to the parlor to receive her guest.

"Amelia dear, to what do I owe such a lovely surprise? If you would like to follow me, I thought we might sit in the garden as it is such a lovely afternoon."

Prudence watched from her vantage point of behind the potted plant at the top of the Kettering's staircase as Amelia followed Ophelia out towards the garden. She released a sigh of relief. At least this should buy her a little more time. And she disappeared back into Clara's room to think on what she should do next.

***

The doctor rose up out of his chair and fetched his hat and bag. He turned to Clara. "Miss Johnson, I fear that it is time for me to check on one of my patients. However, I shall be back within the hour. Please make yourself comfortable and Mrs. Carson shall see to any of your needs until my return."

"Thank you, Doctor." She smiled weakly.

As Doctor Fletcher walked briskly along the street, he turned Clara's problem over and over in his mind convinced that there should be a solution that would be acceptable to everyone. He walked through the gate of Morning View House and smartly rapped on the door. After all, he thought to himself, God does not leave things to chance.

"Good afternoon, Doctor Fletcher." Miss Parker smiled brightly at the young doctor as she stood back to let him in.

"Good afternoon, Miss. I've come to call on Miss Johnson. May I?" He indicated to the stairs.

"Of course, Doctor, Prudence is in with her." Miss Parker smiled to herself as she wondered whether the doctor's visit really was to see Clara. Doctor Fletcher smiled broadly as he strode up the stairs. He stopped at Clara's door and knocked. Prudence opened the door a crack.

"I'm afraid my mistress is sleeping, doctor, would it be possible to return at a more convenient time?" Prudence was shaking, she hated lying, but somehow lying to Doctor Fletcher felt even worse. The doctor smiled at her and leaned in to whisper in her ear.

Prudence opened her eyes wide and at once opened the door to allow the doctor inside.

"Ah, that's better. Now, Prudence, I need for you to collect anything that Miss Johnson would be wearing for a stroll in the park. After which, I need you to dress appropriately and come with me," he said, his eyes twinkling as he regarded Prudence. She nodded and proceeded to dash about the room piling clothes, boots, hat, and parasol into the doctor's large surgical bag, before dressing herself for a lunchtime walk.

She peered out of the door to check that the coast was clear before slipping out of the room and bidding the doctor to follow her. They quickly made their way downstairs and tiptoed out of the front door without anyone seeing them.

The doctor extended his arm to Prudence. Her heart beat a little faster as she took Doctor Fletcher's arm. She could feel her cheeks flushing with color as she looked up at him, wondering what it would be like to be married to such a man. She put the thought from her mind. What right had she to marry such a learned man as Doctor Fletcher.

Upon approaching the surgery, the doctor opened the door for Prudence to enter. She immediately ran to Clara.

"Mistress! Please now will you promise not to go back to that awful place?" she pleaded, tears filling her eyes. Clara looked up at the doctor gratefully.

"You have my word, Prudence dearest, you have my word," she answered wearily. Doctor Fletcher clapped his hands signaling a job well done.

"And what of my second patient? Has she regained consciousness yet?" he asked Mrs. Carson.

"Not yet sir, no. She has been murmuring in her sleep and her fever has dropped, but I have not been able to get even a spoonful of water into her, sir." She shook her head sadly. The doctor nodded as he handed his bag to Prudence. She understood immediately.

"Ma'am, I have brought a change of clothes. Are you able to stand and let me dress you?"

Clara nodded, grateful to be out of Isabelle's itchy, woolen dress.

"We must hurry, mistress. Miss Orm is currently taking tea in the garden with Mrs. Kettering believing you to be safe in your bed."

Clara's eyes widened in horror at the thought of what her guardian would say should she find her missing.

Doctor Fletcher took his leave asking Mrs. Carson for a basin of warm water, soap, and yet more towels. The aging woman shuffled off, happy that she had someone to care for other than Doctor Fletcher.

Prudence and Mrs. Carson bathed and dressed Clara quickly, paying close attention to her fingernails and golden hair. But there was nothing they could do about the facial bruise.

"But what of Mary?" Clara asked, concerned. Mrs. Carson smiled kindly.

"You need not worry, ma'am. I shall take care of the young lady in your absence."

"Thank you, dear, kind Mrs. Carson," she said as Prudence took her arm.

"Excellent!" exclaimed the doctor as he took the other. "We are going out for a stroll, giving you some fresh air and exercising your leg Miss Johnson," he said as he winked at Prudence making her blush. "I shall be back shortly Mrs. Carson. If the young lady, err, Mary was it?" He looked at Clara, she nodded.

"If Mary should wake before my return please try to keep her calm and offer her some water."

"Very good sir." Mrs. Carson smiled as the little party of three made their way out of the front door and off towards Morning View House.

Chapter
Fifteen

"Prudence? Clara? May we come in? I have Amelia here with me." Ophelia waited but when no reply was forthcoming she pushed on the door. "Please, forgive us but is Clara feeling unwell?"

As the door swung open, Ophelia could see that Clara's bed was empty. Letting her eyes sweep the remainder of the room it was clear to all present that neither Clara nor Prudence were there.

"Clara, dear? It's Amelia, are you indisposed? Should we come back later?" She called. But again, no reply came.

Ophelia turned and crossed the room to tap on the interconnecting door between Clara and Prudence's rooms. Without waiting for an answering call, she pushed the door and entered.

"Pardon me, ladies. However..." she trailed off as once again, the room was empty. Clara and Prudence were missing.

Ophelia came striding out of the rooms, clearly unsettled. Amelia followed her out as she called for Miss Parker.

"Miss Parker?"

"Yes, ma'am." Miss Parker put her head out of the kitchen door to answer her employer.

"Have you spoken with Prudence today?"

Miss Parker was shocked at Ophelia's unusually abrupt tone.

"Why, yes ma'am. I informed her of Miss Orm's arrival ma'am." She looked confused. What had happened that could have put the usually calm Ophelia in such a state? "Is something wrong ma'am?"

Ophelia's hand flew to her temples.

"Clara and Prudence appear to have vanished," she said, clearly upset.

"Perhaps Doctor Fletcher took her back to his surgery with him ma'am," Miss Parker replied, her brow furrowed in a deep frown. Ophelia stared at her cook in disbelief. Doctor Fletcher? What did she mean?

"I have no knowledge of Doctor Fletcher having called when was this?" she demanded, feeling more and more perplexed by the second. Miss Parker frowned as she tried to remember all the details of the doctor's arrival.

"Shortly after I had served tea in the garden. The doctor arrived to check on Miss Johnson and he asked if he may be permitted to attend her room. I allowed him in and he spoke with Prudence." She stopped as she saw the look of panic rising in Ophelia's eyes.

"Did I do wrong ma'am?" she asked timidly. Ophelia flashed her a thin-lipped smile.

"Not wrong, Miss Parker, no. Did the doctor or Prudence raise any alarm that Clara had been taken ill and needed urgent medical attention?"

Miss Parker was just about to reply when the door sounded. She rushed to answer it as Amelia turned to look at Ophelia.

"Ophelia, do you suspect that Doctor Fletcher has been forced to admit Clara to the surgery for urgent treatment?" she asked as visions of Clara laying on her deathbed rose in her mind.

"'I must admit, Amelia dear, that it is a strong possibility."

"Ma'am, Miss Orm?" Miss Parker interrupted their panic laced discussion as she approached them, a wide smile on her face. "I believe that Miss Johnson has a surprise for you. If you would be so kind as to step out onto the front lawn." She led them outside to where Clara was walking stiffly up and down without any aid whatsoever.

Amelia let out a little sob of relief as Clara walked out from behind the large magnolia tree completely unsupported.

"Yes, my dear Miss Johnson, I do believe that your leg is ready to be exercised daily. But you must rest if you become too tired." Doctor Fletcher turned his attention to the three ladies on the Kettering's front lawn.

"Mrs. Kettering. Miss Orm," he greeted them. "I am pleased to inform you all that Miss Johnson has no further use of me. All that is required now is to strengthen that leg."

"Goodness child!" exclaimed Amelia as Clara moved closer to her and she was able to get a good look at her damaged face. "What in God's name has happened to you?" Amelia's hand flew to her mouth as she gasped in despair.

"The doctor has informed me that my bruising is superficial and shall fade of its own accord so there is no need of any worry." Clara held up her hands in a bid to waylay the fears of her guardians. As she did so she wobbled a little and it was agreed that Clara was perhaps tired after so much exertion and she should be put to bed immediately.

Doctor Fletcher bid Mrs. Kettering and Miss Orm a good day. He then turned his attention to Prudence.

"Delightful to see you again, as always my dear," he said, turning Prudence's cheeks a deep crimson as she blushed furiously. But when he took her hand and kissed it, the poor girl almost swooned. It was then decided that perhaps both Prudence and Clara should retire to Clara's room for tea.

As Prudence made Clara comfortable in a clean nightdress and sheets, Amelia brought in her gift.

"Clara dear, I felt that you have suffered such misfortune this past month that a small token may help to lift your spirits," Amelia announced as she placed the beautifully wrapped hat box on Clara's lap. Excitedly Clara tore into the paper and opened the box. She gasped with sheer delight.

"Oh, Amelia. It's simply beautiful!" She exclaimed as she pulled the bonnet from the box and admired it.

"I took your tired bonnet to Mrs. Bloomindale and this is what she fashioned."

Clara beamed at Amelia. She loved her deeply. She beckoned for her to come closer and planted a kiss on her face.

"You sweet, lovely, thoughtful dear," she cooed as she replaced her surprise present back within its box to protect it.

"I shall wear it at the very earliest conceivable moment," she proclaimed as Amelia, and Ophelia turned to leave the room so that Clara could get some rest.

"Well, I believe that we have some very good news to take back to the Reverend," said Amelia. "Oh, and I almost forgot. Alexander sends his best regards and is very much looking forward to seeing you again upon your return," she added.

Clara blushed excitedly at the thought of spending more time with Alexander. From his recent visit, she could tell that he was as much fun as she remembered him to be. And he had certainly grown into a very handsome gentleman.

"Lovely, thank dear Alexander awfully for his regards, and I shall look forward to rekindling our friendship," she grinned.

"Try and get some rest Clara dear, Prudence should be arriving with your tea things shortly," Ophelia added as just at that moment, Prudence appeared carrying a tray of scones, cream and strawberry preserve.

Clara waited until she was sure that her guardians were out of earshot before relaying the day's actions to Prudence. Settling back with her cup, Clara finished her tale.

"But I wish you to bear witness to this Prudence dearest. Mr. Griffiths shall be gone from his post within days of my learning how I should go about achieving it," her eyes narrowed as she thought of her assailant. "To think that they have been using my good name as an excuse to get away with...well, you just wouldn't believe it, my dear," she added crossly. She sat there, fuming.

"I wish now I had revealed myself to be Miss Johnson herself. That would certainly have given him something to think about," she stopped as she saw Prudence's look of horror.

"Mistress! Had you done that then the entire workforce would've set upon you!" She gasped in dismay. "And that is if the foreman had believed you," she shuddered at the thought of what could have befallen Clara.

"You are right Prudence dear. I shall just have to discuss it with our family lawyer," Clara sighed. She turned her thoughts to Mary. What was to be done about Mary?

"Begging your pardon ma'am, but if Mary's injuries are as substantial as you describe, she shall not be of use to a foreman. I am feared that Mary may lose her job," she informed her mistress sadly.

Clara gasped in dismay. Although the job was terrible and

the pay incredibly poor, Mary's job was all she had. If her employment was terminated then she would not just lose her salary but her home too. It was clear that Clara had some thinking to do.

"God will find a way ma'am," said Prudence thoughtfully as Clara sat, her face screwed up in an expression of deep thought.

"I do beg your pardon dearest heart, I was lost in my own world. Would you be so kind as to repeat what you just said?"

Prudence looked into Clara's eyes, an earnest and sincere look on her face.

"God will find a way," Prudence smiled before continuing. "For example, ma'am, if Mr. Cavendish had not damaged your leg, you would not have come here to convalesce and I would not have met you..."

"And I would not have missed Florence's wedding, nor been there to save Mary's life," Clara picked up where Prudence had left off. Her eyes grew wide as she realized that everything that had happened up to that point had been as a direct result of her injury.

"God found a way ma'am," smiled Prudence as she watched the realization dawn on Clara's face.

***

At that very moment, in Doctor Fletcher's surgery, Mary

suddenly sat bolt upright.

"Where am ah?" She mused as she scanned the room for something familiar.

"Ah, you are awake, miss," Mrs. Carson shuffled over to Mary to help her down from the table and across to somewhere more comfortable. "Do you feel any pain or unpleasantness, Miss Mary?"

"Who are you and how do you know me?" Mary asked suspiciously as she followed Mrs. Carson gingerly into the parlor, wincing with the effort.

"Forgive me, dear. My name is Mrs. Carson, I am Doctor Fletcher's housekeeper. Do sit down and make yourself comfortable."

Mary cocked her head to one side, clearly still confused.

"Doctor Fletcher? Ah dun know no Doctor Fletcher," she said suspiciously. Mrs. Carson sighed as she prepared to explain.

"Miss Johnson informed Doctor Fletcher where you could be found and he fetched you back here to mend your arm," she indicated to Mary's fresh bandages. Slowly Mary's memory of the past few hours started to come into focus as she remembered Isabelle telling her that she was going to fetch the nurse.

"Listen, it ain't like ah'm not grateful, but ah dun have the money..." she started. At that moment Doctor Fletcher strode into the room.

"Ah, Miss Mary, I see that you are awake. Excellent. Do you feel any pain or sickness anywhere?"

Mary looked at Mrs. Carson, shocked and a little suspicious of the strange gentleman who had suddenly appeared.

"Doctor Fletcher," Mrs. Carson mouthed as Mary started to catch on.

"Thankin' you kindly doctor but ah'm a'feared ah dun have no money fer no fancy surgery or nothin'," she looked at her feet expecting the doctor to call a policeman or kick her out. But instead, he brushed this aside with a wave of his hand.

"No matter my dear, let us just say we share a mutual friend," he smiled.

"Where's Isabelle?" She asked as she sank down onto Doctor Fletcher's soft daybed.

"Isabelle? I'm afraid we don't know anyone by that..." Mrs. Carson stopped as Doctor Fletcher put up his hand.

"Am I to take it that Isabelle was the name of your companion who alerted me to your medical emergency?" He asked. Mary nodded slowly, not entirely sure what everything he had said meant, but she got the general gist.

"Yes, I'm afraid that your Isabelle is actually Miss Clara Johnson, heiress to the factory that employs you as a spool girl," he finished. Mary's mouth opened wide as the realization hit her hard like a speeding train.

"B-b-but, why was she there a'workin' on the factory floor?" Mary was confused, this challenged everything that they had been told about Clara Johnson. The young, funny, friendly girl that she had met was about as far from the stern, aging, uncaring spinster that the foreman had told them about as you could get.

"No, Clara Johnson is a horrid old witch who hoards all of the money ah make for her and cares nothin' fer the folks in her factories. We're dyin' in there an she dun come an sees us or nothin' never no-how," Mary jumped to her feet in flustered desperation. She contorted her face in pain as she thought better of it and carefully lowered herself back down. Doctor Fletcher steepled his fingers as he leaned his elbows on his knees.

"Hmmm, well, I don't know about that young Miss. However, I know the young lady who fell against my gate in a dazed stupor this afternoon to be Miss Clara Johnson."

"It dun matter much now anyhow, ah can't go back there," Mary clutched her sore arm. Doctor Fletcher regarded the skinny teenager, looking at her intently before suddenly making up his mind. He sprang from his seat and reached for his medical bag. Pulling out his suturing set, he grabbed his jacket. He handed the bundle to Mary.

"Are you at all able to use your hand on that arm, miss? Just momentarily," he asked. Mary grasped at the jacket, wincing slightly, but her hold stayed fast.

"Do you think you can sew the small hole in the pocket, Miss Mary?"

What? Repair a hole? Was that all she had to do to repay the doctor for possibly saving her life? She grinned. "Ah can but try," Mary carefully threaded the needle with the thread in her good hand and the needle in her bad. She set to work, steadying her work by running it against the length of her arm as her hand would not work properly.

Doctor Fletcher watched her intently as her fingers nimbly closed the gap between the seam and the pocket. After several minutes, she had fixed the hole. The doctor examined her work seeming pleased with what she had done.

"Miss Mary, I am in need of an assistant. The work will be unsociable and dirty and will involve a large number of sleepless nights. I can offer you five pennies a week and room and board."

Mary was shocked. Her big, soft, brown eyes widened as Doctor Fletcher beamed at her. "You ain't tryin' ter trick me are yer?" she asked uncertainly.

"No, my dear, I can assure you I am indeed serious," he replied. Mary looked around the room.

"Mah own room? With mah own wash stand?" she asked.

The doctor nodded. "Of course, dear lady."

Mary seemed to make up her mind. "Sir, you got yourself an assistant," she grinned happily.

***

Clara's cab clattered through Queens Street pulling up

smartly outside St. Michael's vicarage. She took the cabbie's hand, gingerly alighted, and waited by the front gate, supporting herself on the gatepost as the cabbie unloaded her luggage onto the roadside.

Suddenly, the door swung open and Alexander came dashing out of the house. "Clara my dear, how wonderful to have you home. Please, allow me." He took her arm and gently guided her inside, seating her in the parlor as he returned to collect her bags and pay the cabbie. She watched through the window as he gathered up her things in his big strong arms and carried them indoors.

"Where shall I deposit your luggage dear lady?" Alexander asked, just as Amelia came hurrying down the stairs, anxious to see that Clara had traveled well. Clara smiled warmly.

"If you would be so kind as to return Clara's belongings to her room Mr. Cavendish and I shall unpack them presently," Amelia threw over her shoulder in her haste to get to Clara.

"Certainly, Miss Orm." Alexander made his way to the stairs, the hint of a jaunty smile playing about his lips.

"Amelia dearest, although I have been cared for beautifully by Mr. and Mrs. Kettering, it does feel heavenly to be back home." Her smile faded a little as she remembered her emotional 'goodbye' with Prudence. "Marred only by my having to leave dear Prudence." She smiled gratefully as Amelia took Clara's hands in hers.

"I can guess how you are feeling child, but you must remember that Prudence is in the employ of Mr. and Mrs.

Kettering and it simply would not do to deprive them of their housekeeper simply because you are feeling a little lonely," she said and placed her fingers under Clara's chin and gently lifted her face to meet her own. "And anyway, I am sure that Prudence would be allowed leave to come and visit every now and again." She smiled as she saw Clara's eyes light up with hope.

"Oh, thank you, Amelia, that would be wonderful. I shall write to her the moment I have a chance."

"I have placed Clara's things on her bed, Miss Orm, I do hope I have done right," Alexander said as he strode into the room and took a seat opposite Clara. He let his eyes drift over her lovely visage but recoiled in horror at the sight of the ugly bruising to the side of her face. "My darling Clara! Forgive me for not having noticed sooner but how did you come by such an angry disfigurement?"

Amelia glanced at Alexander, his hands clenched tightly into fists. Clara absently touched her blackened cheekbone. "Oh, I was reckless and attempted to run before I could walk and fell against a footstool," she answered with a sigh and quickly changed the subject, lest any more awkward questions be asked. "Is Uncle Anthony at home today? I need to speak to him on a matter most important." She turned to face Amelia.

Her old governess regarded her thoughtfully. "And what might this matter be Clara dearest? Are we able to assist?" she asked as she wondered what on earth must be so important.

"I believe he is currently at choir practice, but I remember him mentioning that he would certainly be back for supper." Alexander beamed at Clara as he thought of the entire day stretching ahead and almost all of it to be spent in her company. Amelia watched with interest as Clara returned Alexander's admiring looks.

Alexander rose to his feet and crossed the room to stand beside Clara. "Clara my dear, would you accompany me for a light stroll in the garden before supper if you are not too tired?" he asked.

Clara took his proffered hand gladly as her heart quickened at his touch. "Thank you, Alexander, that would be most welcome," she replied as Amelia and Alexander helped her to her feet. She turned to Amelia. "That would be alright, wouldn't it? If I promise not to overexert myself?"

Amelia looked a little uncertain.

"Mr. Cavendish..." she began but stopped when she saw the crestfallen expression on Clara's face. She sighed. "I suppose I could allow you a ten-minute stroll, but remember, Doctor Fletcher has prescribed light, moderate exercise as that leg is still weak," she cautioned.

"Of course, Amelia dear. I shall take the utmost care," assured Clara as she allowed herself to be led, gingerly across the room to the French windows and out into the pretty vicarage gardens.

Amelia watched from the window as Alexander set a nice, slow, steady pace to walk Clara around the dainty beds of petunias and poppy flowers. She allowed herself a little smile as she remembered the giddy way that Alexander used to gaze at Clara from across the nursery when they were children. Perhaps it was time that she and Anthony had another chat about Clara's betrothal.

"Clara it is a delight to be able to spend a pleasant afternoon in your company." Alexander sighed as they approached the old twisted tree at the bottom of the garden. He grinned as a cheeky thought suddenly occurred to him and he abruptly reached up and grabbing the lowest bough pulled himself up and inside the foliage of the great tree. Clara burst into fits of giggles.

"Oh, Alexander you silly thing!" she exclaimed as Alexander poked his head out from between the leaves and branches and dropped carefully back down beside Clara, brushing bits of loose bracken from his jacket. He drank in Clara's delightful giggles as they continued their stroll. But it seemed that their afternoon together was to be cut short as Mrs. Dimbleby came marching across the lawn towards them.

"Begging your pardon sir, miss, but there is a Doctor Fletcher here to see you."

Clara frowned at the cook in confusion. Why would Doctor Fletcher be calling on her now? He had discharged her with instructions to exercise gently and rest when tired. Puzzled and a little concerned, Clara allowed Alexander to lead her back across the garden and into the parlor where Doctor Fletcher was standing. He turned to smile at Clara as she entered.

"Good to see you looking so well Miss Johnson," the doctor greeted as Alexander guided Clara to a seat and carefully lowered her into it. "I felt it necessary to introduce to you my new assistant and you may find what she has to say very interesting." He turned and winked at Mary who was sitting on Reverend Cavendish's parlor daybed. Clara looked from her to the doctor in horror, worried that her secret would be revealed. But Doctor Fletcher just smiled as he took a seat beside Mary.

"May I introduce my new assistant Miss Mary-Anne Tyler. She used to work for your late father I believe but she has some shocking information about the current state of affairs in the factory that I feel you should be aware of." He turned to Mary. "Go ahead, my dear."

Mary looked up at Clara, her eyes wide with a mixture of disbelief and sheer admiration for what Clara had endured to learn the truth about her factories. She cleared her throat importantly.

"Well now, ah've been workin' in yer father's factories for nigh on ten year or more now and ah've seen things you won't believe Izz... Ah mean, Miss Johnson." She glanced at the doctor in panic, but he just continued to smile as though nothing had happened. She turned back to Clara and carried on. "The doctor here felt that maybe if ah come and told yer, then somethin' could be done ter help those as left in there." She smiled awkwardly.

"Go on miss, I can assure you, you are not in any trouble," Alexander said and smiled warmly at Mary, mistaking her wild-eyed glances at Clara to be fear of her superior rather than awe. In actual fact, Mary herself had wanted to make this trip to see with her own eyes whether the woman that she knew as Isabelle and the woman described to her by her new employer as Clara Johnson were one and the same. It was clear to her now that this clean, respectable lady was indeed the scruffy little orphan that she had befriended in the factory. Clara spoke jolting Mary back to the present.

"Thank you, Miss Tyler, for bringing this to my attention. I am anxious to hear what you have to tell me." She smiled as Mary's soft brown eyes grew even wider as she compared Clara's well-educated polite manner with that of the strange Isabelle Crofton. No wonder she hadn't recognized the accent.

Mary imparted to Clara and Alexander everything that Clara had already found out for herself and finished with the story of how her arm had come to be broken and how hers was by no means the first accident that had happened in the place and that fatalities were commonplace. Clara fought back tears as she remembered the horrific screams as Mary had pleaded for her life. She bit her lip in anger and disgust.

"Miss Tyler, I can assure you that I had no knowledge as to what was happening within my father's mills and, as I inherited Daylight Cottons when only an infant, the entire estate has been handled for me." She stopped and looked at Mary, pleading with her to believe her. Mary's face relaxed into a warm smile as she nodded her head slightly.

"Thank you, kindly ma'am. But in a strange way, if ah hadn't have had mah accident, then I would not be workin' for Doctor Fletcher here, so maybe God had other plans fer me." She winked at Clara who turned to Alexander.

"Forgive me, this is Mr. Cavendish," she started, but Alexander interrupted.

"I am Miss Johnson's newly appointed lawyer and I shall be looking into the matter further now that it has been brought to our attention." He winked at Clara making her blush wildly. She fought to regain her composure but it was too late, Doctor Fletcher had already seen.

"And with that dear lady, sir, I believe we shall bid you a good day as Miss Tyler and I have many rounds to make this morning. Continue to exercise that leg and I shall remember you to Prudence when I see her next." He smiled fondly as he thought of the next time he was to call upon Prudence. Clara grinned to herself, secure in the knowledge that Prudence would be blushing with awkward embarrassment at the thought of her feelings for the doctor being common knowledge.

"Please do, although I have been home only half a day I do miss her terribly," she replied as Doctor Fletcher got to his feet.

"Goodbye sir, I consider it fortunate that you were privy to the conversation and wish you well with your legal endeavors into the matter," he offered his hand to Alexander who shook it heartily.

"Thank you, sir, for bringing this unfortunate business to our attention and I can assure you Miss," he said, turning his attention to Mary. "That I shall do everything within the law to see that those responsible are brought to justice." He bowed his head slightly to Mary as she dropped her gaze and clutched at her useless arm.

"Thank you, kindly sir." The doctor and his assistant took their leave, leaving Clara to marvel at the doctor's quick thinking. Without his intervention, she would not have had a legitimate reason to ask her Uncle Anthony for help in firing a foreman she should know nothing about. Oh yes, the good Lord really did work in mysterious ways.

She turned her thoughts to Mary and how beautifully things had turned out for her as she knew that the doctor would take good care of her. She smiled to herself, but it faded quickly as she thought of Mr. Griffiths and the grim matter of relieving him of his post. She glanced up at Alexander who was deep in thought.

So, he thought to himself, *Daylight Cottons eh?* Wasn't that the name of the sponsor he had secured for the museum? He turned to Clara, a look of worry etched across his face. "Clara my dear, I must inform you. I have, in an attempt at gaining funding for Lawrence's museum, secured a sponsorship from the very company in question." He looked down at Clara before continuing. "Daylight Cottons have agreed to sponsor the museum for a moderate amount of advertising space on the premises."

Clara stared open-mouthed as realization dawned on her. "So, am I to understand that my company is helping to fund Lawrence's museum?" She asked.

Alexander nodded solemnly. "I do apologize, Clara, had I known that the company belonged to you, I would, of course, have asked you directly as it is clear to me that decisions are being made for you without your consent." He looked at her, a worried frown plastered across his cheeky, boyish face. Clara threw her head back and let out a long, loud laugh.

"My dear sir!" she exclaimed through tears of laughter. "You have done me a far greater service than you know. It has been a wish of mine to support Lawrence's endeavor and I am overjoyed that I am able to do so in a legitimate fashion." She smiled at Alexander who, upon realizing that he had, yet again made her happy, grinned in response. "But how are we to proceed? I have no knowledge as to whom is running the mills in my absence," she asked, just as the supper gong sounded.

Alexander offered his arm to Clara to escort her into supper. "We furnish ourselves with answers, my dear." He led her into the dining room and seated her beside himself. Amelia entered on the arm of the Reverend Cavendish.

"Ah, Clara my dear. Welcome home." Anthony beamed at his young ward fondly as he seated Amelia. "I trust you are recovering nicely and I feel I am not alone in expressing that it has not been the same here without you. You have been missed." He kissed the top of her head before seating himself at the head of the table and clasping his hands together as the signal to all that he was about to say grace.

As Clara raised her head after the last of the 'Amen' had been said, she plucked up the courage to approach the subject with her Uncle. "Uncle Anthony, who is in charge of my late father's cotton empire?"

Anthony looked up, startled by such a question. Clara had

not ever shown signs of interest towards her inheritance before. "I believe that all property and management responsibilities have been left to your family lawyer. A Mr. Samuel Farnsworth." He stopped and thought for a moment before continuing. "Why the sudden interest child?" he asked, leaning forward to help himself to a crusty roll. Clara glanced across at Alexander who smiled and nodded.

"Well, today I received a visit from Doctor Fletcher." She relayed the earlier conversation with occasional input from Alexander. Anthony sat back, his eyes wide with fury.

"Clara, I had no idea. Please accept my apologies, my dear." He turned to Alexander. "What do you suggest we can do about this?" He regarded his nephew carefully as Alexander pondered the question. Eventually, he spoke.

"I suggest that we send for Mr. Farnsworth and hear what he has to say on the matter," he replied as he broke open his potato and smeared the inside with butter.

Chapter
Sixteen

Samuel Farnsworth sat bolt upright on the very edge of his chair, shuffling his hat nervously around in his hands. It was clear that he wanted to be anywhere but there. Amelia cleared her throat nearly making the poor man jump out of his seat.

"Sir, I hardly feel that it is a difficult question," Anthony said and leaned forward in frustration. "Are you directly responsible for the appointment of staff at Daylight Cottons?"

Samuel darted his eyes from Anthony, across to Alexander, then glanced over towards Clara, and then back down at his clammy hands, still fidgeting with the brim of his hat that sat on his lap. "S-s-so sorry sir, but no. I hired Mr. Griffiths to do the... err... hiring and managing of... err... staff as h-h-he knows far more about it than I," he stammered.

"But forgive me, sir, you are deemed responsible for the general running of the factory, as set out in the terms of the original trust. Have you not at least been to the premises to check up on Miss Johnson's assets in thirteen years?" Alexander asked as Samuel proceeded to fumble with his hat.

Put that way it did sound dreadful. Samuel shifted his weight uncomfortably as he squirmed in his chair. "I-I-I left all that up to Mr. Griffiths," he stuttered. If the truth be known, Samuel Farnsworth was terrified of Mr. Griffiths and the further away he could be from that horrid man the better. Clara looked across to Anthony who nodded encouragingly.

"Mr. Farnsworth," she started. "I regret to inform you that as of now you are relieved of any duties to my family and I am transferring all responsibilities to Mr. Cavendish." She glanced across at Alexander who smiled at her reassuringly. She stifled a blush as she turned her attention back to the stunned Mr. Farnsworth.

"Furthermore sir, I have it on good authority that Mr. Griffiths has been abusing his power and mistreating his workers badly." She paused before continuing. "And that he has been using my own name to justify and excuse his actions and that is something that I cannot forgive," she finished.

"Therefore, sir, if you have nothing further to say in your defense I suggest you take your leave," and with that Anthony got to his feet and rang for Mrs. Dimbleby to show the now shaking Mr. Farnsworth to the door. Alexander leaned into Anthony.

"I feel that the sooner we remove this Griffiths fellow the better." He turned to Clara. "If you are in agreement Clara my dear, I shall make the trip to relieve Mr. Griffiths of his position immediately."

Clara pondered this for a moment. After all, it was her mill, and it was she who had risked everything in order to learn for herself what it was like to work for Daylight Cottons. She made a decision. "Thank you, dear, kind Alexander for all your help. But I really do feel that I should remove Mr. Griffiths myself." Clara stopped as Amelia interrupted.

"Dearest, I understand how you feel but you are still convalescing and I would not wish for you to open yourself up to infection from a factory environment. Besides, the trip may tire you. I should feel happier if you were to stay here with me and allow Mr. Cavendish to go alone." She looked Clara squarely in the eye, but Clara had made up her mind. She was not the child she had been before.

"Amelia dear, I really do feel that this is important to me as it is my factory and I am the responsible party. I need to make amends for the dreadful way the staff in my employ have been treated. And, I also need to clear my good name," she added quietly.

Amelia could see that to argue would be pointless and cause a large amount of unpleasantness. Instead, she allowed Clara to make the trip with Alexander and Anthony with strict instructions that she was not to overexert herself. And so, Clara found herself heading back towards Daylight Cottons and the liberation of a workforce that had been oppressed for far too long.

The cab trundled up to the wrought iron gates of Daylight Cottons. Alexander alighted and helped both Clara and his uncle out before asking the cabbie to wait for them and heading towards the main entrance. As they approached the huge wooden door, Alexander knocked and waited as the sound of a heavy bolt slid back and the door creaked mercifully on its hinges revealing the tobacco chewing gateman. His eyes grew wide as he looked the party over.

"We wish to speak to Mr. Griffiths the foreman. Do you know where we might find him?" Alexander shouted above the noise of the machines inside. Anthony took Clara's arm to steady her as the unpleasant little man disappeared inside and beckoned for them to follow.

As Clara walked the familiar walkways to the filthy office of the foreman, she looked down at the giant mechanical beasts. She shuddered as she remembered poor Mary. The gateman grunted at them to wait by the door as he disappeared into the gloom beyond. After a few minutes, he reappeared and, again, beckoned for them to follow. He showed them into the foreman's office and pointed over to the man himself, seated behind his desk of mounting paperwork.

"Can ah help you, folks?" he wheezed as they moved further into the room. Clara broke away from Anthony as he gave her a reassuring smile and rose to her full height. She stood at the end of the desk allowing Mr. Griffiths to get a good look at her face.

"Mr. Griffiths, my name is Miss Clara Johnson and, as you are no doubt aware, I am the owner and proprietor of this establishment." She paused to let the weight of this sink in. His eyes grew as wide as dinner plates as he began to recognize who Clara was. "And I am hereby relieving you of your post as factory foreman," she finished as Mr. Griffiths started to raise himself threateningly from behind his desk.

"Now see here little lady. Ah don't know who yer think yer are, but ah've told yer afore, in here, ah'm in charge." He stopped as Alexander produced a document and brandished it under his nose.

"This, sir, is the legal deed of ownership of Daylight Cottons to Miss Clara Johnson. I am Miss Johnson's lawyer and do hereby give you twelve hours to remove yourself from the property before you are forcibly removed by the police."

Mr. Griffiths' face grew red as he turned and pointed a grimy, tobacco-stained finger at Clara. "You! You nasty little maggot! You'll pay for this outrage!" he spat.

Clara built up all her courage and leaned in close to the foul man. "I warned you, Mr. Griffiths," she whispered. "I warned you."

Alexander quickly moved between Clara and Mr. Griffiths, truly believing that he might strike her. "How dare you sir, I demand you apologize to Miss Johnson," he hissed through gritted teeth as the filth-laden foreman clenched his fists.

"Ah dunno where she's got that get-up from, but that ain't no Miss Johnson," Mr. Griffiths growled.

Anthony stepped forward. "I can assure you, sir, that this is indeed Miss Johnson as I have been her guardian ever since her parent's untimely demise."

Mr. Griffiths whipped his head round to glare at Anthony. Then, without warning he lunged, swinging his fist to connect with the side of the reverend's head but Alexander had already anticipated his move and, spinning on his heel, he spun around, catching the man mid-blow and tackling him to the ground. Mr. Griffiths' thin, spider-like limbs splayed out in all directions as he fought to keep his balance against the much younger, much fitter Alexander.

"Ah'll 'ave yer. Ah'll 'ave yer all fer this, you see if I don't!" he roared as he threw a badly aimed punch towards Alexander who deflected it with ease, pinning the gangly man to the floor. He brought his face in close to Mr. Griffiths' ear.

"I came here today hoping to find that the accusations raised against you were unfounded sir, but judging by your actions I fear that every word of it is true." He kept his voice, calm and even as though talking to a child mid-tantrum. "I admit that I expected that you would attempt to land a blow on me, but to have struck a man of God." He paused, shaking his head in mock disbelief. "I would not have believed it had I not seen it for myself." He pulled the man to his feet before shoving him back down again into his chair.

"Now," he continued, brushing the dust and debris from his jacket. "I suggest that you gather your things and leave forthwith before Reverend Cavendish exercises his legal right to have you prosecuted and I hardly think you, nor indeed any one of us here, would wish for you to be spending the night in the provost." He turned to Clara. "My apologies my dear for that despicable display of wanton violence." Then he marched across to the door and opened it, indicating to Mr. Griffiths that the matter was closed.

Trembling with fury, the foreman reached into his desk drawer and pulled out a bottle of whiskey which he promptly secreted somewhere about his person. Then, glaring madly at

Clara, he slunk across the room and out past Alexander who closed the door sharply. He turned to his companions.

"I truly am dreadfully sorry Clara, my dear, that must have been an awful spectacle," he started, suddenly ashamed that his beloved Clara should have seen him in such a light. But to his surprise, Clara took his arm, beaming.

"What a dear, brave thing you are," she gushed. "Had it not been for your quick thinking, Uncle Anthony could well have suffered at the hands of that dreadful man."

"Indeed sir," Anthony put in. "I am forever in your debt."

Clara glanced down through the grease-smeared windows into the factory below. "But what are we to do now without a foreman?" She asked. "There are children amongst the workforce and there are a great many changes that need to be made."

Alexander followed her gaze down to the factory floor where he too could see children working at their machines. He turned suddenly and headed for the door. "Well first my dear, I think we need to 'rally the troops'," he said as he led the way back across the narrow walkways and down to the center of the factory floor. He pulled a large crate across and stood on it.

"Sir! I fear that none shall hear you above this unearthly din!" Anthony shouted as Alexander tried in vain to call the workers to a meeting. "We need to shut down the machines!"

Alexander glanced about him. Spying a large box on the wall, he crossed over and opened it. Inside was a lever. He pulled it down and, with a heavy clanking sound, the steam was shut off and the machines began to wind themselves down. He crossed back to the crate and waited. After a while, the noise level had dropped enough that he felt certain his voice would be heard and so he tried again.

"Could I have your attention please?" he bellowed. After another short wait, curious faces began to appear from behind the huge iron monstrosities as men, women, and children all moved towards the crate.

"Excellent!" Alexander beamed at them as they congregated around him, confused and cautious. "I should first like to introduce myself and my companions. I am Mr. Cavendish and I have replaced Mr. Farnsworth as the legal representative of this establishment." He looked down at Clara and beckoned for her to join him beside the crate. "I should like to very much for my companion to introduce herself as I believe she has a few words to say to you all." He smiled at Clara as he pulled her up onto the crate beside him.

Thank you," she started. "I know that Mr. Griffiths has already informed you that your employer is a Miss Clara Johnson." A series of hisses and spitting sounds rose up at the sound of Clara's name. Anthony stepped forwards as Alexander placed his hands on Clara's shoulders protectively, ready to speed her away should the crowd turn hostile. "But I feel that you should be aware that you have been lied to. For I am Miss Johnson and up until recently—"

She squealed in surprise as Alexander suddenly darted across and batted something out of the air in front of her.

She looked down in time to see an empty spool clattering across the factory floor. She looked up at Alexander in horror. He pulled her in closer as he surveyed the crowd.

"I understand your feelings and you have every right to feel upset but—" He stopped as another projectile came hurtling at Clara. Again, he threw himself in front of her and staggered a little as a small boot came whizzing past Clara's ear to strike him a hefty blow to the side of his head. Clara looked at him in dismay as he seemed to brush off his injuries. He cleared his throat to start again.

"Ladies and Gentlemen please, I realize you are all angry for your mistreatment and you believe Miss Johnson is to blame, but I can assure you that she had no knowledge of the terrible conditions of her mill." He paused as a few startled gasps went up from the factory floor as one or two of the workers recognized Clara for the first time. He continued, "Mr. Griffiths has been relieved of his post and Miss Johnson shall be hiring a foreman as soon as she is able, however, in the meantime, I shall need a responsible fellow to oversee things."

A low murmur rippled amongst the gathering as a few of the braver ones raised their hands.

"Please sir, Willard's yer man," a voice piped up and was immediately followed by a chorus of half-whispers, all in agreement.

"Capital. And would Willard step forward and make himself known?"

After a short amount of reluctant shoving and shuffling of feet, the crowd parted and the large, burly frame of Willard came trundling forward. He stopped short before Clara, his eyes fixed on the floor in terror. Clara recognized him at once but said nothing as she and Alexander jumped down and Alexander clapped his hand on the youth's shoulder.

"And are you willing to accept the post, Willard?" he asked.

The boy shuffled his filthy feet in the dust of the factory floor before nodding his head silently, still terrified to catch Clara's eye.

"Excellent my dear fellow. I shall leave the day-to-day running in your capable hands." He turned again to the waiting crowd.

"Any and all problems are to be brought to Willard who shall, in turn, inform myself. Any decisions that need to be made shall be left to Willard." He climbed back up onto the crate for one final address. "Miss Johnson has had a number of issues brought to her attention and over the coming weeks, we shall endeavor to address these. Thank you." He got down from the crate and crossed to Willard. "It is down to you now sir. I shall furnish you with the address of my lodgings and I shall expect a weekly report of any and all goings on within the mill."

Clara gazed at Alexander, her eyes full of admiration and awe at the way he had not only taken charge but how he had saved her from injury twice. Not to mention how he had calmed the mob before it had turned into something far nastier. The problems that had weighed heavy on her mind had all been solved thanks to him. He turned to find her looking at him and winked at her. She felt her heart beat a little quicker as her cheeks flushed with color.

Alexander broke away from the main crowd and came to join Anthony and Clara who were still standing beside the large crate Alexander had used as his make-shift stage. "Well, young Willard has agreed to take charge for now, but he lacks the ability to read or write but one of the others has offered their assistance." He looked at Clara, his face suddenly full of concern. "My dear, I do apologize, I have not given a single thought to your condition. Uncle, I feel that we can be of little assistance here now and our best course of action should be to take Clara home."

Anthony nodded and together they escorted Clara from the factory and out to their waiting cab. As they moved off, Alexander pondered on the bravery Clara had shown in standing up to Mr. Griffiths and he began to wonder if he had been a little too domineering in taking charge. He clenched his fists tightly as he thought of that insufferable ape Griffiths. How dare he speak to his Clara that way. He gazed at her, enchanted by the way her golden curls bounced as the cab trundled along the cobbles.

She turned, aware that he had been looking at her. She smiled warmly as he blushed suddenly embarrassed at being caught staring. This wonderful creature, this captivating beauty, his Clara that he had held close to his heart all through childhood. In that instant, he made up his mind. He would speak with Uncle Anthony this afternoon, he couldn't wait any longer.

***

"Come."

Alexander took a deep breath and pushed open the door to his uncle's private study.

"Ah, Alexander my dear boy, come on in and have a seat." Anthony beamed as Alexander crossed the room and seated himself opposite the desk. "And what can I do for you, sir?" Anthony asked.

Alexander looked him square in the eye, unsure of how to phrase what he had to say. After a few minutes, he seemed to have made up his mind.

"Uncle, I wish to talk to you about Clara... err... Miss Johnson," he started. Anthony leaned his elbows on his desk and steepled his fingers, surveying his nephew over the top of his spectacles.

"Oh yes?" he asked, encouraging Alexander to continue. Alexander took another deep breath to calm his nerves.

"I am an active partner in my father's law firm and a fully qualified lawyer as you know and I feel that I am now in a stable financial position," he blurted out. This wasn't going how he had rehearsed it at all. He looked up into his uncle's kind eyes.

"Let me make this a little easier for you, shall I?" he asked.

Alexander heaved a relieved sigh. "Yes, thank you," he breathed.

Anthony smiled. "I believe that you have come here today to present to me your excellent credentials as a sound businessman within a fine upstanding family firm, is this correct?"

Alexander nodded before trying again. "Uncle, I have fallen in love with your ward Miss Johnson and I wish to make her my wife," he managed. He relaxed his body a little. Anthony rose to his feet and moved around his desk to face his nephew.

"Sir, I can think of no one more suited to Miss Johnson than your good self." He paused as Alexander raised his face to look into his eyes. He smiled warmly before he continued, "And it is with great pleasure that I give you my blessing."

Alexander grinned at his uncle and he got to his feet heartily shaking Anthony's hand. "Thank you, sir, you have my word that I shall do everything within my power to keep Clara well and happy," he said as he made his way towards the door, still beaming happily as he let it click closed behind him. Anthony let out a little laugh to himself. But now there was the matter of Lawrence and Miss Baxter. He smiled. The good Lord really does find a way.

Chapter
Seventeen

"Ah yes my dear, that one belongs here I believe." Lawrence gently lifted the ancient fossil from Sophie's hands and placed a tag around it before carefully wrapping it in cotton and replacing it in its wooden box. Sophie gasped in awe as another box was opened and more fossilized remains were lifted out, examined, given a tag and returned to its wooden casing.

"It is almost unbelievable that your museum is set to open on Thursday next," Sophie giggled excitedly as Lawrence finished tagging an antiquated stone pot. She glanced down at the remaining boxes. "There are still many left to catalog though. I do hope we shall be ready in time."

Lawrence stopped and smiled at her. "We shall be ready my dear, fear not. I shall enlist the services of my cousin Alexander to unpack and display each item." He gazed at her as her face broke into a smile.

"Miss Baxter," he started.

Sophie put down the framed butterflies that she herself had donated to his effort. "Yes, Mr. Cavendish?" she replied.

Lawrence looked flustered and hot. He shook his head, suddenly feeling that perhaps now really wasn't the right time after all. "It's nothing my dear lady, please, put it from your mind." He smiled nervously. "I shall speak with you about it at a later date."

Sophie nodded. "Very well, I shall look forward to it," she said with a smile. Lawrence felt his heart thump in his chest as he returned her captivating smile. She let out a contented sigh as she slid the lid off another box, eager for it to give up its secrets.

Professor Baxter came shuffling in and placed another three boxes on the pile. "I say, sir, I do believe that we shall have quite a collection to open with next week." He surveyed the list of already tagged items.

"Oh Father, there are some truly beautiful pieces that put my watercolors and butterflies to shame," Sophie said, holding up an early example of a metal clasped brooch. She turned it over in her hands, admiring it happily. Lawrence watched her, delighted that she should get so much pleasure from these things as he did.

"Your watercolor studies are delightful and your butterfly collections shall be an excellent addition to our natural history section Miss Baxter." He grinned as Sophie's cheeks flushed with color as he praised her work.

"I agree with Lawrence my dear, your watercolors are exquisite and you should be proud of them," Professor Baxter said to his daughter. He glanced across at Lawrence as he continued to gaze at Sophie. She picked up another box and set it carefully down onto the table where she opened it and examined its contents before passing it over to Lawrence. As he watched, the professor noticed that there seemed to be a natural rhythm between the two of them and he wondered how long it would be before Lawrence came to talk to him about their future together. He smiled as he rang for his housekeeper.

"You rang, sir?"

"Ah Mrs. Prost, I wonder if you would be so kind as to provide us with a tray of refreshments," he asked.

"Very good sir," she replied. "Tea or coffee sir?"

"Lawrence, would you take tea or coffee?"

Lawrence reluctantly pulled his attention away from Sophie and their little production line to answer the professor. "Oh, a cup of coffee would be most welcome, thank you." He turned back to Sophie. "And you my dear?" he asked.

Sophie chuckled. "I'd like coffee too please Mrs. Prost," she replied.

Mrs. Prost nodded and shuffled off to prepare drinks and sugar biscuits, smiling to herself as she went. Oh yes, Miss Sophie certainly had an admirer there, it was clear to her that Mr. Cavendish was smitten.

"And what of the invitations sir? Are they all prepared for the opening ceremony?" The professor asked.

Lawrence nodded earnestly. "Indeed, so sir. I have sent out several dozens and I am expecting a good many of them to attend," he replied happily. Everything was coming together at last. If only he could ask his beloved Sophie to be his wife. He thought back to earlier conversations on the matter with his father and shuddered. He wished to avoid another confrontation of that nature if at all possible. But surely now his father must have seen just how perfect Sophie is? And what of Clara? Was she still expecting to marry him?

"Are you feeling unwell, Mr. Cavendish?"

Lawrence started guiltily as Sophie's voice startled him out of his worries. He smiled at her concerned expression. Dear, sweet, thoughtful Sophie. "No, my dear, I assure you I am perfectly fine," he replied.

***

Alexander walked the length of his bedroom floor, turned at the wardrobe and came back again to the bed on what must have been the seventieth time that hour. He stopped and glanced out of the window. The warm afternoon sunshine was filtering down through the trees leaving a mottled effect on the lawn below. He took a deep breath, filling his lungs with the heady aroma of sweet honeysuckle and roses. Yes. Today was the perfect day. His plan was a simple one. He would ask Clara to take a little exercise with him in the garden and when they stopped to rest at the swing he would declare his feelings.

Taking one last look out of the window, he turned and walked briskly out of the room, hoping that Clara was feeling rested enough for a stroll. He turned and took the stairs two at a time, anxious to get ahead with the thing now that he had talked himself into finally doing it. He found Clara sitting at the window in the library, thoroughly absorbed in a book on ancient civilizations.

"Clara my dear, it is a most beautiful afternoon. Would you care to accompany me for a stroll about the garden?" he asked.

Clara flicked her eyes up to look briefly at his face before dropping them back down to the book in her hands. "Of course, Alexander, that would be delightful. However, I would ask for just a few moments longer to finish this chapter. It should not take more than a minute or two," she replied as she turned a page.

Alexander regarded her thoughtfully, wondering how much growing up with Lawrence's influences had shaped her taste in literature. He smiled to himself as she casually brushed a stray hair from the side of her face, never once taking her eyes from the page.

"Certainly, my dear," he said as he carefully lowered himself onto the seat beside her. She snapped the book closed and placed it on the seat.

"I am so sorry for making you wait but I the ancient Mayans were a fascinating people." She got to her feet. "However, I am ready now," she said with a smile.

Alexander jumped up to take her arm and lead her gently out of the library and through the parlor to the garden. "My dear, you grow ever lovelier each time I see you," he complimented and allowed himself to gaze upon her as they stepped out into the sunshine.

Clara blushed and giggled. "Thank you for your kind words, sir," she managed as they took the path that led to the large old tree swing at the far end of the lawn.

"I have enjoyed our afternoon walks together immensely and I feel that accepting uncle's invitation to stay was probably one of the soundest decisions I have ever made," he stopped at the swing and lowered Clara into it. She sat down gingerly, moving to one side to leave room for Alexander to join her, but instead, he sank down on one knee. Clara could feel her heart quicken as he took her hand in his.

"My darling Clara," he began. He had expected to be nervous, but it all felt too perfect, too right. He looked deep into her eyes as the words flowed easily through him. "I have admired your grace, poise and exquisite beauty since childhood but it is only now that I am able to find the right words to convey to you my feelings," he continued to gaze into her deep blue eyes as a smile started to form on her lips. "From the days of sitting at the feet of Miss Orm listening to tales of wonder and far off places to the recent days spent strolling in the garden you have had me spell-bound," he paused as to clear his throat for he wanted to make sure that what he was about to say next could not be misheard or misconstrued.

"Miss Johnson, would—"Clara cut across him.

"Alexander, please." She looked down at his face as her

eyes began to fill with tears. "I am dreadfully sorry but I feel unwell." Her voice cracked as she tried to hold back her sobs. Alexander rose and helped her to her feet.

"Of course, my dear, I shall escort you back to Miss Orm." He took her arm and began to lead her back towards the house. Clara looked at her feet, her heart threatening to break in two with the weight of her guilt.

Alexander brought her back into the parlor and seated her carefully on the daybed before dashing off to find Amelia. Clara sank to her knees and clasped her hands before her as she addressed God in his heaven.

"Oh Father, why must I love Alexander if I am to be married to Lawrence? You know that I love you and I will always follow you but it seems so cruel that I can hardly stand it." She dropped her eyes as she let her tears run down her cheeks. "Please, I pray to you to give me the strength I need to be a good wife to Lawrence and deny my feelings for Alexander." She bowed her head as she whispered her closing to God before pulling herself back onto the daybed, grunting a little as her stiff leg refused to go where she wanted it to. As she sat contemplating the divine, she heard a light tap on the parlor door.

"Come in," she called with a sniff, expecting a concerned Amelia to come bustling across to her. She looked up in surprise as Anthony gently lowered himself beside her and took her hand in his.

"Clara my dear, forgive me but I could not help but bear witness to your stroll in the garden with Alexander just now," he said softly. Clara looked up at the reverend, her honest eyes wide with worry. "Is there anything you wish to talk with me about my dear?" he asked.

Clara finally succumbed to her sobs as she poured out her heart. "Oh, Uncle Anthony. You will think me a wicked child for I knew what Alexander meant to ask me and I wanted with all my heart to say yes, but..." she trailed off as another sob choked her.

Anthony nodded his head. "But you still feel that a union between yourself and Lawrence is God's wish?" he finished her sentence for her. She nodded, grateful that she hadn't had to explain. Anthony tilted Clara's chin up so that her eyes matched his. "My dear, the good Lord speaks to us in many ways and it is up to preachers such as myself to interpret his will." He paused as Clara let out a soft sob. "But," he continued, smiling softly. "Even seasoned members of the clergy such as I sometimes misinterpret his signs."

Clara's eyes grew wide as she realized what Anthony was trying to say.

"So, a union between myself and Alexander..." she trailed off as Anthony nodded his head slowly. A large smile lit up Clara's face, but it quickly turned to worry as her eyes filled up again. "Oh, but Alexander will be terribly hurt and I fear he shall not ask me again," she whispered as her tears began to fall anew. Anthony squeezed her arm softly as he rose to his feet.

"Leave that to me," he smiled knowingly as he left the room.

***

As it turned out, Clara did not need to wait long as barely an hour had gone by before Alexander entered the parlor with a look of nervous apprehension. He crossed the room to seat himself awkwardly beside Clara. For a short while he said nothing but simply sat looking out of the window. Clara kept glancing towards him, unsure as to how to go about starting a conversation. But before long he spoke.

"Clara dear, shall we try that again?" he asked as he turned and flashed her a smile. Clara nodded with relief as he slid down onto one knee and took her hand in his. "Miss Johnson, would you do me the honor of becoming Mrs. Alexander Cavendish?"

Clara could feel her heart wanting to explode out of her ribs and soar up over the trees. She placed her hand over her chest in a bid to keep it in. Then, taking a deep breath she regarded the handsome man before her. A huge smile broke out across her face as her eyes filled with tears in a mixture of happiness and immense relief.

"Oh Alexander, of course, I will," she whispered as tears of joy tumbled down her cheeks and splashed onto her hand, still clasped in Alexanders. He beamed at her as he helped her to her feet, relief flooding his system as he breathed a huge sigh. "And please accept my sincere apologies for..." She couldn't finish as Alexander placed a finger delicately to her lips.

"Already forgotten," he whispered.

As Clara left the parlor she was just in time to see Amelia going up the stairs. She called out to her to wait. "Amelia dearest! May we speak with you?"

Amelia retraced her steps back down into the hallway to find Clara and Alexander standing beaming at her. She already knew what they may want to speak with her about but she didn't want to spoil their moment. After all, how many times are you able to announce your engagement?

"Of course, Clara," she answered and smiled at her warmly, delighting in watching Clara almost dancing with excitement.

"Amelia dearest heart, we are to be married!" Clara exclaimed. Amelia took her arms and pulled her in, embracing her tightly.

"That is truly wonderful news my dearest. Congratulations!" She beamed as she released Clara and turned to Alexander. "We shall, of course, look forward to welcoming your parents to a formal dinner once you have informed them, Alexander," she smiled warmly as Alexander bowed his head to her.

"Thank you, Miss Orm. I shall write to them this very afternoon," he replied.

"Indeed. And I too have a considerable amount of correspondence to attend to," Clara added, "but not before I have informed Uncle Anthony and Mrs. Dimbleby!" And with that, she dashed from the room. Her slight limp barely slowing her in her rush to tell the world of her betrothal. She knocked on Anthony's study door and waited.

"Come," he called. Clara pushed open the large wooden door and poked her head into the room.

"Pardon me, Uncle Anthony, am I disturbing you?" she asked. Anthony smiled to himself.

"Not at all child. I am always rather glad of distractions as this sermon is proving a rather difficult lesson to write today." He placed his pen back into the holder on the desk and gestured for Clara to sit. "How can I help you, my dear?"

Clara opened the door completely and crossed into the room followed by Alexander. Anthony sat back in his chair, looking forward to discussing their upcoming nuptials with him.

***

Lawrence kicked the gate open with his foot as he tottered up the vicarage steps carrying a large package. He set his load down on the top step to open the door when suddenly, the door flew open and Alexander almost fell out on top of him.

"Dreadfully sorry old fellow didn't see you there." He gasped as he steadied his cousin. Lawrence brushed it off.

"No, my fault entirely. Would you be so kind as to help me in with this parcel?" He indicated to the package on the floor.

"Only too glad," Alexander replied and he took one end as Lawrence picked up the other. "Where would you like it?"

"The library if it's not too much trouble."

The two men carefully carried the box to the library and set it down with the others that were still waiting to be cataloged ahead of next Thursday's grand opening. Alexander tipped his hat to Lawrence and, whistling happily turned to go but Lawrence stopped him.

"You seem in good sorts today sir," he said as Alexander beamed at him.

"Indeed, I am, sir. For the delightful Miss Johnson has agreed to marry me."

Lawrence's smile spread from ear to ear as he clapped his cousin heartily on the back. "Oh, congratulations Alexander! That is wonderful news. And I can tell you, sir, that I couldn't be happier for you." He grinned.

"Thank you kindly. I believe Clara is in the drawing room dealing with some rather urgent correspondence." He winked at Lawrence who nodded knowingly. "Which reminds me," he continued, looking at the envelope in his hand. "I really must mail this to Father and Mother. I shall be along after supper to help you catalog this lot." He waved his hand towards the pile of boxes.

"Thank you, sir, I shall of course go and offer her my heartfelt good wishes on your upcoming nuptials." The two parted company with Alexander hurrying off to catch that afternoon's mail and Lawrence making a beeline for the drawing room. He knocked politely and waited.

"Do come in," Clara called from within. He pushed on the

door and stepped inside.

"Clara dear, I have just intercepted Alexander and he has told me the most wonderfully good news and I thought I must share it with you." He grinned at her confused expression before continuing. "He is to be married you know. Some girl named Clara has actually said yes to the silly thing and now he is dancing about with wings on his feet." He mimicked a pirouette as he crossed the room towards her.

"Oh, Lawrence you are silly sometimes," she chided and smiled warmly. She was certain now that the feelings she had for Lawrence could not ever be the love that she felt for Alexander. She cared deeply for him, of course, she did, and he would always hold a place in her heart, but as her silly older brother, not as her husband.

"I couldn't be happier for you both and I look forward to the big day in earnest," he said, bowing his head slightly and as she looked up at him standing there with a silly grin on his face, she suddenly remembered what Prudence had said. God had found a way after all.

"Have you told Father?" he asked as he crossed back over to the door.

Clara nodded. "Of course. He was one of the first to know," she said as she turned back to her desk. She looked at her unfinished letter to Florence and smiled as she remembered seeing her descending the stairs to be presented to her father at the bottom. Suddenly a thought struck her and she reached for a clean sheet of paper.

Lawrence left her to her work and quietly clicked the door closed. He turned and marched off to Anthony's study, his heart flying high. Finally, he would be able to ask his beloved Sophie for her hand. On reaching his father's door, he knocked and waited. But when no answer came, he pushed on the door, calling out to Anthony in case he had fallen asleep.

"Father? Are you home?"

But having again received no answer, he headed to the kitchen to help himself to a coffee before he started the long task of cataloging the last of the items before their transfer to the museum building tomorrow morning.

"Ah, Father," he said as he walked into the kitchen to find Anthony at the table talking with Mrs. Dimbleby. "Is it a good time to speak with you?"

"Yes of course," he replied. He turned his attention back to Mrs. Dimbleby. "So, I was rather hoping for one of your delectable apple pies Mrs. Dimbleby." He looked at his cook hopefully. "Do you think that would be a possibility?"

Mrs. Dimbleby tittered as she looked at the expression of hope on Anthony's face. "I already have one in the oven sir." She grinned.

"Excellent!" Anthony turned to Lawrence. "Now my boy, what was it you wanted to discuss with me?"

Lawrence poured two cups of coffee and cream and handed one to his father. "It is a little delicate Father," he replied, gesturing to the door.

Anthony nodded and got to his feet. "Please excuse us Mrs. Dimbleby and I shall look forward to supper immensely," he said as he followed Lawrence back out and into the hallway.

"Father, my museum is set to open on Thursday and I intend to ask Miss Sophie Baxter to be my wife at the party and it is my fond hope that you..." he trailed off.

Anthony smiled warmly at him. "Sometimes even priests have difficulty in understanding the mysterious ways in which God moves," he said as he watched Lawrence's face begin to light up. "I wish you and Miss Baxter every happiness in your upcoming engagement and I look forward to reading the banns for both yourself and Clara."

Lawrence beamed at his father as he felt the weight lift from his chest. All that was left to do now was to ask the professor and hope that Sophie felt the same as he did. "Thank you, Father," he breathed happily.

***

"Amelia, may I have your opinion, dearest?" Clara crossed to Amelia carrying the letter she had just finished.

"I feel that you are maybe a little old for me to be checking your grammar and spellings now Clara dear," Amelia joked as Clara handed her the paper.

"Don't be silly, Nursie." Clara grinned, two could play at that game. "I was hoping you would read what I have written and give me your opinion. That was all."

Amelia took the letter and scanned it. She looked up at her

young ward with a look of pride. "I believe that is an excellent idea dearest heart and that he shall be only too glad to oblige."

The letter read as follows:

Dear Mrs. Kettering,

I hope this epistle finds you and your family well. I am writing to inform you of some wonderful news. I am to be married to Mr. Alexander Cavendish and as my father has since passed on, it is my fond hope that Mr. Kettering would agree to 'give me away'. I look forward to your response in earnest.

Yours expectantly,

Miss Clara Johnson

Chapter
Eighteen

"And it gives me great pleasure to declare this museum open on this, the twenty-third day of the month of May in the year eighteen twenty-four." Mayor Geddes held up the bright yellow ribbon in his left hand and carefully cut it through with the silver scissors given to him ten minutes before his speech by Professor Baxter. A cheerful round of applause rose up from the guests as Mrs. Dimbleby and Mrs. Prost circulated with trays of refreshments.

"I think that went rather well don't you Clara dear?" Alexander asked as he helped himself to two glasses of orange juice as Mrs. Dimbleby sailed by with the tray. He handed one to Clara who took it gratefully.

"Indeed so." She smiled. Suddenly, she spotted someone she knew over the other side of the yard near the steps to the back entrance. "Would you accompany me, Alexander I wish to speak with Prudence," and she gestured to where a very nervous Prudence was hanging off the arm of Doctor Fletcher.

"Of course, my dear," he replied as he offered Clara his arm and allowed her to lead him over towards her friend.

"Prudence dearest, so lovely to see you, are you well?"

Prudence smiled warmly at Clara. "I'm very well, miss. Thank you," she replied but her face fell a little when she saw the look on Clara's face.

"Prudence dear, we are *friends*. You are no longer serving me so I would very much prefer you to call me by my name." Prudence shot a panicked glance at Doctor Fletcher who smiled at her.

"She's right my dear," he said cheerily. "And if that is how Miss Johnson would prefer to be known then that is how you should address her."

Clara smiled at her friend as Prudence nodded shyly. "Very well then, Clara," she murmured quietly, as though terrified that merely using Clara's name would land her in trouble.

Doctor Fletcher threw his head back in a hearty laugh. "What a shy little mouse you are," he said through chuckles. "If you are going to address Miss Johnson, I think you need to do it loud enough to actually be heard, my dear." He turned his attention to Alexander. "I hear congratulations are in order sir," he said and offered his hand to Alexander who took it.

"Thank you, sir, you shall, of course, receive an invitation to our garden party to announce our betrothal officially," Alexander replied as he shook the doctor's hand. "I don't believe we have been formally introduced," he continued. "Alexander Cavendish."

"Issac Fletcher. Delighted to make your acquaintance dear

fellow."

***

Lawrence took a deep breath to steady his nerves as he approached his old college professor. Professor Baxter was currently deep in conversation with his father and Lawrence felt that this might be the perfect opportunity to speak with him.

"Excuse me Father but may I have a quiet word with Professor Baxter?" he asked.

Anthony nodded. "Of course, my boy. I shall take my leave as I was hoping to speak with Doctor Fletcher before he left." He turned his attention to the professor. "Fascinating as always sir."

Professor Baxter smiled and nodded as Anthony excused himself and went to seek out the doctor. The professor looked at Lawrence expectantly. Lawrence cleared his throat and absently fiddled with the buttons on his waistcoat.

"Sir," he started shakily. "I have, for some considerable time now, been in admiration of your charming daughter and now that I..." He stopped short as Professor Baxter interrupted him.

"Say no more, my dear fellow. I would deem it an honor to have you as a son-in-law. I have been expecting this conversation ever since your graduation and I am certain that Sophie shall very much enjoy a chance to indulge herself in matters of a botanical nature, albeit a historical one." He grabbed Lawrence's hand and vigorously shook it taking

Lawrence by complete surprise. He pushed his glasses back up onto the bridge of his nose as the professor loosed his grip.

"Thank you, Professor. I shall endeavor to do my best to make Miss Baxter happy," he said solemnly.

The professor laughed. "My goodness me, how serious we are." He clasped Lawrence's shoulder. "All I ask sir is that you allow Sophie the chance to continue her studies and I am secure in the knowledge that she will make you a fine wife."

Lawrence smiled thoughtfully as he wondered what the future held for him and his dear Sophie. He swept his eyes over the assembled crowd. Many were walking around the exhibits, seemingly very interested in his collection. He smiled to himself proudly as he realized how wonderful it felt to share his vision with others. Shifting his gaze from his guests, all gently circulating around the artifacts he let his eyes rest upon two women, their heads bent together in active conversation. He smiled warmly as he made his way over to join them.

"Clara, my dear, I see that you have taken an interest in our wonderful collection of watercolors. May I turn your attention to the beautifully detailed poppy study?" He gestured to the appropriate frame proudly.

"Indeed, I have Lawrence, I was just saying as much to Miss Baxter. The level of intricacy is astounding. Where were you able to procure such delightful paintings?"

Lawrence puffed out his chest proudly as Sophie shyly

dropped her eyes. She clasped her hands in front of her in a display of awkward modesty. "These are the work of Miss Baxter herself. A fabulous botanist and wonderfully creative artist, would you not agree?"

Clara looked in astonishment from Lawrence to Sophie, who was gazing fondly at Lawrence as he boasted about her talents as though they were his own. "My dear Miss Baxter!" Clara gasped. "These are indeed beautifully produced. Why I believed them to have been scientific studies." She squinted at the cut section of a daffodil. "Truly lovely, you have a great gift and I must admit to being the tiniest bit envious. I should like to possess such a talent." She smiled warmly as Alexander sidled up beside his fiancée.

"Miss Baxter delighted to see you again." He bowed his head slightly to Sophie before turning to Lawrence. "So sorry to interrupt sir but Miss Orm has expressed her concerns regarding Clara's injured leg and wishes for her to rest for a while." He turned to Clara. "Are you feeling tired my dear?"

Clara looked up at him, her face full of adoration and gratitude for his kindness. It was then that she realized she had not thought about her injuries now for days. Amelia had been cleaning and dressing the scars but they no longer hurt her as they had and she believed her limp was beginning to subside too.

"Alexander you dear, sweet thing. I feel fine, honestly. I have not even suffered the slightest twinge." She slipped her arm into his before changing the subject. "Miss Baxter has crafted these exquisite watercolors, they really are very fine." The conversation turned to the study of botany, something which it seemed Sophie was also surprisingly gifted with.

Lawrence watched, captivated as she spoke animatedly about her interests. Indeed, he believed he could have stopped the conversation and proposed to her there and then, but he knew that this was not the time nor the place. Even he knew that a delicate matter such as this was best done privately. After all, he did not wish to embarrass Sophie or the good professor in any way.

"Clara, my dear, there is something I would like for you to see," he said grinning widely. "If you would all kindly follow me." Offering his arm to Sophie, he led them outside and round to the side of the large building onto the busy main road of Meeting Street. He stopped and gestured up to the wall.

"There. What do you think of that?" he asked as the party all looked up as one. Clara gasped as there on the side of the building, picked out in bold lettering ten feet tall were the words 'Charleston Museum of Antiquities are proud to be sponsored by Daylight Cottons Ltd'. She gave Alexander's arm a little squeeze.

"I think that God found a way," she murmured to herself. "I think it is wonderful Lawrence and I thank you for it," she said aloud as Alexander insisted that she take at least a small rest on a nearby bench.

The story of Clara and Alexander's great victory at the factory had quickly become common knowledge and Anthony had delighted in telling anyone who would listen about how his nephew and adopted daughter had acted as local heroes in liberating the factory. Indeed, he had used the subject in the weekly lesson as an example of helping those less fortunate than yourself.

Lawrence glanced over and smiled warmly to himself as he watched Alexander gently seating Clara down and caring for her tenderly. Perhaps it had been God's intention that she wed Alexander all along. He shot a glance out of the corner of his eye at his darling Sophie, a glimmer of excitement forming in the put of his stomach at the question he had burning inside his heart. He held out his arm and together the two made their way back into the museum, busily discussing what new artifacts could be added to their natural history section.

***

Mrs. Prost opened the door stifling a smile as she greeting a nervous looking Lawrence. "Back so soon?" she asked. "Miss Sophie is in the parlor sir," she winked knowingly as Lawrence bustled in behind a bouquet of Peonies and red tulips.

"Thank you, Mrs. Prost." He breathed as he took a deep breath to compose himself. "Before I go in, I would value your opinion ma'am." He held up the flowers for Mrs. Prost to inspect. She grinned.

"I should say, sir, that the rarity of the tulips as an expression of your feelings over the more obvious choice of roses shall impress Miss Sophie greatly," she leaned in to whisper in Lawrence's ear. "And peonies are her personal favorite."

Lawrence sighed with relief as Mrs. Prost took his hat and shuffled off to the kitchen to prepare a vase for Sophie's flowers. He took a deep breath and knocked politely on the parlor door.

"Come in," Sophie called in her bright, trill little voice. Lawrence pushed open the door, carefully holding his floral message behind his back to obscure them from Sophie until the right moment. She looked up, her face breaking into a big smile as she saw him standing in the doorway.

"How lovely of you to call Mr. Cavendish. My apologies though, Father has been called to the college on a matter quite urgent." She looked up at Lawrence as he brought himself further into the room. He lowered himself onto the sofa beside her being careful not to crush his delicate surprise.

"Miss Baxter," he began nervously. When he had planned this out in his mind yesterday it had all seemed easy and straightforward, but now that he had actually come to ask her his mind was filled with doubt and worry. What if she did not want him? What if this declaration of love ruined the wonderful friendship he had with her? He swallowed hard, trying with all his will to push these doubts from his mind as he slid himself off the sofa and down onto one knee. Sophie gasped as it dawned on her what he was about to do.

"Miss Baxter," he tried again. "From the moment we met I have been enamored of you. Your beauty, your talents." He paused as Sophie giggled helping to relieve some of his tension. "And your delightful giggle," he added as he pulled the flowers from behind his back and presented them to her.

"And I would consider myself to be the most honored man on God's earth if you would consent to become my wife." There, he had said it. He held his breath as Sophie gathered up the flowers in her hands and stared at him.

"Tulips and peonies," she remarked with a bright smile. "I would love nothing more than to be married to you."

Lawrence released his breath as he took Sophie's hand in his. A polite knock came at the door. Lawrence quickly raised himself to sit beside his bride-to-be as the kindly old Professor Baxter came striding into the room.

"Excuse me my dear but I wonder if you..." He stopped in mock surprise. "Ah, Lawrence, delighted to see you, sir." He smiled.

"Father!" Sophie exclaimed happily. "I should very much like you to be the first to know." She glanced across to Lawrence who was still smiling broadly. "Lawrence and I are to be married!"

Professor Baxter beamed at his daughter as he crossed the room and kissed her tenderly on her head. "That is truly wonderful news." He turned to Lawrence and offered him his hand. "Congratulations dear boy and welcome to the family and may I say how proud my dear departed Martha would've been had she not have been taken from us when she was, for I feel certain that she would definitely have approved of you, sir."

Lawrence smiled happily as he realized that God had answered his prayers but that the solution had benefitted, not just himself and Sophie, but Clara and Alexander too. And Father had got what he had wanted also, the Cavendish family and the Johnson family would now be forever joined. He looked up to Sophie, but his expression of joy turned to one of concern.

"Father," she said slowly, her eyes narrowing at the old man. "I believed you had urgent business at the college."

Professor Baxter threw his head back in hearty laughter. "I believe you have rumbled me, my dear," he said breathlessly. "I admit, I had seen young Lawrence here approaching with his bouquet from the upstairs window and felt that I may have been very much a third wheel as they say."

A big grin broke out over Sophie's face. "Am I to understand then that you were, in fact, hiding Father?" She started to giggle as the professor nodded.

"Mrs. Prost secreted me about the kitchen!" He clutched his stomach as he roared again with laughter. Lawrence couldn't help himself at the ridiculous idea of Professor Baxter hiding in his own residence. He burst into fits of merry laughter as Sophie did the same. He could tell that he had made the right choice and that his marriage to Sophie would indeed be a thoroughly enjoyable affair.

***

Amelia looked up from her writing desk to watch the drops of rain roll down her window, collecting on the pane to form a long channel of water. She sighed heavily as she thought of the many lonely hours she faced once Clara and Alexander were married and it crossed her mind that she may need to find herself another position. As she was pondering her future she noticed a figure walking up the path towards the front steps. Rising from her desk she crossed the room and out to the landing in time to hear Mrs. Dimbleby answering the front door.

"Good morning, please would you inform Miss Johnson that Mrs. Baxter is here to see her?"

Amelia descended the stairs to find Florence taking off her bonnet and handing it to Mrs. Dimbleby. "Florence my dear, how wonderful to see you. Are you well?" she asked as she crossed over to kiss Florence's cheek.

"Indeed, I am." Florence beamed. "I had to come as soon as I received dear Clara's letter."

Amelia smiled as she saw how excited Florence was for her friend. She turned to Mrs. Dimbleby. "I shall show her in Mrs. Dimbleby thank you."

Mrs. Dimbleby smiled. "Very good ma'am," she replied and took herself off to the kitchen to heat a kettle.

"I believe Clara is currently in the library. Mrs. Dimbleby has her looking through cake designs."

Florence grinned as Amelia knocked politely at the library door before pushing it open gently. "Clara dear? I have Florence here to see you," she announced as she swept into the room, holding the door for Florence to follow. Clara was over at the window seat surrounded by cookbooks. A pencil and paper were balanced on the window ledge, presumably for her to scribble down any ideas that appealed to her. She looked up as the two ladies crossed the room.

"Florence dearest heart! How lovely of you to call," she said to her friend as she jumped up to greet her excitedly.

Florence squeezed her arm affectionately. "Now dearest, I want to know everything. Every last detail. Don't leave a single thing out or I shall sulk terribly." She treated Clara to her very best pout. Clara giggled at her excitable friend. Florence joined in and soon the two ladies were busily chatting about Alexander's proposal. Amelia smiled to herself as she turned and crossed to the door. She would give them some time alone as she still needed to finish her correspondence.

"Oh Flo, I have so much to think about now." She paused, remembering that Florence had once been in her shoes. "And what of Owen? Are you enjoying your marriage dearest?"

Florence looked wistful as she replied, "Clara, you shall know when you are married but it is a truly magical feeling being near one who holds you so dear. You must come for dinner now that you are well. You and Alexander are always welcome," she glanced across at a list of things that Clara still had to do. The first word listed was 'bridesmaid'. Florence dropped her eyes to her hands.

"My dearest Florence, whatever is the matter? Are you feeling unwell?" Clara asked, her voice full of concern. Florence reached across and took Clara's hand in hers.

"No, my dear, nothing like that. It's just that," she trailed off finding the words difficult to say. Clara squeezed her hand.

"You can tell me dearest heart, you know that."

Florence looked up into Clara's eyes, tears forming in her own as she choked on what she needed to say. "I'm so sorry if this seems presumptuous Clara dear but..." She paused to take a breath before continuing. "I do hope that you do not ask me to be a bridesmaid as I have already said that I would oblige Sophie Baxter. But then I received your letter informing me of your wonderful news and I feel truly dreadful honestly. If I had received your letter first..." she trailed off as Clara smiled at her warmly.

"Please do not give it another thought dearest. I understand completely and it only seems right that you should be a bridesmaid to Miss Baxter as you are a Baxter now my dear."

Florence embraced her friend tightly, grateful that she had been so understanding of the matter. In truth, Clara had been in something of a turmoil about her bridesmaids as of course, she would ask Florence. After all, she had known Florence the longest and the two shared a closeness that put them more like sisters than mere friends. But then there was dear Prudence. After all, she owed the good health of her leg to her. Not to mention everything that she had done for her and the risks she had taken getting her into the cotton mill.

Clara looked into Florence's eyes. "Of course, I would've asked you dearest, but I do understand and I am certain that you will be a wonderful bridesmaid to Miss Baxter. After all, she was a wonderful bridesmaid to you when you needed one," she said solemnly. Florence fished her handkerchief from her waistband and dabbed at her puffed eyes. "Now, let us consider the matter closed. It is fortunate that you called today as I would value your opinion on flowers."

Chapter
Nineteen

Clara smiled warmly to herself as she took in the familiar scenery. The cab click-clacked over the cobbles as they turned into East Bay street and along the brightly colored houses along the seafront.

"Morning View. East Battery ma'am," the cabbie called out as he brought his horse to a stop. He climbed down and opened the door to help Clara out.

"Thank you, sir," she said as she paid for her ride and walked up towards the Kettering's front door. But before she had time to ring the bell, the door opened to reveal Prudence standing smiling at her on the doorstep. Clara returned her smile as she crossed over into the Kettering's hallway. Prudence took her bonnet and cape and showed her into the parlor.

"Mrs. Kettering is in the orangery, miss. I shall..." She stopped short as Clara interrupted her.

"I am here to see you actually dearest. Although I should like to see Mrs. Kettering while I'm here."

Prudence showed Clara into the orangery where Ophelia

was busy tending to her plants. She glanced up from her work as Clara walked in behind Prudence.

"Clara my dear, how wonderful to see you looking so well." She glided effortlessly across the room to kiss Clara's cheek. She gestured to a chair as she crossed the room to ring for Miss Parker. "Do sit." She turned to Prudence. "You also Prudence my dear as I should imagine that Clara has come to call predominantly on you."

Prudence nodded and awkwardly lowered herself to perch on the edge of the chair. Clara giggled.

"Prudence dear, make yourself comfortable. I do not believe that you are taking liberties. After all, I have invited you to join the conversation," Ophelia said and smiled at Prudence but wondered if it would not be easier for her housekeeper if she were to visit Clara in future. She put it from her mind.

"You rang ma'am?" Miss Parker asked politely as she smiled warmly at Clara. Prudence caught her eye and she winked at her. It had pleased Miss Parker immensely that Clara had befriended her. What with Clara and the growing relationship with Doctor Fletcher, Miss Parker felt that soon the Kettering's would be looking for a new housekeeper, and although she would miss Prudence dreadfully, she couldn't help but feel happy for her.

"Yes, Miss Parker, a pot of fresh coffee. Oh, and a plate of your delicious sugar biscuits if you would be so kind." Ophelia delicately sank into the chair opposite Clara.

"Very good ma'am," Miss Parker replied and with that, she

marched briskly to the kitchen to prepare the refreshments ordered.

Ophelia turned her attention to Clara. "Now, let me first congratulate you my dear on your wonderful news. And also, to apologize for not having yet responded to your letter." She smiled. "To say that Joseph would be honored with such a role would be a huge understatement. He shall, of course, give you away my dear and he thanks you sincerely for thinking of him."

"I am so glad that he has agreed and I feel strongly that my late father would be very happy with the arrangement." She beamed.

Ophelia smiled at the memory of Joseph's reaction to Clara's letter. "And to what do we owe the pleasure of your visit this afternoon?" she asked as Miss Parker set down the tray of coffee and biscuits on the table in front of her. "Thank you, Miss Parker," she added.

Prudence sat silently, feeling very awkward in the unfamiliar setting. It wasn't that she didn't want to receive a visit from Clara. She had been overjoyed to receive Clara's letter telling her that she was planning a visit to see her. And it wasn't that she wasn't grateful to Mrs. Kettering, but she felt that it wasn't at all usual for a housekeeper to find herself in such a position and she didn't really know how she was expected to behave. Her eyes grew wide as Ophelia passed a cup of hot coffee across to her. She took it gingerly.

"Th-thank you, ma'am," she replied as she set the cup down on the table.

Ophelia flashed her an apologetic smile. "I understand that this is difficult for you dear and that your situation is rather unusual." She paused as she considered what to say next. "Perhaps, under the circumstances, once I have finished talking with Clara, you and she might retire to the parlor to continue your visit in private?"

Prudence looked at her kind employer gratefully. "Thank you, ma'am," she replied. Ophelia nodded as she poured herself a hot cup of coffee, creaming and sugaring the drink before taking a sip.

"So, Clara my dear, you were telling us the reason for your visit," she reminded her and smiled as Clara set her coffee cup back onto the saucer.

"Yes, of course. As you know, I am to marry Mr. Cavendish. However, Lawrence is also to be married to Miss Baxter the week before." She paused to take another sip of her hot drink letting the creamy, bitter liquid glide down her throat before continuing. "I had intended on having two bridesmaids, with Florence being one of course. But as that will no longer be possible, I have decided on having just one bridesmaid."

Prudence looked from Clara to Ophelia, wondering what on earth she could possibly add to the conversation. She frowned as she looked at Clara. "Pardon me, erm, Clara," she murmured, still unused to using her name in such a familiar fashion. "But if Mrs. Baxter is not involved with your wedding, then why..." she trailed off as Ophelia tutted and rolled her eyes.

Clara giggled. "Oh, Prudence. Can you not guess dearest? I

had wanted both you and Florence to be my bridesmaids, but Florence shall be busily assisting Miss Baxter." She grinned at her friend. Prudence's eyes grew wide as her jaw dropped open. Her? Clara wanted *her* to be her bridesmaid? Overcome with emotion, Prudence allowed two tears to roll down her scarred cheek and plop into her lap.

"Clara," she whispered. "I would be honored."

Ophelia smiled broadly and set her now empty coffee cup back onto the tray. "Good," she turned to Clara. "And with that settled, I should imagine that the two of you now have plenty to discuss—"

"Pardon me Mrs. Kettering but there was one more thing." Clara clasped her hands in her lap, realizing that she was about to ask a very large favor of Mrs. Kettering and she was unsure as to whether it would be met with good grace.

"Yes, my dear?" Ophelia lowered herself back down into her chair as Clara awkwardly struggled through what she wanted to ask.

"As there will be dress fittings and a fair amount of planning in which Prudence shall be involved." She took a deep breath before continuing, "Amelia feels that it may be best if Prudence comes back with me on an extended stay, however, we do understand that you will lose your housekeeper and I do not wish to add undue stress on Miss Parker."

Ophelia smiled broadly. "Of course, my dear. It is an excellent notion and one that I feel would benefit Prudence far more than having to travel between two houses." She turned to Prudence. "What do you think Prudence?"

Prudence could hardly believe that this was happening to her. She looked across to Mrs. Kettering gratefully before turning to Clara. "I would like very much to stay with Clara to help with her wedding ma'am," she whispered quietly.

Ophelia nodded. "Very wise," she rang for Miss Parker to come and collect the tray. "I think then Prudence that you should go and pack your personal things and prepare yourself for the journey to St. Michael's vicarage."

Prudence excused herself and dashed from the room. Rushing out she passed Miss Parker coming out of the kitchen and making her way to the orangery to answer Ophelia's bell.

"Careful there Pru, what's the big rush?" she asked, catching Prudence in her arms before she collided with her.

"Sorry, Miss Parker," she said excitedly, "but I have to prepare my things. Clara has asked me to be her bridesmaid and she is taking me back with her to stay." Her eyes filled up again with tears. "As her *guest* Miss Parker!" she exclaimed. Miss Parker chuckled as she pulled a clean napkin from the stack by the kitchen door and handed it to Prudence.

"And to think that some people would believe a machine in the face would be a bad thing," she said. Prudence gently stroked the scar on her cheek as Miss Parker continued. "God has marked you, as a shepherd marks his flock. That scar is to remind you that the good Lord only gives us what we can handle and sometimes, great things come from the bad. God works in mysterious ways after all," she grinned cheekily. "And I guess that the next time your young doctor comes to call, we shall have to tell him where to find you."

Prudence felt her cheeks flush with color as she put up with Miss Parker's teasing. Smiling happily, and thanking the good Lord for all he had given her, she made her way up to her room to pack.

***

Alexander smiled warmly as he took Prudence's luggage up to the room Amelia and Mrs. Dimbleby had prepared for her.

"Now dearest, you are here as my guest. As of now you are my friend and my equal and no one will be treating you as anything other," Clara said as Mrs. Dimbleby waited patiently to take their bonnets and traveling capes. Prudence blushed and nodded. This was going to take some time to adjust to. Clara giggled as she thought how funny it all was. "Think of it as a complete reversal of the time you were instructing me in working-class etiquette," she said. Prudence chuckled.

"I suppose that's true," she mused.

"Excuse me, may I come in? I'm here to see Miss Johnson."

Clara spun round to find Sophie standing on the step outside, peering in through the front door, still open as Alexander paid the cab driver.

"Of course, Miss Baxter what an unexpected surprise.

Please do step inside," she invited. Sophie smiled as she crossed over the front step and made her way into the vicarage entrance hall. "We have not long arrived ourselves and were just on our way to the parlor. Would you like some tea?" She gestured towards the parlor door as Sophie removed her bonnet and cloak and handed them to Mrs. Dimbleby.

"Thank you, tea would be most welcome," she replied as she followed Clara into the parlor.

"Do forgive me, I don't believe you have met. This is my dear friend Miss Crofton." She turned to Prudence. "Prudence, this is Lawrence's fiancée Miss Baxter."

Sophie beamed at Prudence who smiled self-consciously, worried that Sophie's dress was far grander than her own, simple black frock. "Delighted to make your acquaintance, Miss Crofton. I believe we met briefly at the museum opening."

Prudence nodded.

"Wonderful. Tea ladies?" Clara offered as Mrs. Dimbleby placed a tray of tea and cakes down on the coffee table. "Please help yourselves to cake."

Sophie took her cup from Clara and sat back in her chair. "Thank you, dear," she said. "The reason I have come to call is that I have hit upon a notion that you may be interested in," she paused to take a sip of her tea.

"As we are to be married within a week of each other, I wondered if you would like to combine our weddings into one ceremony. That way, as we shall be inviting many of the same guests, and attending the same church, all the preparations can be made together and long-distance family and friends need only make one trip." She reached over to help herself to a sponge finger.

Clara looked at her in amazement. "Miss Baxter, that is a wonderful idea," she replied with a grin. "And I have to say, how lovely of you to want to share your special day with me."

Sophie smiled, pleased that Clara had taken to her idea. Prudence looked between the two brides. She took in Clara's plain, vibrant colored dress with matching ribbons. Then she turned to look at Sophie's subdued floral print with frills and lace. The two girls could not have looked more different.

***

"Thank you for coming it was a pleasure to see you again," Clara, Alexander, Sophie, and Lawrence flanked the front door as one by one their guests bid them good night and took their leave. It had been decided that, as the weddings themselves were to be combined, it also made sense to have a joint garden party to officially announce the engagements. And, as much of the planning for the event had been done by Mrs. Prost and Mrs. Dimbleby, the party had been a tremendous success.

"Delightful soiree. We have had a truly wonderful time dearest, thank you." Florence clasped Clara's hands on her way to the door, stopping also to thank her husband's cousin.

THE COURAGEOUS BRIDE OF CHARLESTON

"Thank you for coming. We shall look forward to welcoming you to the wedding," Sophie replied happily as a long line of friends and family filed out. In fact, almost all of their guests had at long last taken their leave and gone their separate ways. Only the good doctor was left, still sitting in the garden chatting with Prudence, under the watchful eye of Amelia.

Suddenly, a small, dark-skinned girl pushed her way through the throng of people. "S'cuse me, comin' through. The doctor is needed, it's an emergency. Pardon me, ma'am."

"Out of the way Rebecca, can you not see that this child needs to get through?" Mr. Heeley pulled his wife to one side as Mary squeezed through the doors and dashed up to Clara.

"Ah need Doctor Fletcher quick," she said and panted, breathless from having dashed all the way on foot. Alexander took her by the arm and quickly whisked her into the garden. Doctor Fletcher was standing beside Prudence who was sitting, gently rocking the swing to and fro.

"Doctor sir! You are needed most urgently!" Alexander called across the lawn as Mary sprinted towards the swing.

"It's Mrs. Kildare's youngest. She's bin coughin' up blood for the best part of an hour sir. Ah gave her what yer said, but it ain't done nothin'!" Mary screamed as she reached the doctor.

Doctor Fletcher's face turned white. He turned to Prudence. "My apologies dear lady but I am needed." He leaned down and quickly kissed Prudence's hand before darting off after Mary. As he sped down the hallway Clara was already holding out his hat and bag. "Dreadfully sorry. Lovely time. Emergency!" he garbled as he pushed his way through the throng of party guests.

"Comin' through, doctor on call!" screamed Mary as Doctor Fletcher hailed a cab and threw himself and his assistant into it and was gone into the night to deal with the sudden emergency.

Prudence came in from the garden on the arm of Amelia. She began to imagine what each day, and night for that matter, would be like being married to a doctor. In the middle of dinner, or at the theatre, or even just sitting enjoying each other's company, as they just were. It wouldn't matter what they were doing. If a doctor was needed, then he would have to drop everything and attend. Was that something she could live with? She put the thought firmly from her mind. She was a housekeeper and he a doctor. It was all very well striking up these friendships, but when it came down to it, the doctor would never marry so far beneath him and she would have to get used to it.

Clara, having seen off the last of her guests, came and took Prudence's hands in hers. "I am so sorry dearest heart, but that is the way with doctors," she stated and looked at Prudence who smiled proudly.

"Yes," she replied. "Selflessly saving others at the expense of his own enjoyment."

Clara smiled at her soft-hearted friend. How noble of Prudence to think of others before herself. She led her off to the parlor with Alexander and Anthony to allow Lawrence and

Sophie to say goodnight privately.

Lawrence kissed Sophie's hand tenderly. "Good night my darling Sophie. You have managed this party admirably and I am so very proud of you."

Sophie's cheeks flushed with color as she let out a little giggle. Her father waited outside, reminding her that the time was well past ten o'clock and that in order to get a good night's rest for the busy days that lay ahead.

"Good night, dear sweet Lawrence. I am looking forward to working with your sister on our wedding. I have some wonderful floral ideas that I am sure she will love," she said as she stepped outside towards the waiting cab.

Lawrence waved them off and closed the front door. Everyone was starting to come out of the parlor and head to their separate rooms ready for bed.

"Wonderful do wouldn't you say so?" Anthony asked as he headed for the stairs. "And very good I thought of the doctor agreeing to be best man to you both," Anthony smiled at the thought of a good old-fashioned family wedding.

"Indeed Father. And with Sophie and Clara working together this will give them both the perfect opportunity to form a long-lasting friendship." Lawrence smiled as he thought of the future. Everything was looking perfect.

Chapter
Twenty

"Oh, my Miss Sophie," the housekeeper gasped as she dabbed at her eyes with the corner of her apron. "If only your dear mother was here to see you..." she trailed off, overcome with emotion. Sophie smiled at her kindly housekeeper.

"There, there Mrs. Prost, please don't take on so. Mother has the best seat in the church and shall be smiling down upon me I'm certain of it."

A polite tap at the door indicated that Sophie's father was standing in the hallway. Mrs. Prost crossed to the door to let him in. He drew in his breath as he saw his daughter. Her bright white silken gown seemed to glow through the floral lace sitting on top. He beamed at her as tears filled his eyes.

"My darling Sophie," he whispered. "I have something for you my dear and it would honor me if you would wear it today." He fished in his pocket and pulled out a small velvet box. He handed it to Sophie who opened it.

"Oh Father, it is simply beautiful," she said and gasped as she carefully pulled the gold and mother of pearl heart-shaped brooch from its box and held it up to the light. The old professor dabbed at his face with his handkerchief as he let the tears flow freely.

"I gave this same brooch to your mother on the eve of our wedding. I hoped that it would be your 'something old'," he breathed through his tears. Sophie threw her arms around her father hugging him tightly and enveloping him in silk and lace.

"I will treasure it always," she whispered. And with that she allowed her father to secure his gift to the bodice of her dress.

***

Amelia came striding in holding an old box. "Clara dearest, it was my wish to have had something of your mother's to pass on to you on this, the most important day of your life." She paused as she fingered the box nervously. "However, the day your mother and father left for their summer house was the eve of their wedding anniversary. Your father had planned several surprises for your mother, and so she took with her a number of dresses, bonnets and, of course, her jewelry box." She cast her eyes down to the box in her hands. "All of which were destroyed in the fire," she continued. "I have but one heirloom to give to you." She opened the box and pushed aside two layers of tissue paper so old that it crackled and crumbled under her delicate touch. Clara gasped as Amelia held up the most precious thing she owned.

"This barrette was my grandmother's. My mother wore it on her wedding day and now, with no children of my own, I am passing it on to you." Her voice cracked as she choked back tears. "It is all I have for you Clara," she whispered, worried that Clara would not want such an old-fashioned gift from a family that was nothing to do with her own. But instead, Clara reached out and carefully took the barrette from Amelia's hands, her eyes filled with tears at such a touching gift.

"Amelia dearest heart. I have *never* considered myself motherless," she told her and looked deeply into Amelia's eyes remembering all the times that she had done the work of a mother *and* a father. "I am not only honored but deeply humbled that you should pass your beautiful treasure to me." She held out the clip for Amelia to secure it in her hair. "I shall wear it with pride." She beamed as Mrs. Dimbleby dabbed gently at her face with a clean handkerchief.

Amelia's heart nearly burst as she considered Clara's words. Offering her arm to Clara and collecting her train, she led her out onto the landing and down to Joseph.

***

Sophie took her father's hand as he helped her step carefully from the carriage and down to wait outside St. Michaels. Florence dashed up.

"Oh, Sophie dear, you look an absolute dream!" she exclaimed happily. "Mr. Cavendish should consider himself truly blessed."

Sophie giggled happily as her bridesmaid fussed about her. She glanced up in time to see Clara's carriage arriving. Joseph stepped out and helped Clara to alight.

Prudence gasped as she caught sight of Clara. Her beautiful golden curls tumbled down to the shoulders of the simple white silken dress she had chosen. The sunlight caught the white gold and diamond barrette in her hair giving Clara's visage a golden glow. In her hand, she clasped the same bouquet as Sophie, a collection of white roses, peonies, and baby's breath, all twined together with a long length of green sage green ribbon. She looked so beautiful that Prudence felt a sudden surge of pride for her friend.

"Clara," she started as her eyes filled with tears. "I do believe that no one has ever looked lovelier," she whispered. Clara leaned in and kissed her friend's cheek warmly before taking Joseph's arm as he led her over to where Sophie was waiting with her father. Prudence looked from one bride to the other and thought again about how different Sophie was from Clara and how awfully strained her marriage would have been to Lawrence.

Clara turned to Sophie, a sudden feeling of gratitude swept over her for she knew that Sophie was suited far more to Lawrence than she could ever have been. She smiled broadly at her. "You look truly beautiful, Sophie dearest," she whispered.

"As do you Clara dear, an absolute vision." Sophie beamed.

"Are we ready my dears?" asked Joseph with a proud smile. Sophie nodded shyly as Joseph winked at her and, clutching her bouquet tightly, took her father's arm once more to fall in beside her soon to be sister-in-law.

"Yes sir," said Clara happily as the church doors opened

and the booming opening chords of the bridal march could be heard.

Prudence and Florence took up the trains of their brides and the little party walked beneath the lynch gate and up towards the imposing white spire. The grand entrance pillars, which were now decorated with two large flower arrangements, held in place with large swathes of sage green ribbon, marked the welcoming entrance hall of the house of God.

As they made their way into the nave, Clara looked up at the raised pulpit. A comforting and familiar sight, but today, decked out as it was in fresh flowers of white and green, it was as if she had never seen it before. She smiled as they approached the altar with its breath-taking tiffany style window gracing the chancel. She remembered all the times as a young child she would stand in front of this very window speaking her fears, her hopes, her dreams as though it was the window to God himself. Maybe it was, maybe, even today, he was watching her through that window. She bent her head slightly as she mouthed a heartfelt 'thank you'.

Lawrence glanced across at his cousin as he stood nervously in front of his father. For the umpteenth time that morning he adjusted the sleeves of his light grey mourning jacket revealing the golden cufflinks beneath. He and Alexander were both suited in light grey and white. Lawrence watched as Alexander clinked the golden chain of his fob watch nervously. He smiled, relieved that he was not the only one.

Alexander looked at his cousin. "Nervous old fellow?" he

asked, as he pulled his watch from his waistcoat pocket to check the time. He glanced at the golden case as he flipped it open with his thumb.

Lawrence feigned confidence as he brushed his cousin's question aside. "Not at all, sir. Yourself?" he asked with a weak smile.

Alexander slid his watch back into his pocket before looking up at the altar. "I do believe I have never been more nervous of anything within my entire life," he replied truthfully as Anthony looked proudly at his son and nephew and gestured with his head towards the back of the church.

Lawrence and Alexander turned as the congregation got to their feet. Alexander could feel his heart beating wildly in his chest as around the corner of the first pew, Joseph led his beloved Clara. He watched, breathlessly as the sunlight filtered through the church and glinted off her golden curls giving her the appearance of an angel in his mind. His heart fluttered as she glided through the church towards him, unable to take his eyes from her. She seemed to shine as brightly as the sun as she came towards him. Her beautiful smile lighting her entire being and at that moment, he knew that there had never been anyone he had wanted more.

Lawrence let out a little gasp as Professor Baxter slowly swept Sophie around the back pew and into full view. She was a vision to him in subdued white and traditional lace, her shoulder length hair pulled up on one side and secured with a peony as soft and as delicate as she was making her the picture of purity and grace. She caught him gazing at her and smiled showing her beautiful dimples. Lawrence sighed, unable to look anywhere but at his beloved bride.

Joseph brought Clara to a stop beside Alexander and waited as Sophie arrived next to Lawrence. Anthony looked down at both couples. He turned first to the professor.

"Who gives this woman to this man?" he asked, his voice echoing around the church. Professor Baxter puffed out his chest proudly as he took Sophie's hand.

"I do," he declared as he placed his daughter's hand into Lawrence's. He clapped his soon to be son-in-law on the shoulder as he made his way to sit next to Mrs. Prost on his side of the church. Anthony turned his attention to Joseph.

"And who gives this woman to this man?" he asked again. Joseph took Clara's hand and gave it a little squeeze as he placed it into Alexander's. Clara looked up into the eyes of her groom, her heart overflowing with warmth and love. She knew that she could never have married Lawrence. This all felt so wonderful, so perfect and so right that it was clear to her that this was God's true will. She smiled as Alexander beamed at her.

"I do," Joseph said cheerily as he bowed slightly to the altar before taking his place beside his enchanting wife.

All eyes were on the couples as they solemnly promised to love each other and support each other with the help of God. All eyes except Doctor Fletcher's. His eyes were fixed on Prudence. Her slight frame and willowy figure were highlighted beautifully by her simple ivory gown. Her short hair was pushed back from her face beneath a circlet of flowers to show off her big, beautiful, baby blue eyes.

As Amelia bowed her head in prayer she realized that God had answered her own prayers long ago and always had. She absently touched her stomach. She thought back to when she was a child and had fallen from an open window. Everyone had expected her to die. For three days she lay at the mercy of God. She was spared, but at a price. She would never be able to raise a family of her own. Having wanted nothing more than to be a mother she had prayed each and every night to the good Lord for a miracle. She raised her head as the last of the 'Amens' echoed around the church. She looked at Clara, tears forming in her eyes. Standing at the altar, clothed in white and now wearing the bright golden band signifying her union with Alexander, stood Amelia's miracle.

Epilogue

The carriage clattered through the cobbled streets, slipping and sliding on the water strewn roadways, the driver working his horse hard. He cracked the whip, forcing his charge on into the driving rain as the carriage wobbled and careered past the Exchange and Provost, his passenger smashing against the sides of the coach but he hardly cared. What mattered was getting there in time. Skidding into Queen's Street, the driver pulled back hard on the reins letting his horse rest for a moment as the carriage screeched to a stop. The young passenger threw himself out of the cab into the pouring rain.

"Please wait for us sir!" he shouted to the cabbie, anxious to be heard above the downpour.

He sprinted through the gate and up the steps to hammer repeated on the front door. After what seemed to him like an age, the door opened a crack and the tired face of Anthony squinted out into the dismal night.

Alexander shouldered his way inside, pushing past his uncle, in what would be considered a rude manner under normal circumstances, but tonight was far from normal.

"Alexander, dear boy, what on earth is going on?" Anthony

asked, confused from being woken suddenly and shaken from Alexander's rough shove.

"Please forgive me uncle but you and Miss Orm must come immediately!" he exclaimed, grabbing the reverend's cloak and hat and calling up the stairs for Amelia.

"Whatever for, it is the middle of the night..." Anthony started but could not finish as Alexander cut across him.

"Clara is in considerable trouble and we fear we may need a priest." He bundled Anthony's clothes into his hands and began to dart up the stairs to hammer on Amelia's bedroom door. He stopped short as she sailed down the stairs, her dress pulled on over her night things.

"What has happened Alexander, where is Clara now?" she asked, concerned that he may have brought her in the cab.

"Please, Miss Orm, she is bedridden and soaked in blood. The midwife is with her but after five hours of laboring, she says that there is nothing more she can do. I have sent for Doctor Fletcher but Clara insists on you being with her Miss Orm and in the event of..." he trailed off, fearful to say the terrible words aloud. Amelia grabbed Anthony's arm and pushed them all out of the front door and down the steps to the waiting cab.

"East Bay Street and please, drive your horse hard for we may already be too late!" Alexander screamed.

The cabbie cracked his whip once more and tore off into the miserable night with Amelia, Anthony, and Alexander holding on for dear life in the back.

***

Amelia hammered on the door which was immediately thrown open as a dark-haired girl ran past. She darted up the stairs carrying towels and soap. Amelia flew up the stairs after her.

"Where is Clara! Can I see her?" she demanded as the girl kicked open the door to Clara and Alexander's bedroom. She jerked her head over to where Clara was screaming and sweating into her pillows, the sheets were dripping with blood. Doctor Fletcher was standing at the foot of the bed, his arms beneath the covers while the shaking midwife held Clara's convulsing body as firmly as she could.

"No, the child is wedged. And there is a danger it will suffocate. And as it is the mother is losing too much blood. Mary, I shall need my forceps and second delivery bag."

The dark-haired girl nodded as she dashed past Amelia, her face contorted with panic and worry. Amelia immediately ran to Clara.

"Clara dearest, it's Amelia. The doctor is with you dearest heart," she crooned as she held Clara's head as she sobbed. Suddenly Clara's back arched and she screamed out in pain as the midwife and Amelia tried to calm her. Doctor Fletcher reappeared from under the covers, his hands and lower arms covered in Clara's blood.

"Miss Orm," he said and kept his voice as calm and professional as he could. "The child is not quite breech but sitting across the pelvis, I need to shift it slightly to give the forceps access to the head. Try and hold her legs as still as you can."

Amelia nodded and grabbed Clara's ankles, holding her legs as high as she could while Clara screamed and squirmed. Amelia closed her eyes as she whispered to the Lord above to protect Clara. From beneath the sheet, Doctor Fletcher gave one almighty grunt as Clara's legs flailed and kicked as she fought against Amelia's grasp. He reappeared, sweat dripping from his brow.

"She's torn but not badly. I have the room I need," he informed Amelia. "Keep holding her legs if you would ma'am as I want to minimize the risk of the child slipping back." Through all the commotion the doctor remained calm as another contraction wracked Clara's body sending her thrashing about.

"You are doing well Mrs. Cavendish. We will get to your baby I promise," the kindly old midwife told her and stroked Clara's hair as she sobbed.

Mary crashed through the door holding up the bag the doctor had sent for and a strange contraption sealed in sterile cloth. Doctor Fletcher unwrapped the large scissor-like tool and instructed Mary and Amelia to each take a leg and hold her still. Clara let out a piercing scream as the doctor inserted the forceps to get a good grip around the child's head. Steadying his foot against the bed he pulled, trying to time each pull between the natural rhythm of convulsions as Clara's body reacted to the contractions.

The sound drifted down to Alexander and Anthony as they

waited anxiously in the hallway. Alexander paced back and forth as he tried not to think of his beautiful wife upstairs. Anthony strode up and fell into step beside him.

"The good Lord only gives us that which we can cope with," he said softly as Alexander came to the drawing-room door and stopped. He looked into his uncle's wise eyes.

"Thank you, sir," he said breathily before turning and striding back up the tiled hallway to the front door. Here Anthony stopped him. He clutched his shoulders and lowered him gently to sit on the bottom step of the staircase.

"Two blind men once approached the Lord Jesus Christ and asked him to heal them for they had heard of a dead girl that Jesus had resurrected and had risen from her grave," He paused and looked at Alexander. "Jesus asked them if they wanted to be healed and if they had faith that Jesus could do it. The men declared that they did indeed have faith in Jesus and so, Christ touched the men and they were healed." Anthony put his hand on his nephew's arm. "Have faith and trust in the Lord for those who have faith are healed," he said.

Alexander smiled. Grateful for the words of comfort. He thought about his faith in God as Anthony clasped his hands together and bowed his head.

They began to pray and Anthony led them. "Lord, we ask thee to bless this house and that your daughter Clara be guided through the difficult journey of childbirth. We thank you father for your son Jesus Christ and his healing powers that taught us to have faith in your love. Amen," he finished.

He looked across at Alexander, his head still bowed as he whispered his own prayers. Anthony smiled as he left Alexander to practice his faith in peace. He allowed himself a glance upstairs as another scream echoed down to them.

"I need you to keep as still as you can and push hard for me Clara. As hard as you can!" Doctor Fletcher shouted to Clara over the top of her screams as he slowly inched the child out.

"I-I-I cannot! Amelia! I cannot!" Clara screamed as Doctor Fletcher pulled again. "Please!" She sobbed. "Please! Help me!"

Amelia's heart nearly collapsed at the sound of Clara's desperate pleas and she nearly released her grip on her leg to go up to her head, but instead, Mary called out.

"The Lord is my shepherd; I shall not want," she started. Amelia recognized psalm 23:1-4 immediately and joined in.

"He makes me lie down in green pastures. He leads me beside still waters. He restores my soul. He leads me in paths of righteousness for names' sake. Even though I walk through the valley of the shadow of death, I will fear no evil, for you are with me," Mary and Amelia chorused in unison. The stirring words of the familiar psalm seemed to give Clara new strength as Mary called out again.

"Ah'm clingin' on Clara. You know you can do it! You push with me now y'hear?" She called as she started to count. "One, two, three, push!"

Clara bore down burying her chin in her chest as she

roared with all the effort of pushing out the child.

"OK now, again. One, two, three, push!" Mary called again and again Clara pushed. Instead of grunting, her body began to go limp as her head flopped backward in a dead faint. Doctor Fletcher continued to hold the baby's head as he instructed Mary what to do.

"Take the smelling salts from my bag and attempt to rouse her. We need her awake!" he instructed as he gently pulled at the child again.

Mary darted to the bag to retrieve the bottle of salts and, pulling out the stopper shoved the entire thing underneath Clara's nose. Clara's eyes flickered as she started to come to.

"She is exhausted. We may lose her," the doctor continued to ease the child's head as Mary once again waved the salts in front of Clara's face. Suddenly, with a cough and a little scream, Clara came to once more.

"Now Clara, I need you to give me one final push my dear. Can you do that?" the doctor called as Clara summoned up all her strength and pushed as hard as she could. Doctor Fletcher pulled hard as the child came free. Clara's body, her energy spent, collapsed back onto the bed, limp and lifeless.

Amelia dropped her leg to rush to Clara's head, she picked her up and cradled her, crying into her hair. After a few moments, she began to realize that Clara wasn't moving. She looked up and called to Doctor Fletcher.

"Doctor! There's something wrong! Clara is not responsive!" she sobbed. Doctor Fletcher passed the baby to Mary who looked down at the sorry looking thing. Its limbs and head were black and misshapen from the forceps, she knew that was to be expected for she had seen a forceps delivery before, but in every case, the child had cried out or made some noise. This baby did not.

With tears forming in her eyes she picked up the blanket from the crib and swaddled the child, cradling the little creature in her arms hoping to at least keep the thing warm. But she already feared that Clara's laboring might have all been in vain as the tiny bundle had not moved once. Clara suddenly threw her head back and gasped for air before again screaming out as her body convulsed again. Doctor Fletcher sped to the foot of the bed expecting the afterbirth but what he actually found was far more worrying.

A second head was birthing but he was certain that Clara would not have the strength to labor a second time. Assessing the situation, he sent the midwife down to speak with Alexander. Mary sidled up to the doctor and whispered in his ear. His eyes grew wide as he looked down at the lifeless child Mary held in her arms.

"Place the child in the crib and fetch Reverend Cavendish. Tell him we may need his services," he murmured quietly so that Clara would not hear. She nodded and carefully laid the child down before following the midwife downstairs.

As she got nearer to the hallway she could hear the end of the conversation.

"The doctor is doing all he can. I am so sorry Mr. Cavendish. He has said that Mrs. Cavendish is suffering from exhaustion and blood loss," the midwife said solemnly as she looked into Alexander's usually bright eyes, now dull with the pain of worry and anxiety. "Please have faith, sir. Doctor Fletcher is one of the best and I know he will do all he can to save your wife."

Alexander smiled weakly as he spied Mary on the stairs. She crossed to Anthony.

"Ah'm mighty sorry sir, but the doctor is in need of your services. The young'un..." she trailed off as she caught sight of Alexander's face and could not bring herself to finish. Anthony nodded and followed her up the stairs to Clara's room where it was clear that everything was not at all as it should be.

Amelia had both of Clara's legs now, fighting against her thrashes and kicks. He looked across at the doctor who was again, down under the sheets pulling a second child from Clara's spent body. Mary tugged delicately on Anthony's sleeve as she handed him the little bundle. He held it gently in his arms, close to his body. Praying and willing for the lord to spare their family.

"Is it... Was it a boy or a girl?" he asked quietly as a tear ran down his wizened cheek. Mary looked up at him, her face filled with sorrow.

"A little boy sir," she whispered.

Anthony nodded as he continued to keep the child clasped to his chest, whispering the Lord's prayer. Clara screamed again as yet another contraction shook her frail body.

"Please! Dear Lord! Have mercy! Please!" she sobbed, as her back arched again as another wave of pain hit her. Doctor Fletcher called out to Mary to come and support the second child as he continued his firm but steady pull.

"You are nearly there Clara my dear! You are very nearly there!" the doctor called out to her as she lay back on the bed sobbing.

"You can do it Clara Ah knows it!" Mary called out as with one last herculean effort from a body that had nothing left to give, Clara pushed.

Mary grabbed the child's back as the baby came free. Looking down at the slimy little being in her grasp, Mary watched with relief as the child's mouth opened and it let out a high-pitched cry.

"Clara! Clara, you did it! Ah've got yer baby! An she's as beautiful as you!" Mary cried as she carefully wrapped the second child in Alexander's dressing gown. She went to pass the child to Clara but again, her eyes were closed and she was barely breathing.

Anthony continued his blessing of the first child as his sister screamed and cried. But as he looked down he thought he saw the child's mouth open and close. He stared at the baby, waiting for him to do it again. After another few minutes, he did just that.

Mary walked up and down cradling Clara's daughter as Doctor Fletcher set about resuscitating Clara for the second time. As Mary brought the screaming child closer to Anthony, her brother started making snuffling sounds. Mary moved past and the child snuffled louder. Anthony walked alongside Mary so that he could watch the child reacting to his sister's bawls. And, sure enough, after a few moments, the child in Anthony's arms screamed out along with his sister. He bent his head down in prayer, thanking the good Lord for his miracle. He turned to a stunned Mary, tears in his eyes and a bright smile on his face.

His smile quickly turned to worry, however, when he saw Clara's lifeless form lying in the knotted sheets, still wet and sticky from her blood. He looked up at Amelia who was clutching Clara's hand and sobbing. He lay the child back down in the crib and raced down to fetch Alexander.

"Alexander! Alexander! Come quickly!" he urged as his nephew looked up at him, his face streaked with tears. He got to his feet quickly and dashed up the stairs.

Entering the room, he looked down at Mary who had both babies on her knees, each one screaming out loudly. Alexander smiled at her as he choked back his tears, but Mary shook her head sadly. He let his eyes slide up towards the bed where his beautiful wife lay pale and unconscious.

Slowly, as though he were in a dream, he crossed over to the side of the bed and bent down. He kissed his wife's clammy cheek as he let his tears flow freely. Doctor Fletcher tried one last time to massage Clara's heart, desperate to get her breathing again.

"There is a faint pulse!" he declared as Alexander stared at him. He bent down level with Clara's ear and whispered to her.

"Clara darling? We have two fine children and they need their mother. I know you are not lost to me. I know that you are there." He reached down and squeezed her hand.

"Come back to me, my love." His voice cracked as he surrendered to his sobs. "Come back to me." He squeezed her hand again. Suddenly, he brought his head up and stared intently at Clara's face. Had he felt it? Had he really felt it? He squeezed her hand again and this time there was no mistake. Clara squeezed his hand back as her eyes flickered. Alexander looked at the doctor. His eyes full of gratitude as Clara slowly began to regain consciousness.

***

Clara sat a little dazed and clearly tired as Amelia, Mary and old Mrs. Chandery the midwife, stripped and cleaned the bed. Mary fluffed the pillows as Alexander carefully lifted her back beneath the sheets.

"How do you feel my dear?" he asked as he kissed her cheek. Clara looked up at her husband shakily, clearly confused.

"I-I-I do not know," she replied as Amelia brought her son and placed him in her arm. Mary leaned over with her daughter and placed her in her other arm. Clara looked down at the two children before looking up at Alexander a frown on her face.

"T-two?" she stammered. Alexander nodded.

"Twins," he said and smiled at her. "A boy and a girl."

Doctor Fletcher, now clean, came across to check his patient. He looked at her pale skin and dark sunken eyes with concern. He turned to Alexander. "I am not at all happy Alexander. She has lost a considerable amount of blood and will need plenty of water and to rest. Two things that I am not confident your two new additions will allow her to have." He looked down at the sleeping children in Clara's arms before continuing.

"She will need the water to make new blood, but her body will use it for making milk. Now I realize that she will want to have fed her children herself, however." He paused and looked across at Amelia. "Under the circumstances, I feel that it might be better for her to allow her milk to dry."

Clara held up her hand to try to protest. "Dear Doctor, I feel that I have more than enough milk for two. I am certain of it." She stopped as the doctor held up his hand.

"I have no doubt as to your capability Clara, it is your health I am worried for." He looked at her again before making up his mind. "In fact, Clara, I forbid you from feeding your children as I am convinced that you are in need of more blood," he turned to Alexander.

"There are formula powders but they are expensive. The alternative is to hire a wet nurse..." he trailed off as Alexander shook his head.

"If Clara cannot feed her babies then I shall. Money is no object, sir. Please inform me as to where we can obtain such powders and the equipment that we shall need." He raised himself from the bed in readiness to fetch his children whatever they needed. Doctor Fletcher nodded and scribbled the name of the concoction and which pharmacist to approach. Alexander leaned over and kissed his wife tenderly on her head.

"I shall be back momentarily my dear," he whispered as he dashed off down the stairs.

Amelia crossed the room and took the doctor to one side. "Doctor, will there have been any permanent damage done to Clara? And shall she be bedridden?" she asked, her voice full of concern. Doctor Fletcher smiled.

"Temporarily yes as the bleeding will need to slow, but otherwise, once her strength returns Clara shall be fine," he told her and adjusted his jacket sleeves.

"We are forever in your debt for what you have done for us this night. Please forward your bill to us and we shall pay it as soon as we receive it." Amelia looked up at the good doctor. He smiled at her.

"Ah now, yes, my fee." He walked across to Clara and carefully checked on the two sleeping twins before returning to Amelia. "Clara and Alexander are dear friends and I feel that their happiness is reward enough." He leaned into Amelia and whispered in her ear. "And I feel that the lovely Prudence may soon be needing Clara's attention." He winked at her as he collected his cloak and hat. He gestured to Mary who nodded and crossed to Clara.

"Ah have finally managed to repay you for saving mah arm." She smiled at her friend before reaching down and tickling the two babies under their chins. "They are fine lookin' young'uns, Clara. You did a mighty fine job back there."

Clara looked at Mary through her tired eyes. She stifled a yawn. "Forgive me, dearest, I really am not myself," she murmured. Mary smiled as she left Clara gazing down at her two little bundles.

"I shall be back tomorrow afternoon to check on you all. But as for now, I suggest these two new mouths get a good feed and the rest of you a good night's rest." He tipped his hat as he ushered Mary out.

Alexander returned, breathless from having run the entire journey. He held a large bag out to Mrs. Chandrey. "I assume that you will have a far clearer idea than I dear lady," he said as she shuffled across and took the bag. He removed his cloak and hat and eased himself down beside his wife and children. Anthony pulled his chair a little closer so as to speak to the new parents.

"Well now, we shall have to start making plans for the christening," he said and beamed. There were two aspects to Anthony's calling that he particularly enjoyed: the Sunday school Easter production and Christening celebrations.

Alexander looked into his wife's eyes as he realized that they had not yet named their offspring. Clara smiled warmly as she felt a wave of pure love sweep over her. "My darling Clara," Alexander began. "What would you like to call our children?"

Clara pulled her babies in closer to her chest, cuddling them into her as she thought about what names she liked best. Then suddenly it hit her and nothing seemed more appropriate. "If it is acceptable to you dearest, I should very much like to call them Willis Edward and Joslyn Cornelia."

Amelia gasped at the mention of Clara's parents' names. Her hand flew to her mouth as tears formed in her eyes. Anthony leaned back in his chair, a big smile spreading across his face. Alexander beamed at his beautiful wife as tears began to form in her eyes.

"They are wonderful names, my dear."

Clara chuckled as she cradled Willis and Joslyn in her arms. Amelia leaned down to kiss Clara's head.

"I believe that you have named them perfectly my dear," she said as Clara held out her children for Amelia to see. She looked across at Alexander who nodded and smiled. She turned back to her old governess.

"Miss Orm," Alexander started formally. "We should very much like for you to be our new governess. If you are in a position to accept the post of course," he smiled as Amelia beamed.

"My dear Mr. Cavendish, I shall be only too glad to take up the post offered," she replied in the same formal tone as Alexander before letting out a burst of laughter just as Mrs. Chandrey returned carrying two bottles of feed. She handed them to the new parents and showed them each how to hold and feed the babies. Clara looked up happily at her little family. The good Lord had certainly provided and she offered up her thanks for the mercy he had indeed shown her in her labor.

***

Alexander pushed open the door to the nursery and crossed to where his wife was busy changing a rather smelly diaper. Alexander wafted the smell from his nose with the paper he was holding. "I believe I have arrived at a rather unfortunate moment," he said with a chuckle as Clara cleaned and powdered her little girl's behind.

"Would you just place your finger there please Alexander? I fear that I am not yet completely proficient at securing the diaper pin," she admitted as Alexander helped her.

"My dear, I have, this very morning, received a letter from my parents informing me of their intention of coming to stay within the next two weeks," he said as Clara picked up their daughter and carried her back over to where Amelia was busy feeding Willis.

"Wonderful my dear. I shall look forward to seeing them," she replied as Alexander leaned down and tickled Willis' feet making him squirm.

"Oh, and Willard has informed me that the extension building to the dining hall is moving along splendidly." He paused to pull a letter from his bundle. He handed it to Clara who scanned it.

"His letters are getting clearer and clearer. Why I do believe he has written this one entirely himself!" she exclaimed smiling.

Every week, without fail, Willard had sent word on the development of the factory. Things had improved dramatically. The new dining hall was the latest in a long line of changes that Alexander had instigated, with the approval of his wife of course. The first being the introduction of two new looms he had imported from England which had a special shut off valve. Yes, there were to be no more injuries or fatalities at Daylight Cottons. The next stage was to build a brand-new village on the land behind the main mill building for the workers and their families.

"I think it might be time to appoint him official foreman my dear, what do you think?" he asked.

Clara nodded and grinned. "I believe that is an excellent idea Alexander."

As Alexander made his way out onto the landing, he suddenly heard the doorbell ring. And, as today his housekeeper was at the dentist with a dreadful toothache, he left his family and descended to answer his front door. Standing on the step were Lawrence and Sophie. He greeted them warmly.

"Lawrence dear fellow and the delightful Sophie! Please, do come in," he said ushered them inside. "Clara is currently in the nursery. If you would like to seat yourselves in the drawing room I shall inform her of your arrival."

"No, no need to disturb her just yet Alexander old boy. We

were just in the neighborhood and we thought we might... err... drop in. Is that not right my dear?" He turned to Sophie who giggled.

Alexander apologized to his guests as he explained about their housekeeper. "However, I believe I can remember how to boil a kettle," he remarked with a grin. "Would you like a pot of tea or coffee?"

"My apologies Alexander, but do you think I might have a small glass of water instead?" Sophie blushed as Alexander looked at her in surprise.

"Certainly, my dear," he replied, a little taken aback. "I do hope you are not unwell."

Sophie looked at Lawrence before replying, "I just feel a little queasy."

Alexander made his way to the door, just as Clara walked in.

"Lawrence! Sophie!" she exclaimed happily. "To what do we owe this unexpected pleasure? Please let me fetch Amelia. We have just settled the twins for a nap." She slipped from the room to fetch her governess.

Lawrence placed his hand on his wife's arm and gave it a little squeeze of affection as Clara came back followed by Amelia.

"Good morning Mr. and Mrs. Cavendish," she smiled. "It is so lovely to see you both looking so... um... well," she finished lamely as she glanced across at Sophie. The poor girl looked anything but well. If anything, she looked a little green.

Alexander came back with a tray and handed a glass of water to Sophie. "There we are, my dear. I do hope you are not sickening for something," he said as Sophie took the glass gratefully. She smiled.

"I shouldn't think so sir," she sipped her cool drink slowly as Lawrence looked around the faces in the room.

"Sophie and I have an announcement," he declared. "We shall soon be joining you as parents!" He beamed with joy and excitement as Clara jumped up and ran to fuss around Sophie.

"Oh, my dear, that is wonderful news!" she exclaimed as she kissed Sophie's cheek.

Amelia grinned at Lawrence. "Congratulations to you both. I shall look forward to your child immensely."

Sophie giggled excitedly as Clara slipped her arm in hers and led her off to check on her sleeping children. "Tell me, dear, have you told Uncle Anthony yet?" she asked as she pushed the door open quietly, tip-toeing into the room to check on the two cribs, indicating for Sophie to follow her.

Sophie gazed down at her husband's niece and nephew and wondered what her baby will be like. She stroked her midriff absently, absorbed by the serenity of the sleeping infants. Clara took her arm and the two ladies crept back out of the room and onto the landing.

"Not as yet Clara dear, Lawrence insisted we inform father

first and Amelia. We shall call upon him this afternoon." She smiled as she thought about her father as a grandparent.

"Well, if there is anything that you feel I can help you with my dear, just let me know." She paused as she thought of something. "Although, I shall be very busy for the next few weeks," she continued, a huge smile plastered across her face. Sophie looked at her expectantly. "I have promised dear Prudence I shall be a bridesmaid at her wedding to Doctor Fletcher at the end of the month!" she exclaimed as she turned towards the stairs.

Sophie smiled as Clara made her way back down to the drawing room where Lawrence and Alexander were listening to Amelia's hushed tones.

"And then she said 'I have finally repaid you for saving my arm.' What do you suppose that means?" she asked, just as Clara entered the room.

"It means, Amelia dearest, that God found a way."

THE END

But before you go, turn the page …

(turn the page)

Also by Chloe Carley

Thank you for reading **"The Courageous Bride of Charleston"**!

I hope you enjoyed it! If you did, may I ask you to please **write your honest review on Amazon**?

It would mean the world to me. Reviews are crucial and allow me to keep writing the books you love to read!

Some other best sellers of mine:

His Stubborn Sweet Bride

A Debutante for the Rancher

A Cowboy to Save Esmeralda

The Frontier Gambler's Lady

Also, if you liked this book, you can also check out **my full Book Catalogue on Amazon**.

Thank you for allowing me to keep doing what I love!

Made in the USA
Lexington, KY
12 November 2018